DOTTIE FOR YOU

DOTTIE FOR YOU

SEASON 1, VOLUME 1
(EPISODES 1-3)

REGINA WATTS

PAINTED BLIND
PUBLISHING
LITERARY ALCHEMY

Dottie For You Season 1, Volume 1
© 2023 Regina Watts
ISBN: 978-1-957469-03-4

Text: Regina Watts
Book Design: M. F. Sullivan

Regina Watts Online: hrhdegenetrix.com
Painted Blind Publishing: paintedblindpublishing.com
Join Regina's mailing list for three free stories!

A FRIENDLY WARNING
FROM AUTHOR REGINA WATTS

This is not a billionaire romance. *DOTTIE FOR YOU* is my answer to the unfinished masterpiece of the Divine Marquis, *120 DAYS OF SODOM*. It is a means by which to explore all the erotic/grotesque aspects of modern human sexuality— as many as can be explored in a consensual setting between two (or more) adults. In such a scenario activities may be so abstracted that they do not resemble sex. All things become transmuted to sexuality within the pages of such a book, whether the author finds it personally sexual or not. In my opinion this is a horror novel, a work of transgressive fiction with erotic elements; due to its extreme adult nature, it is being marketed as erotica, but please take that label and the sexuality depicted with a grain of salt. It is, like a Francis Bacon painting, a study in the extremity and violence of the human desire for intimacy.

True authors are mere court reporters, captive to the interactions of their characters. They strive to be honest and fair in their depictions. They do not necessarily condone the behaviors of the characters they explore, and I am no exception. Harold and Dottie are two strange people: this is the story of a strange love, a satirical exploration of society's notion that consent makes everything acceptable. It is not a story meant to encourage anyone to do or try anything, except perhaps to write more far-flung pieces of transgressive fiction that require an opening advisory. Please keep this in mind while reading, and please understand: while this series may not be for you, somebody out there is enjoying the hell out of it.

EPISODE 1
FEELING DOTTIE

1.

BEFORE KNOWING DOTTIE, Harold Fleetwood was a pathetic man. Not that he was any less pathetic for knowing her. If anything, knowing her put him in intimate touch with his wretched nature. This self-knowledge, this awareness of his own unsuitability, occurred to him with Dottie in a different way than it did when setting eyes on other beautiful women. Dottie was very different than even the most beautiful of beautiful women, but he didn't find that out until after the first time he fucked her.

There had to be something special about Dottie. After all, his life didn't lack for beautiful women. Harold, described by his late mother to disappointing blind dates as the "quiet, intellectual type," was the CEO of a Fortune 500 company. It didn't matter which one: by this point in his career, nested in the midst of his fifties, "career" had become an abstraction. Money poured into his life and was transformed into real estate, objects, fine food, books, artwork. Mostly he spent money on the last two. Traditional artworks of course—paintings, say—but what made Harold a pathetic man in his own estimate was his dirty little secret.

Harold was very wealthy, obscenely wealthy, ridiculously wealthy. He could have courted the sexiest super-models and the tightest athletes. Any hot little bitch in all the world would have fallen back and spread her legs if he threw around the money. Some women did try, but after a while people began to speculate that he was gay and gradually the flirting dialed down. Finally he married a woman named Molly, had no children, and divorced her four years later, all of this taking place in the overlap between the ages of forty and fifty: a treacherous period where people are prone to depressing mistakes. From the outside, this sequence of events only cemented his reputation as what was once, with an Oscar Wilde wink, called "a confirmed bachelor."

But he was not gay—well, not exclusively. Harold loved women. Was obsessed with women. Oh, women. Women, women. He saw them wherever he went. God! There was not a one among them that was not, in some way or at some point in her life, in possession of the capacity to shoot him through the gut with sharp, cruel pain. Women, women! They were so beautiful, and even with bank accounts, bonds, stock portfolios and collections of precious paintings and preserved old books, oh, wretched Harold Fleetwood would never be worth a second of their private time. He felt it every time he was alone with a woman, the weakness: as if he was plagued by some diseases, some reemerging parasite that bloomed to life in the private audience of a female.

Did he hate women for it? No, of course not. He hated himself. Hated this insane desire to fall to his knees and bury his face in a beauty's skirts like she was his own mother; hated his compulsion to kiss and caress and bruise with love every smallest facet of splendid feminine bodies. But most of all—most of all, he hated all the other things he wanted to do. He hated his urge to enfold them in his arms until their bones snapped to pieces in his grip; hated his desire to beat them bloody, strip them down and whip them and rub their wounds with burning ointment like the Marquis de Sade, whose books Harold reread more often than even the Bible. It would surprise no one who knew his private fantasy life to learn that Harold was a devout Catholic, but his shame for his own inner world of sin was so great that it had been years since he'd been to Confession and subsequently years since his last Eucharist. No flesh of God here, which was ironic.

The problem with what Harold wanted to do to women was that it did not stop with the Marquis de Sade's tamer fantasies. The problem with Harold was that he was a fan of what was referred to on the Internet as "Dolcett," which was, he supposed, better than actual snuff. As a matter of fact he refused to watch actual pornography with actual people because he was positive his tastes would escalate beyond all reason. One trip to Pornhub on a weak night and soon he'd be spending swaths of that vast fortune shipping nubile young women to some obscure private island for him to shoot and kill and eat like wild pigs.

That was what Dolcett illustrations were about, roughly speaking—women who were (generally consensually) eaten by, oh, far-flung societies where females were raised for meat, or sororities whose hazing routines somehow involved someone being eaten, who knows…it was all nonsense, all silly excuses to produce a framework for horrific fantasies. The subculture got its name from the artist who founded it, and although now many other artists had joined the community, their art was all described as Dolcett. Harold knew one such artist, someone who drew Japanese influenced illustrations inspired by the aesthetic referred in that country as "erotic grotesque," and paid her routinely for her drawings because she was just so good at bringing his ideas to life. This was, if nothing else, after the divorce. At least he wasn't also hiding those expenditures from his wife.

He was embarrassed, Harold. So ashamed. He could not control himself, or had so decided long ago—and once one makes a decision like that, one's life begins to take a certain form. Harold's life had taken a lonely form because the idea of bringing a woman into that life frightened him. Molly had found him a very boring man with nothing to say but this was because the things on his mind not related to business were inexcusably profane. She was five seconds out the door when he was already thinking about cannibalism again. Now to bring a woman into his condo, oh, what a mistake that would be! Say she should discover his private collection of images, those marvelous commissioned works? Or, Heaven forfend, the chatlogs, long into the night, between himself and the artist with whom he would sometimes fantasize for hours. Dear God. Any woman who stumbled on those in her husband's or boyfriend's computer would be rightly frightened—worse, far worse, she might get a real sense for what the slime that coated Harold's very soul. That repugnant barrier between himself and any possibility for real intimacy. The women of his imagination were safer. Loving. Enthusiastic. And that, ultimately, was why he fell so hard for Dottie: in these qualities, she was beyond even his wildest imaginings.

Dottie Shipman was frighteningly cute. Of all the women filling the company offices, Dottie (hired as the assistant to Harold's assistant) was the one who most obsessed him. This was not until around Christmas, this physical obsession with her beauty, but even before then he had noticed she was lovely almost beyond compare. They were introduced upon her hiring and he shook her delicate little hand: it was so soft, so warm and smooth, that he at once wished to cut it off at the wrist and keep it in a box forever. God! So soft. To kiss that hand—oh, she was gone. Off to work. Yes, another workday.

And another, and another. Every day Dottie was a little different. Sometimes her black hair, long straight streams of it, sat in a ponytail at the back of her head. Sometimes it was in a strict schoolmarm bun that drove him wild when paired with those stern spectacles she lowered down her nose while typing away at work. Once or twice it was curled, oh! He loved it curled. He loved her, loved her as people loved birds, and she had the same effect on his crippled old soul. After Christmas especially, on those instances when the girl would come through his office to deliver some paperwork he would sit, breathless. Watching her without watching her. Saying nothing, crawling out of his skin to say everything. To touch her. Oh! God, just to touch her.

He was miserable, Harold. Truly miserable. And his misery only increased when he realized Dottie was not nearly as wowed by his wealth as everyone else in the office. It was his only commendable quality in his own estimate, and those who managed to see through it surely knew they were studying a very rotten man. Dottie knew. That pouting mouth he loved so dearly, one day while passing by the break-room he heard it laughing. He stopped to listen, hand to his heart and face pressing to the jamb of the door, glad he had covered that sensitive beating organ when he realized what she laughed about.

"He really is such a weird dude," she told someone, anyone, everyone, didn't matter. Might as well have been everyone for how it wounded him. "Like, I guess it's nice he doesn't get any ideas—try to grab my ass, or something—but any time I walk by his desk it's like I can hear his pants shrinking, you know? I wish he would try to contain himself…ugh, men are so gross, and they're so much worse when they're rich. They think they can do whatever they want. Like that stupid book, that *Fifty Shades of*—"

Harold went home early that day. In fact, he took a few days off. Oh, God. Nobody understood. He worked so hard to contain himself. No one knew suffering like this—to be so full of cravings impossible to consummate. Well…not safely, anyway. Not without great horror, great shame. No: Harold would never have hurt anyone, not really. Not without consent, and even then only to a point.

But, oh! Within the realms of his mind, he was awful. Simply awful. Though he disliked the low standard of art and writing prevalent in the Dolcett and horrotica communities, Harold was grateful for their existence, because it all made him feel less alone. Besides, not all the artists were bad. A few were really quite good, painterly almost, although the one he chatted with routinely was his favorite. She never burdened him with talk of the past or trying to pressure him for personal details, and he never did the same. They talked about books and movies and artworks, not just cannibal-themed ones but many more innocuous ones too. But they discussed, also, many, many cannibal-themed pieces of media, and all the fantasies that overflowed from their dark minds.

He knew for sure she was a woman because she once live-drew on a video stream in their cannibal fantasies chatroom once and that feminine hand kept edging into camera. The delicate curve of her demure wrist proved infinitely more titillating to Harold than even the most detailed illustration of a woman being eaten by tribal savages or butchered up for sale. After the drawing stream ended he sent her their first private message and commissioned a drawing, and soon it was a regular expenditure. Mostly he pined for illustrations from existing works: for instance, the libertine near the end of *Justine* whose interest was focused on the severing of girls' heads. Her comedic rendering of the eponymous character's narrow escape from the scenario was his favorite commissioned piece to date, and that was impressive because it didn't even pertain to cannibalism. Just beheading. It was something in her style: the fabulous facial expressions, the suffusion of details everyone one looked, Justine's immense fright as visible in pupils rich with two-dimensional panic. So believable and so erotic despite stylization that left it nearer to a cartoon than a woodcut print.

Yes, the illustrator had a distinct style. He could have recognized it anywhere, and was so unprepared to see a rendering in this fashion resting on the edge of Miss Shipman's desk one slow afternoon that he almost dropped his briefcase. He had been on the way home but now hesitated, lips parted in shock as he bent to examine the smiling hula girl. Work-safe, certainly. Charming, of course. His Dolcett artist?

It had to be.

Harold could not believe it. He was terrified by it, this discovery, and looked around to see if someone played a prank on him. Back down: yes, the width and proportions of the thighs, the forearms, the trapezoid of the illustrative grin, then—

"Can I help you find something, Mr. Fleetwood?"

Jumping, Harold whipped around to find Dottie behind him, those green eyes over her low-set glasses piercing as poison darts. "Ah—" He stepped back, pale, trying to laugh, failing, oh, God, get him out of here! "Ah—no, I'm sorry, I just—just happened to notice your drawing."

"Oh!" Shocked, visibly embarrassed, the girl lowered smoothly to her seat and flipped the hula girl face-down. It pained him. "I promise, I wasn't goofing off at work…I drew her at lunch and just—"

"No, it wasn't that. I was just thinking how cute she was." Harold studied the flush-faced girl who reached up to unfix her ponytail from the back of her aptly spotted blouse. Now, the true shape of things coming together in his mind, he was almost breathless as he asked, "Did you really draw that?"

"Well—well, yes…"

She was uneasy with his attention, that much was clear. For once faint confidence rose in his breast. Harold even smiled, difficult for him to do in front of women because he was so painfully shy. "You're really very good, you know."

Those glamorous eyelashes batted in lurid surprise, tantalizing him without ever intending to. Look at that! Even smiled back, oh! She'd never smiled at him before. Not enough to show those little dimples on either side of her pink mouth. "Gosh, thank you!"

"How long have you been drawing?"

"Oh, a long, long time."

"Did you go to art school?"

"For awhile…I dropped out." The girl grinned a little, adjusted her glasses, began to turn back to her quote-un-quote real work. "It just wasn't the environment for me."

"You must do something to practice, as good as you are…" He searched her face and, when she glanced back at him, he held her eyes in his stare. "Do you ever post your drawings on the Internet, maybe?"

Was it his imagination? No: the color discernibly drained from her face and though her smile remained it struggled to do so. "Oh yeah," she said uneasily. "Sometimes, yeah."

His heart raced until he was dizzy. How was a thing like this possible? God was good, very good—or very, very cruel. Perhaps he needed to hurry back to the confessional soon. "You know"—What to say? Should he say anything at all? Just walk away, go home?—"I think I might have seen your work around online before."

The widening of her eyes was distinct even behind her glasses; the face that once paled now flushed again instead. "O—oh! Uh! Really?"

"I think so."

"Wh—where'd you see them?"

Glancing back to the blank side of the hula girl, he said, "Around. I'm sure you know how it is, browsing the Internet."

"Uh—yeah." So taken aback that the effect was physical, she leaned away from him in her seat. "Yeah, you see a lot of—a lot of stuff. On the Internet."

"Yes, you do. You aren't going to do anything with that hula girl, are you?"

"Oh! Uh—" God, he'd never seen her so much as stutter. All

her woman's confidence drained to girlish anxiety so charming he wished at once to crush her skull in his hands. Ah! To kiss her brain until its tissue ruptured. Clearly exposed—and clearly wondering if she was going mad or being called out on the carpet—Dottie looked down at her drawing, managed a laugh, and at last put herself back together enough to shake her head. "Uh, no, I'm not going to do anything with her." Such a gay, carefree little grin, a touch of slyness! He loved her, yes, it was impossible to avoid admitting it. A man couldn't look at such a girl and not love her, not wish to kiss her until the lips fell off her beautiful face. "Do you want her?"

"I'd love her," Harold said, the words almost a whisper. Dottie's smile widened. With one of those delicate, infinitely perfect hands, she flipped the hula girl upright again and slid the drawing to him. He smiled tenderly down at the image, carefully lifting it toward him, but with a belated gasp, Dottie said, "Oh!" and caught Harold by the wrist.

His body! His whole body was caught in a blaze by that gentle hand, that soft hand. The first time he had felt Dottie since meeting her. Harold almost trembled while, oblivious to his suffering, Dottie slid the paper from his hand and bent her grinning head over it. "I have to sign it!"

Poor Harold had to take another day off after that.

2.

OH, DOTTIE, DOTTIE. Dottie all day long, unsettling his mind. The day Harold stayed home he examined himself, conscience and body, and found both unworthy of her. The inside of his mind was too rotten. He couldn't get it up without imagining any one of a number of variously depraved scenarios. Sometimes he called on the services of a reliable network of working girls, a few of whom having graduated over the years into madams to acquire him more working girls. All the women who saw to him were treated very well and paid very highly in exchange for the opportunity to treat them quite unkindly for awhile, and sometimes return the favor. In the style of the Marquis de Sade—or at the very least one of his fictional villains—Harold kept a cozy country *maison* some ways away from the city where he and his company made their home. Every once in a while he would hire a few girls for a fun weekend party, give them a lot of money and a lot of food and a lot of drugs, maybe film a few fun things, then send them all back on their ways quite a few thousand dollars richer. He found curiously that he was not able to watch the films produced by his exploits with these hired women. They were more like collectors' items—there if he needed it, if he ever became an invalid incapable of even being entertained by professionals. Maybe because of this deep dread of age he was compelled to film the interactions—sometimes even script them—and store them away in a vault in his closet as if they were truly depraved.

And they were, essentially, but they were not *really* depraved. Nobody was really being hurt. The girls he hired, though he thought of them as girls owing to the age gap between him and them, were always at least eighteen years and vetted for their birthdays, backgrounds, and conviction histories long before they made it to Harold's secret house. They were not really hogtying one another and shoving apples in each other's mouths and dusting one another with flour or cooking oil or fragrant herbs with any ill intent. All good fun, all of it. None of them were actually interested in cannibalism at all. They were bored to tears by Harold's fantasies and were all immensely grateful he didn't talk about anything with them but things that seemed to activate their interest, like sex or celebrities or money.

That was what made the working women safe, you see. Their interest in money. Harold understood that, then—understood what they wanted. The relationship was clear and safe and it was in the best interest of these women to keep matters very quiet. He was an odd man, Harold, and while his sexual tastes were beyond perverse he was nonetheless a cherished client in that he could be relied upon to be up-front, to pay, to make no negotiations for anything extra, and to never try to turn it into some kind of romantic situation. He struck all the girls as very romantic as a person—in fact, he struck his staff members that way, too, and most of American high society across the board, though he did not get out much to anything in years. The divorce was just a convenient excuse there. He had never much been wild about public appearances or any other form of getting out.

Dottie got out, though. He noticed this after the hula girl, when his attention for her became so honed it was like nothing in the office existed but this one exquisite girl. Monday morning Dottie lay flushed and sighing in her desk chair, drinking bottle on bottle of water and, bless her heart, struggling through her work. He refrained from teasing her—refrained from saying anything (What could he bear to say? That precious hula girl danced at him from his entryway's mirrored key hook, where it was stuck with a magnet.)—and went about his day. Night came. For the first time in a few days he had interest and daring enough to go to his chatroom, where his arrival interrupted a conversation between the artist and a few other regulars of the room. A few lines of the conversation prior to his arrival loaded when he entered: he scrolled up a bit to parse together her lines.

<drawswift> i don't know dude, i've just been feeling super stressed lately
<drawswift> probably im' just depressed bc i'm hungover but you know how it is
*<drawswift> *i'm*
<drawswift> yeah it's like i work super hard all the time and still barely make rent
<drawswift> i'm really upping my commission hustle and it's working but it's like ugh
<drawswift> i hope i can take more time to draw for myself soon

Guilt struck him through the heart in the same instant that his private message box pinged with a note from her.

<drawswift> hey!!!!!!!!!!!!!!! where have you been?????

<eattherich> Home sick, sorry to be unavailable to entertain you.

<drawswift> you should be sorry! omg ok so here's a story
<drawswift> so i think my boss is into dolcett??

Despite himself, Harold laughed and polished the lens of his glasses before responding.

<eattherich> What on earth makes you say that?

<drawswift> i drew this little cartoon at work the other day
and he recognized my style lol
<drawswift> what a dirty old man! i knew he was a pervert

Yes, he was. Harold's hand rested upon his heart, his whole being basking in the gentle glow of shame as normal men basked in praise. He would have given anything for her to praise him, of course, but that was the problem…he didn't deserve praise. It was enough to be demeaned. More than enough. Dottie, Dottie—God, this was Dottie. His typing fingers trembled.

<eattherich> I'm sure he'd be humiliated to know you were on to him.

<drawswift> yeah what a weirdo! he'd probably like it
<drawswift> did i tell u he stares at me

<eattherich> Does he really?
<eattherich> Well, if he really is a member of the community,
who knows what he's thinking at a time like that?
<eattherich> Better be careful of those quiet types.

So very careful. Harold thought of the girls that he knew, and the people that all those girls knew. He could interact with those people to an extent. He could talk to people at parties. He could talk to the press. But—opening himself, really opening himself? He couldn't do it. Couldn't do it on an intimate level with a woman he adored and, sad to say, he adored Dottie, to whom he meant less than nothing, nothing, nothing.

Tuesday. Dottie looked better. Wednesday. Even better. Thursday, her hair was in his favorite style, curled and pulled up too, and she sat at her desk snacking on the glistening jewels of pomegranate seeds that stained her fingers bloody red. Jesus Christ, he wanted to marry her.

Friday came somehow, and near the day he paused to fix up his appearance in the wall mirror. He was by no means a bad-looking man and was well aware of that fact, yet somehow suspected—feared, at least—that the horrors of his proclivities were visible, oozing out somehow upon the sculpture of his senatorial visage. He tried not to talk to women in a personal or private way because he feared ultimately that his thoughts would turn down these dark corridors—that they would somehow divine his nature, as if his fascination for violence might burst out of him.

Might it? No. No, no. Harold was a pleasant man. A quiet, thoughtful man. He fought hard for his company and hard for a comfortable life. As a result both had excelled beyond his wildest dreams: beyond a company and comfort into a corporation and opulence. He would not squander it on falling for some trap of animalistic novelty. But—oh, if there were one woman in the world upon whom he could release his consumptive desires…

He had just smoothed back his graying gold hair and straightened his glasses when Dottie, previously sent for, knocked upon the door and leaned in with more anxiety than he'd yet seen from her. No one liked to be called into the boss's office on a Friday afternoon. It was a cruel move on his part, but, well, she was being a little brat, wasn't she? Couldn't let her walk on him entirely…he was her boss, after all.

"Dottie, good afternoon. Why don't you close the door and take a seat…it won't be but a minute, I just wanted to let you know what to expect moving forward."

"I'm not getting a promotion, am I?" The tone was grim, hopeless—braced for bad news. He lowered into his desk and folded his arms over his diaphragm, giving a brisk brush-off wave of his hand far more casually than he might have with other employees.

"No, goodness, you don't need one, do you? You've enough work already. If anything"—God, this conversation was going to be more words than he'd spoken to her in all her time at the company, and his brain rushed high with endorphins of power at his own ability to form more than one sentence in her presence—"it's occurred to me that I'm paying you not nearly close to what I should. Barely entry-level…between you and me, we could do with treating even our least-experienced employees a little more. But particularly you, having proved yourself so valuable, well…I think you deserve it."

The divine moon of her face and all its lovely features expanded with absolute shock, those eyes growing brightening behind her glasses. "Really? A raise, really?" She hesitated, then decided it acceptable to ask, "How much?"

He named a figure and she balked. "Wh—that's almost twice what I'm making now."

"I know! We really have been paying you much too little."

"Well—but I don't understand."

With a pleasant smile, Harold toyed with the nearby fountain pen to disguise his anxiety. "As I said…you've been here some time, and you've become quite a key player in the office. Almost a year already? This is around the time in a young employee's career where they start getting antsy…start looking for other employment. And I don't want you looking elsewhere for other employment."

She studied him so closely, an owl regarding a camper in the night. He couldn't stand it. In a moment of weakness he felt obligated to say more. Obligated to tease her. "Consider this," he fatally said, "my modest proposal that you stay with us at least a few years longer."

Within the green pools of her irises her black pupils expanded like saucers. That same attractive flush that crossed her face during their interaction above the watchful eye of the hula girl now returned, doubled; the redness crept across her nose, her ears, down her neck. He wished he were a vampire, had fangs to puncture that pomegranate flesh and drink the shining blood within. Dottie, Dottie! Sitting across the desk from her, he wanted to scream.

And he very nearly did when, the tip of her soft pink darting out across her lips, Dottie leaned forward. "Is this about that hula girl?"

"Goodness, Miss Shipman, there's a phrase about this involving gift horses and looking them in mouths…I think I've given you more than enough reason for the raise. Or do you think you don't deserve it?"

"No, it's just—it's just, I was just talking to somebody in my art community about—" She faltered, her hand lifting to pat her firm-shut lips.

And he expected her to give up then. To give up and thank him and walk away, and let him keep playing his coy little game. But, oh…Harold should have known Dottie better than that.

"Did you know about me when you hired me?"

"I'm not sure what you mean."

"Quit messing around—who are you? Which one? 'GeinGuy42?' 'Foodchain?'" Her eyes widened. She leaned forward in her seat, her words a breathless whisper. "No—are you 'eattherich?'"

All his power left him. It was like every one of his worst nightmares—yes, just like all that vulgar evil in his mind oozed out to confront him. He could not answer in any way. How could he? He could not lie—no, not to her. But he dared not confirm. Anything else, any more questions—oh, she was staring. How she stared! Watching, waiting. His hand lifted before his mouth as though to shield him from her; he looked away upon the narrowing of her eyes.

"That will be all, Miss Shipman. Enjoy your raise."

"Hey, but—"

"See you bright and early Monday morning."

He took out his phone and looked at his calendar, staring through it, unreading. After a few seconds and an annoyed huff she gave up and left the room, at which point Harold collapsed face-first upon his desk with a groan for the cool wood against his overheated face. God, yes. Absolutely pathetic.

3.

THINGS ONLY GOT harder from there. He abandoned entirely his accounts with the cannibal chatroom and associated burner email address, took a few girls out to the country and tried to pretend he didn't spend every waking second—and many of his fitful sleeping ones—plagued by racing thoughts of Dottie. Dottie, Dottie, Dottie! What was he going to do about Dottie? What could he do?

She was on to him. There was no fighting it. No denying it. Sooner or later he would have to admit his identity to her and then—then, things would escalate. They already were escalating. It might have been selective attention at work but it seemed she was, overnight, volunteering for a great many more tasks around the office. In particular, taking it upon herself to helpfully act as courier between his assistant and himself. The Tuesday before Valentine's Day (the date seemed significant only in retrospect—the holiday at the time was absent from his psyche, as far removed from him as was Venus from Earth) Dottie came upon him taking lunch at his desk and smiled while he wiped off his hands to accept his mail.

"What are you eating for lunch, Mr. Fleetwood?"

His glance couldn't hold her face longer than a few seconds before lowering back down to the envelopes whose return addresses he just couldn't manage to read. "Pork."

"Gosh, that sounds tasty. What kind of pork?"

Don't look at her, don't look at her. "Pulled pork."

"One of my favorites. Say—you don't have to be worried, you know." His resolve faltered. Harold looked up and was petrified by the sinuous daemon who had slithered into his office to tease him with her very existence. The girl smoothed her blue blouse, the hip of her patterned orange slacks propping against the edge of his desk as she said, "About me saying anything, I mean."

"I'm not sure what you mean."

"I'm very discreet…nobody knows about me, either."

Clearing his throat, Harold reached for his nearby letter opener and ignored all the intrusive thoughts bombarding him to touch such an object in her presence. "That will be all, Miss Shipman."

But it was not all. It would never be all. He could hardly sleep that night and the next day came in just a little later than usual, once all the employees were already in. When passing Dottie's desk he couldn't help but think she worked very hard to not look at him, and soon he discovered why. Hidden in a sealed envelope, slipped into the drawer of his desk, was an illustration that made his skull tingle as if pricked by needles. A cartoon damsel in distress—whose pencil skirt and glasses and black ponytail marked her as none other than Dottie herself—tied spread-eagled across a cutting board. Over her a lascivious cartoon wolf licked its chops, brandished a knife, wore a silly chef's hat and, crucially, bore a representation of Harold's somewhat crooked pair of spectacles. After self-consciously straightening his own, he held the drawing to his heart, shuddered, put the envelope safely into his briefcase, and tried to decide how to proceed.

Harold was a man who prided himself on his foresight. He got where he was by seeing patterns—looking into the future of the American market, making decisions no one else could make. Though nothing in life was completely predictable, human behavior on a mass scale generally was. On a personal scale, however…well. Men, fine. Women who wanted money, fine. Women who left him drawings, who were so secretive and evidently two-sided, who were into Dolcett when they weren't at the office (or maybe when they were…he'd check with IT to see her browser history if he wouldn't have been obliged to follow up on anything he found)? This was a completely different, altogether more frightening kind of woman: infinitely more frightening than the kind inclined to be disgusted with his proclivities and break things off. More frightening than the kind he had thought her to be before, the type to jeer and mock and publicly humiliate.

Not that the two were mutually exclusive. Not at all. But that was the problem. Something about Dottie now appeared dangerously changeable. It was as if he had discovered a secret identity of hers, and she, his; and now they were in a kind of perverse stand-off. Who would blink first? Oh, he knew. He damn well knew. And he wasn't just going to blink, either. He was doomed to shut his eyes and lay down in the dirt for her. He knew it, yes—knew he was defeated even before once again calling Dottie into the office at the end of the workday.

This time, she seemed ready for it. Was he hallucinating, or had she unbuttoned the lilac silk of her blouse an extra button? Christ, her skin was so pale. It must have been so impossibly soft—tender. Oh, to just once bury his face in her neck, her bosom! To smell her, gasp himself full of her, sink in his teeth—

"You wanted to see me, Mr. Fleetwood?"

"Ah—yes, I did." He was just deciding how to broach the subject when, bending forward in her seat, Dottie captivated his attention with a pair of clasped hands and a bitten lower lip.

"Did you like my drawing?" Her doll eyes batted above the rims of her spectacles and pumped his muscles full of predatory adrenaline. God, God, she didn't understand what she did to him!

"That's just it, Miss Shipman. While of course your technical skills are very admirable—"

She smiled. "So you did like it."

"—such, uh—such illustrations don't belong—"

"When you like something someone gave you, you're supposed to thank them for it."

He stopped, flustered by her reproach. People did not generally admonish him; and to experience it behind the desk of his office, at the hands of petite Dottie, well! It was something of a shock. Thrown off, he somewhat sheepishly corrected himself. "Well—well yes, of course. Thank you, Dottie." His voice lowered. "I like your drawing quite a lot."

"I'll bet you do, you dirty old wolf. Tex Wolf, howling at girls."

Face flushing, Harold leaned back in his seat and began, "Now, just a moment," but the girl was unstoppable. She had caught him unaware by bringing up the drawing before he did and then chastising him for his failure to appreciate it. The script had been flipped: Harold had the rare sense of being on the losing side of a negotiation and now from this position of stolen power Dottie reamed him like he was a poor employee. No—not an employee. A worm. Nothing. Human garbage. He shuddered as she told him in a voice not soft enough for his liking, "I've wondered! All this time I've wondered why you've been staring at me. I knew you were thinking perverted thoughts…I just didn't know how much of a pervert you really were. Last night I was looking back through some of the things you commissioned from me and I just thought, well, maybe you'd like something new. Sorry if this one isn't gory enough! I wanted to make you something cute and fun." Her eyes seemed as though to flash behind the lenses of her glasses. "The next ones will be more hardcore."

It was one of the first times in his life Harold was at a loss for words. He could not think of a thing to say, even to end the conversation. His heart pulsed in his ears and he fancied he felt faint, but that was really just the effect of Dottie's stare; Dottie's proximity. Thank God for this desk! It was the only thing keeping them safe from each other. Every bone in Harold ached with his immense desire to kiss her—to push her entire body into his mouth, yes, to swallow her whole. A Little Red Riding Hood.

"I don't think this is a good idea," whispered Harold, a miserable man reduced already to pleas. "It may seem like it's fate—"

Oh, that pure, wonderful high-beam smile! He'd never seen her smile at him like that, ever, ever. Didn't know she could smile like that at all. "I'm so glad you said it! It does, doesn't it? I've been thinking the same thing."

"—but some things had ought to remain…unexpressed."

"What do you mean? If I didn't draw, I'd go crazy…I'd be some kind of serial killer. Who knows what you would do with your time if you weren't running this place…you need outlets. It's when you don't express these things, that's when they get bad."

He looked askance, the back of his hand pressed to his lips. "I wouldn't call this career a sufficient outlet."

"You don't sit around thinking about what all your female employees taste like?"

"Just you." He dared look back at her and could not look away again, absorbed by the cherry of her flustered cheeks and aroused lips. "I try not to look at women. I think such vile things about them, all I can do is avert my eyes. But—I can't help but look at you. I've never been able to help it. Maybe something in me recognized your hands." He glanced down at them, then back up to her face. "That time you propped the webcam up and let us watch you draw. Maybe that's why every time you walk past me, I—"

"Stare like a deranged old creep? Think all those bad, bad, nasty thoughts about me?"

His breathing was hard and fast. Harold managed to look away again but the damage was done. Visions of Dottie were plastered all across his frontal lobe: Dottie being stripped, Dottie being fucked, Dottie being killed and dismembered for dinner. Dottie, Dottie, oh, Dottie! His dick was so hard he covered his face and gasped softly into his hand. "Please, Dottie, I'm ashamed."

"I'll bet you are—you should be ashamed, you dirty fucking pervert. Trying to call me in here and chew me out for leaving you a gift when you're the one who should be in trouble." The glitter of her eyes intensified. Dottie crossed her legs and sat up straight. "Come here."

Terror gripped him at the intensity of his impulse to obey. "I can't."

"Don't make me come over there." The girl's voice was low, almost unnaturally firm. Harold tried to look her in the face and found he couldn't even approach her defiant stare. Like an animal, a dog with its tail between its legs, Harold pushed himself up from his seat.

Dottie's eyes narrowed. "Not like that. Lower. Crawl."

Exhaling, unable to help himself, Harold obeyed; this man, this fifty-something man (closer to sixty than fifty in truth), this filthy rich capitalist swine, uneasily lowered himself to his knees with one hand braced upon the desk. In disbelief of his own willingness—nay, his own need—to obey a girl in her fresh twenties, Harold did as he had been told. Head lowered in an effort to hide his shamed face, he crawled around the desk and soon found himself studying the carpet beneath Dottie's crossed feet.

"You like other stuff, too, huh. Not just fucked up cannibalism shit…you fucking psycho." The heel of her purple pump lifted from the floor and Harold moaned to feel it grind into the back of his head. "I'm so mad at you for not telling me who you were sooner."

"I'm sorry, Dottie, so sorry—I didn't know, not until the girl you drew."

"I though you were my best online friend…I guess you can't know anybody over the Internet, not really. 'Eat the rich.'" The girl chuckled darkly and Harold, docile upon the floor at her feet, almost trembled at the contact of her shoe upon the back of his neck.

"You want to be eaten, too, huh…you only talk online about eating women, but what you really want is for some hot little number to come along and cook you up. Stick you in the throat like the dirty pig you are." Her foot lifted away. "Sit up."

Harold did, euphoric, all his troubles somehow gone amid this dark spell in which Dottie ensnared him. This—this was what they spoke of when they spoke of mindfulness, of living in the moment. Plans, stress, existential anxieties, paperwork, global crises: none of it, absolutely none of it mattered. None of it existed there at Dottie's feet.

As though she were a tender little wife to him already, Dottie cupped his face in those hands he so loved. Their contact caused him a shock of pain, the nerves in his cheeks stimulated beyond his endurance by her delicate, ultra-light touch. "You're a dirty pig, Harold. Say it."

He shut his eyes to whisper, "I'm—" but the girl commanded, "Look me in the face."

With a soft gasp, he obediently forced himself to begin again, throbbing in his trousers to make eye contact with her as he whispered, "I'm a dirty pig."

"Louder."

"I'm—I'm a dirty pig, Dottie, I'm sorry."

Her giggling turned up her lips to reveal a winsome hint of snaggletooth: a left cuspid just a touch crooked. A petite fang. "It's okay…you're Dottie's dirty little pig, aren't you?"

"I—"

"And one day"—she lowered her head over his, (oh God, oh God!) so close he tasted her sweet breath on his mouth, a soft cry of terrified desire rising from him—"if you're a very, very good little piggie, maybe you'll get all cut to pieces, and turned into tasty bacon and yummy pork, and then Dottie will eat you all up. Wouldn't you like that?"

"Oh, God—yes, yes, Dottie." His whole body burned with such desire, such tension, that he was startled by the silent slide of her shoe between his legs. It rubbed there and as he relaxed into the inflaming touch she rewarded him with another smile.

"Yeah…you sure would like that…you really are such a dirty, weird old man. But I like you. After realizing who I am, maybe if you still like me—"

"God, Dottie, you're all I think about!"

She laughed in a kind of surprise and, with a schoolgirl's delight, went on coyly, "Maybe we can be friends in real life, too, then?"

Her foot paused its caresses and he saw in her eyes a glittering earnest light of hope. Pure and true and gorgeous beyond any compare. "I'd like that," he told her, cautiously turning his head to kiss one of the hands that still held his face. While she sighed, so did he, almost collapsing against the palm to which he held his mouth. He groaned, inhaling her as if her body flowed with wine until he gave up and lifted a trembling hand to press hers inescapably there. "Oh, Dottie—I'm afraid."

"You're a big, strong man with more money than almost anybody in the world…what do you have to be afraid of?"

She simply took the words from him. He could not speak. He was too busy being absorbed by the experience of holding her hand against his parted lips, the salt of her skin tantalizing his tongue even without contact. "Say," whispered the girl when she decided he wasn't going to respond, her foot beginning to rock into motion again, "will you come visit me in my apartment?"

"When?"

Those dimples reappeared. "Tonight," she suggested. He shuddered, the very tips of his fingers charged with his litany of hungers for her.

"All right," he said. "Whatever you want."

"All right." She removed her foot, releasing his cheek before slipping her other hand out of his desperate grip. "Then I want to see you tonight…and I want you to be ready to give me whatever I want."

"Yes—of course."

"What a good boy you are…for a gross, creepy old pervert."

And then—then, then, then, then—then, Dottie leaned down, and she kissed him. Kissed him! The words didn't do it justice. The soft pillows of her lips pounced upon his unready mouth, which had been already parted in the simple wonder of her closeness. He gasped, choked, eyes falling shut as he flung his arms around her neck like he was the young girl and she the depraved sub-retirement monster craving to strip the flesh off her bones. To swallow the soft, wet tongue that stabbed against his until, with that evil nymph's giggle, she drew away, stood up, smoothed her skirt, then as an afterthought wiped the back of her hand across her glistening lips.

"Wow." She laughed again, his heart. What a girlish delight she was when once she shed her playfully cruel shell! "You're sure…wow." Her grin widened; she shook her head, looking fit to burst before she let herself out and left her boss kneeling on the floor. A literal skip in her step all the way.

Tonight—tonight? Oh, God. What had he just agreed to do? Sense made an effort to return to him but soon had to admit its futility. Drunk, Harold swayed upright, touched his mouth, looked dumbly at the nearest clock. What time was tonight? Where did Dottie even live?

He supposed he could look it up in her file. Ah…in a moment. Unsteadily, Harold crossed back to his customary side of the desk, lowered himself into his chair. He did not even think about resuming work. For the first time in a long, long time, he sat watching the city and smiling at absolutely nothing that could be seen.

4.

ON HIS WAY to Dottie's apartment Harold stopped to get some wine and, upon considering their proclivities, thought anything else—food, say—would be a dangerous invitation. He left it at the alcohol but added a bouquet of flowers and soon after purchasing both sat in his gleaming black car to study the apartment building just down the street from the parking garage where he'd found a space.

306. Apartment 306. Dottie's apartment. Middle floor, neighbors above and below. Thin walls. Not that they were going to make a ruckus, but it was good to know they couldn't. Somehow safer. A controlled environment. Again—not that they were going to get out of hand. Nothing was going to happen. This was what he told himself all the way up the elevator, but when he stared down the hall with an orange carpet reminiscent of *The Shining*, he wondered if this was true. God, let it be true. He had never known anyone like himself in real life and the harder he thought of Dottie—of all the possibilities—the stronger grew his urge to turn around.

Too late. Look: 306. He looked one more time at the label of the bottle. He checked his watch. He smoothed his hair.

Dottie's door flung open before he could knock and he gasped, almost dropping the bottle and bouquet both. The girl, dressed in jeans and a black v-neck that might as well have been the seven veils of Salome, smiled in obvious pleasure. "Hello! I'm so happy you're here! I was worried you wouldn't—" Her eyes fell to the flowers and she gasped. "Oh, Harold! Are these for me?"

"Uh—yes, of course." He smiled and, flustered, initially offered the bottle, then laughed at himself and corrected to the flowers. "They're both for you, of course, ah, but—"

"They're so beautiful, thank you! Oh"—with a click of that unforgettable tongue, Dottie fell back on her heel to let him pass—"this is so wonderful. Nobody's ever given me flowers before."

What a shocking idea. "No one? Ever?"

"Well—I don't know, my dad did once, I guess, but I was young and it was just a nice thing, you know. Here, let me go get something to put them in…make yourself at home!"

Not many places to do that in. Dottie's apartment was small and cluttered, crammed with coffee tables covered in photo books, paintings stacked up in the corners, a bedroom door cracked open to reveal a drawing table covered in papers. A thrill surged in him to recognize it from that drawing stream. The futon, prominently displayed in the living room, was arranged with psychedelic pillows perhaps leftover from a teenage bedroom; and, owing to the tight space, the brick walls were lined with shelves supporting a number of photographs. Little Dottie, oh—very cute, obscenely cute. He had to look away so as not to sully her memories and smiled instead at the tropical fish meandering about beside the living room's one window. "You have a very nice apartment, Dottie."

"Thank you! Sorry it's kind of a mess." With a throaty laugh like the huff of a horse, the girl trotted from the kitchen with a pair of glasses and a corkscrew. "I was thinking before you came over—when was the last time you were even in an apartment so small?"

"Oh, I have a few friends who live in smaller places."

"Really?"

"It's never advisable to cloister oneself in any one group of—oh." He realized with a chuckle that he still held the wine when she sat on the edge of the futon to set the glasses down. Bashful, Harold cleared his throat and edged nearer her, relinquishing the bottle like an offering: the vibration of the air around her was so intense that he recoiled immediately, falling back a step and looking down at himself. "Ah, where should I put my coat?"

"Here! I'll take it, we can put it in the bedroom—you open the wine." The girl sprang up and before he could move away she was upon him, one slim hand catching the lapel to pull it back from his shoulder. The trembling came upon him again. Transfixed by those eyes, holding his breath, Harold watched her realize at the same time as he did that she was touching him. Her motions slowed. The spring lamb of a delicate girl squeezed past him, their bodies sliding together, the area where he stood between the coffee table and futon conveniently restrictive. The blood boiled in his veins. It seemed she twirled around him, dancing, drawing back a curtain, and then his coat was gone and in the same smooth motion she sashayed off to hide it in her bedroom.

Her bedroom! He was on the verge of a stroke. Light-headed, Harold took up the abandoned corkscrew, unwrapped the wine bottle, and was just twisting the sharp implement into the hapless cork (What if this was Dottie's eye, instead? Her tight little stomach? Oh, her pretty—) when his hostess re-emerged, faltered to see him, and, with a wonderful grin, leaned her hip against the jamb of the bedroom door. One hand lifted shyly to her giggling mouth.

"This is so weird," she said over the sound of the cork's

freeing pop. "Oh, this is so weird! You're my boss, and you're eattherich, and you're here…in my apartment. I don't even know what's going on."

"I'm not sure I do, myself." He set the bottle down to let it breathe and, now out of reasons to avoid it, eased himself into the violet cushion of the futon. Sure enough, seeing this, the cunning predator into whose den he'd foolishly stumbled hurried to sit at his side, where she settled down at an angle close enough to ensure her knees brushed one of his.

He was too sick for wine. He was too afraid of this. Something was going to happen here: he felt it in the air like the humid static of a thunderstorm. The act of knowing Dottie was going to change him so sharply that there would be no returning. The act of knowing Dottie reminded him time moved only in one direction and what was done could not be undone. But—the act of knowing Dottie made him recall time would flow forward with or without Dottie.

Since his time was whiling away anyway, wasn't it worth seeing what could happen if he really got to know her?

"I think I'm going insane," he summarized after a few seconds of contemplation, studying the denim-shielded knees prodding his. "Maybe I am. This could all be a dream."

"I feel that way, too…I never could have guess this, not in a million years. Have you ever met anybody from online before?"

"No, God no. It seemed dangerous, given the subject matter."

Laughing Dottie propped her dimpled cheek upon her fist. From that angle he noted with a stab of desire a single freckle at the corner of her eye—a natural beauty mark hidden behind the frame of her glasses and revealed only on close proximity, with the kind assistance of certain angles. Certain lightings. He wanted to kiss that mole—dreamed of nibbling it off as she said, "It's not dangerous…people share fantasies all the time without enacting them."

Frightened beneath the hard light of her gaze, desperate to change the subject as much as to continue exploring the present one, he hedged and found a way to do both. He turned away to pour the poorly aerated wine while asking, "Have you ever met anyone from online before?"

"Oh, a couple times, but never from the Dolcett community. I gave my first blowjob to a guy I met on some dating site." She grinned while she accepted the wineglass from him, his fingers stinging from the brush against hers. "Thank you—I still feel sort of bad for ghosting him, but it was like, 'thanks for the practice, bye.'"

"Goodness. Weren't you worried about meeting a stranger like that?"

"Well sure, but, I don't know…I was in college, you know. Eighteen and super horny." Oh, what a devious little trollop. The simplest word was a weapon on her lips. Her frank language shot through him to leave him shuddering and, knowing it, she grinned into her wine glass. "Not that I'm not still super horny all the time."

"I get that impression while talking to you online, I must admit…" Glancing askance, his eyes again crossing over that shelf of family pictures, Harold felt obliged to deepen his sense of shame by asking, "How old are you, Dottie?"

"Can't you just look it up in my employee file like I assume you did my address?"

It hadn't even crossed his mind, focused as he'd been on getting her address—besides, he was only interested in her age in context. "Women lie about their ages all the time."

"They can't on driver's licenses!"

"Fake drivers' licenses aren't so hard to buy…I have a friend whose license has said 18 for a few years now. She gets another one every year."

With a delightful toss of her head, the merry girl asked, "Really! What a lot of work, who'd want to do that?"

The woman in question was a prostitute and having an ID that claimed she was eighteen was very good for business.

Harold smiled thinly and whitewashed it, saying, "Vanity, I suppose."

"No kidding…well, it makes me feel better to know you know other young(ish) people, but I'm still worried you'll think I'm too young for you." With a wrinkle of her nose and a playful curl of her pouting lips, Dottie said with a bashful look into, then up from her wineglass, "I'm twenty-four."

Harold groaned in agony. It was one thing when it was a prostitute claiming to be eighteen forever, or even actually being eighteen…but when courting an unpaid girl the age gap humiliated him. "More than thirty years between us…what's wrong with me?"

"Yeah, you dirty old man, what is wrong with you?" Her expression sly above her girlishly bitten, wine-stained lips, Dottie hid her jaw behind her glass. "Bad old cradle-robber. You're old enough to be my daddy."

This girl was going to kill him. "Sadly that's true, but—"

"It's not sad." With an aggressive bump of her knee against his, Dottie lowered her glass and let it hang from a hand whose elbow propped against the back of the futon. "Older men and hot young women have been fucking each other since Biblical times…probably since we were living in caves." Then, free hand reaching up to toy with her ponytail: "You do want to fuck me, right?"

"Oh, Christ, Dottie! Yes." The words escaped from him in one fast breath before he could stop them, before he could so much as think another thing. While he sat with his shame Dottie grinned, shielding that grinning mouth with the tip of her ponytail and the pale fingers pinching it. As her knee slid up over his, hooking across his lap to let her leg wind between his limbs, Harold managed to breathe again and used his breath to whisper earnestly, "Yes, yes, very much. I find you very attractive."

"I find you super-attractive, too. Now that I know who you are, anyway…I mean, you've always been good-looking, but a lot of gross, creepy perverts are handsome. But now that I realize you're my friend…" The girl drained her glass and wiped the back of her hand over her lips, banishing the bloody tint of wine as she had earlier the remnants of his kiss. "Does anybody else anywhere know you're into Dolcett? A girlfriend or anything? I thought I read in Forbes that you were married once."

"A few years." Leaning forward, Harold took up the bottle to refill her glass before topping his own off with a few splashes. "Molly never knew. She wouldn't have understood and I was too ashamed."

"Ashamed! Really? Gosh, I'm sorry. For me it's all just—" Gasping, the girl reached out and clutched his now free hand as he sat back in his seat. "Oh," she began while he, reeling, adjusted to the venom in her cobra strike of a touch, "oh, gosh, you know when I call you things like 'dirty' and 'weird,' you know I'm not—I don't want you to think I don't like you, is all."

There was no helping it. The animal in him rose up in those seconds, too great, too hungry. Her hand on his, her brow furrowed with darling concern: he kissed her, an impulse like a slap, his lips brushing hers as hers earlier had so unexpectedly consumed his. The girl's breath hitched and she yielded the inner workings of her mouth in an instant, her wine-flavored lip falling open like a flower to submit the nectar of her tongue. In the commingling of their breaths was born a perfume like none Harold had experienced: consciousness of that splendid scent, that gentle flavor, snapped him out of the passion of the kiss and into the shocking reality of it all. Panting, he drew away, and colored down to her heaving bust by a new scarlet hue, Dottie slowly permitted her eyes to reopen.

"You're really a pervert, though. I really do think you're a pervert." Each whisper cast another alluring puff of breath across his lips and cheeks, each nerve hyper-aroused, eager to receive the slightest stimulation from her body. "But it's okay, because I'm a pervert, too."

"How does a girl so young ever think this way?" Fascinated by her, unable to lean either to her or away, Harold searched her face for some answer—some sign of the true inner workings of her mind. "What are you doing, running around in these depraved circles online?"

"Practicing my drawing, of course." With a roguish lift of her eyebrows and a new, madder grin, Dottie sipped a mouthful of her wine, head titled back so she could part her lips and let him admire the flow of the crimson fluid back over her pretty pink tongue. "If you mean how I got into Dolcett stuff, well—gosh! Now I'm the one who's embarrassed."

"I must love to see you embarrassed then," he told her while she looked blushingly away. "You are so beautiful, Dottie…come now, you've never told me. I'm dying to know how you became so interested."

"Well…I started out—looking for, um." Her eyes rolled with embarrassment. After another fortifying sip of wine, she admitted, "Like, asphyxiation porn."

"Really!"

"Uh-huh…around the time I was in college strangling was super-hot to me"—Imagine a girl like this admitting a thing like that! Ah, his body was hollow, everything replaced with burning, abominable lust—"but I had a really hard time finding good artwork…and obviously videos were out. I mean, girls get choked in porn all the time, but—well. You know what I wanted."

No doubt if he could have seen his own face it would have reflected the bleak aspect of hers, the grim self-knowledge of the horrors that so pleased them. "Yes."

"So I drew my own, but I kept looking. Also, I just didn't have any place to share my artwork… You can't make art in a void forever. Sometime, someday, you want somebody else to see it. Do you draw or anything?"

"Oh, no, no"—Harold laughed at that, a few short bursts of noise like she had told a joke, and as she smiled he wondered if he had ever laughed in front of her before—"no, I'm afraid I'm not very artistic at all. Not very creative with anything except how to make money."

She gasped, almost insulted, sitting up stock straight as if stung by a wasp on that graspable ass of hers. "That's not true! You give me such great drawing ideas all the time. I love drawing for you. You've been my muse since the first time we talked." Another red sip. "Can you believe that was three years ago? Gosh—you talking to me wasn't the reason you had to get divorced, was it?"

"No, that was before." The wine had settled into his body; he was getting braver and (though not without caution, without slow restraint) dared to lower his free hand upon the knee still hooked over his. When the girl sighed, he commenced to gently pet that warm joint through the denim. "Would you judge me if I said something absolutely pathetic?"

"Only if you asked me nicely."

Why was she so hot to him? Christ, an incorrigible brat, that mouth never stopped. It flared his blood again as he confessed, now able to look her in the face with the help of the wine, "I'm not sure I've ever been with anybody who was actually attracted to me. And vice versa. Nobody's ever known who I was, ever."

"God, me neither. I stopped dating last year, around the time I came to work for the company...I didn't have time, working full-time and drawing all night, plus chatting, it was like—well." She laughed. "I'd rather spend hours waiting for you to come online so I could talk to you for even five minutes. I guess I'm pretty pathetic, too."

"No—no, Dottie, oh, you make me feel so good, I—" The air heaved from his lungs in a sigh of longing and Harold looked away, unable to bear her beauty all over again. "It's not fair of me to say that Molly—my ex-wife—that Molly and I never got along. We did. Nor is it fair of me to blame her for not loving the real person I am, because I never let her see that person. I've never let anyone I cared about see that person. It's too—I can't." His hands were numb to say such things aloud. When was the last time he had spoken so much at once? He tossed back the rest of his wineglass, eschewing his usual refinement in such matters as wine tasting, and leaned forward across Dottie's knee to reclaim the bottle. "The consequences could be so high if someone who I thought might accept me could not. And I knew Molly could never accept me."

"Then why did you marry her?"

"Oh, I don't know…people, especially single people in middle age, make stupid decisions. Tell themselves stupid things. "I can control myself," the say. "I can change." "I can settle down and pretend like I'm normal and never acknowledge what it takes to get me off." But living like that—after awhile I just couldn't touch her. To even get it up, let alone to finish, I had to think the most awful things, and whether I was thinking those things about her or about someone else it felt like such an evil thing, such a betrayal of her trust, that I couldn't. I couldn't make myself do it. I couldn't even look her in the eye until she served me the papers. Then I felt for the first time in years like I could think my own thoughts without betraying someone else, whatever it said about me or my soul. Oh, I was relieved."

Had he really said all that? This wine: high proof, dastardly stuff. Yes, dastardly. He checked the label while Dottie, having listened saintly through this pained confession, placed a hand over his chest and caused his heart to miss a beat. As he looked back at her, she said with a kind expression, "I didn't realize you were such a gentle man."

"I'm not, really…that's the problem. I wish I was gentle or sensitive. Inside of my head, though, it's all…Marquis de Sade."

"But you are gentle and sensitive, or you wouldn't feel so twisted up about it! Look—have you ever really hurt anybody? Like, killed them and ate them?"

The very question sent a pulse of desire racing through him but he was forced to confess, "No, of course not."

"Would you if you could? Well, I mean, I guess you could. You have all the money you could ever need—I see your name in the news, attached to charities and donations and whatever, and our company is doing all this philanthropic stuff all the time…so you must have some moral sense, some sensitivity—some empathy, I guess—to keep you from spending your money on bad things instead of good things."

"I wouldn't say all the things I spend money on are good things, but you are right…I try to better people's lives, not to hurt them. I think—you know, when I was looking around online, before I found the Dolcett community, I wasn't very interested in the content I discovered because on a superficial level so much of what I found was depicted as non-consensual."

"Yes!" Enthusiastically, Dottie lifted her head from out of her hand, spreading her fingers and saying, "The consent is the hot part—the desire, the craving to be consumed! Yes, I totally agree."

"Yes…but real life isn't like that, of course. Almost nobody's lining up to be eaten and those that are generally aren't the type one wants to eat…or should eat, anyway. And it's not as easy for even the wealthy to escape the consequences of consensual murder as fiction would have you expect. So, to say I'm putting my money into good works because I am good…I wouldn't say that. I am putting my money into good works for want of anything more pleasurable, more customized, to do with it. Were the universe in which I lived a more depraved one, I cannot say I would not, with absolute glee, throw myself into the sanctioned hobbies of the land."

"Well…you're in a different universe, now." Lip disappearing once more behind those white little teeth, Dottie tangled her fingers into the locks of the ponytail he wanted to yank while he fucked her from behind. "My apartment is totally different place."

"Careful, Dottie."

The crimson of her face deepening at his warning, she continued, listing toward him, "No, really—I want you to feel like you can be totally honest with me. I want to know every filthy, fucked up thing inside your head…I love it when you tell me your ideas." A flare of inspiration illuminating her face, Dottie lowered her voice in the manner of her sagging bedroom eyelids. "How would you eat me?"

The fear again! Sweeping through him, clutching his arms like the cold fingers of death. He grew absolutely still. "Dottie…Dottie, I don't—"

"No!" Her sharp order startled him and he jolted back a degree, the shock sufficient that he yielded the wine glass right off when she took it from his hand. Setting it alongside hers upon the table, Dottie said sternly, "You have to tell me… you have to be honest with me. Now's our chance to be honest with each other. Okay? So you have to—"

"It was the prostitutes," he confessed at that, because she was right, she was right, oh, God, she was absolutely right. He had to tell her now or he would try to hide it forever. At her look of surprise, he studied her colorful fish swimming in the distance and explained, voice softer, "I was spending a lot of money on prostitutes, and Molly noticed. She hired a private detective and the detective—I won't bore you, it's a trite and classic story. However, neither she nor the private detective realized why I was bringing the girls to our country house."

Breathless, her pupils tiny pinpoints of psychopathic excitement evident even in the corner of his focus, Dottie asked, "What were you doing with them?"

"All kinds of things…whatever I couldn't bring myself to so much as think near Molly. Spanking, whipping"—he dared glance at her as he added—"asphyxiation. Bondage." Her pale chest heaved in the black frame of her t-shirt, that small bust accentuated by the fast rhythm of her pumping lungs. As, inch by inch, she used that pre-hooked knee to insidiously slide into his lap, Harold went on in a murmur, "After awhile the ones that were open to the idea got comfortable with letting me work olive oil into their flesh…letting me fuck them with an apple in their mouth." Her hitched breath so stirred him he felt obliged to further admit, "One lets me put her in the oven as long as the other girls are around."

"Fuck." Dottie gasped as, with her now in his lap, his hand boldly rested in the small of her back, then slid down that smooth curve to fit against her rump. Ah! Dottie's wonderful ass, he was touching it, really! His hand seemed close to bursting into flame, a risk all the more imminent as she whispered, "That's super fucking hot, Harold. Why didn't you ever tell me about this during our chats?"

"Too embarrassing to talk about, even online…but you're right. I don't want to lie to you, Dottie. This opportunity—I'd like to feel less alone."

"Me, too, oh, Harold, I don't want to be alone anymore—please—"

Both sets of self-control collapsed, an indecisive waveform realized at last in action. Harold sank his fingers deep into the flesh of her wonderful ass while she lunged up at him in a kiss, each humming, gasping in primal desire for the other's taste. Her teeth (perfect pearls, by God) scraped his lip and he cried softly into her mouth, then again in sorrow as she lifted her head away. Somehow in the scramble she had managed to straddle his lap and now knelt over it, one hand on each of his shoulders, the predatory loveliness of her face hovering mere inches from his.

"Are you farsighted," she asked, "or nearsighted?"

He laughed at the oddity of the question, answering, "Nearsighted," to which the girl beamed while removing her own glasses.

"I figured, since I've never seen you without them. Me, too! That's good—I want to see your eyes while you tell me how you've been thinking about eating me."

Again, he froze: now that she was free of her glasses, oh, no…no, no, he almost couldn't stand it. Her perfect, naked features. Jove! Like seeing the face of God unclothed. The vision seared his eyes, the shades of her lashes black as the beauty mark now unhampered and aggressively glamorous. Nascent crows' feet appeared with her smile and oh, oh! He loved her smile! It hypnotized him: he cringed in surprise when she reached up and, with careful fingertips, eased the corrective frames from his face.

Silent, still smiling, Dottie looked into his face; her smile widened and, tongue playfully jutting through her teeth, she turned away, reverently folded his glasses to set beside hers. Then, turning back to him, her hands lifted into her long black hair to let it tumble, untamed, from its ponytail. "What do you want to do to me, Harold?"

"I want to fuck your screaming little body until you bleed, Dottie."

"Oh"—an astonishingly sexual moan, as if she had been penetrated by his very words; his cock throbbed in his trousers while the girl, still poised above, ran her fingers through her liberated locks—"just before you kill me, Daddy?"

"Christ—ah, before—" He gasped, not just to be thus called by her but to see her face half-hidden by her hair. Unable to help himself, he reached up to run his fingers through those wonderful locks, to press them to his lips and nose and inhale, eyes squeezed shut while she laughed at his wretched pleasure. "Before and, yes, maybe even after. You would be sexy even as a corpse, oh…I don't know if I could help myself."

"Fuck—yeah, all drained of blood and *mutilated*, oh, oh Harold! How would you kill me?"

"I'd strangle you to death with my bare hands." The little strumpet moaned and pushed his face away from her hair to remove her shirt, leaving Harold so staggered by the sight of her bust and tempting, tight stomach that he had to cover his mouth as he extolled, "Watch that pretty tongue of yours thrash in your lips, your mouth, oh, Dottie! I want to eat your tongue—all of you, oh, Christ, your cheeks, your thighs, your hot, ripe little ass."

"Yes, yes! Oh, tell me, please, please—help me out of these fucking jeans, Harold, I can't stand it—"

Neither could he. While their panting lips again made contact and Dottie contorted to remove her bra, Harold's fumbling fingers managed to make quick work of the button of those tight jeans. "You're a fucking disgusting, sick piece of shit, Harold! Oh, I love it. How would you cook me?"

"So many ways, oh, Dottie, Dottie—ah!" Her bare breasts were so soft and pale, still so pert—none of the girls he paid were so agonizingly beautiful. Dottie made him wish to weep. His hands fit to her tight waist while his head lowered to permit him to bury his face in her breasts, where every gasp filled his lungs with the Circe odor of her bosom and left him more and more an animal. "A tender rump roast, a marvelous little roast carved out of that pretty body of yours. Have to hang you upside down first, of course, before the carving, drain out all the blood. What would I do with all of that? Bathe in it, maybe."

"Harold, Harold, Harold, I love your fucked-up brain— oh, Christ, I wish I could cut open your head and lick that dirty fucking frontal lobe in there."

Her jeans were down around her thighs, and, with a dry sob, he clutched her body to him. Harold leaned her back to permit his kisses down her bosom, over taut nipples, along the curve of her ribs peering through the veil of her flesh—an anticipating bride. While she gasped and he pushed her aside, out of his lap and down into the futon so he could pull her jeans completely off of her, Harold whispered hoarsely, "I wish you could, too. I wish you could open my head and I could watch—that I could watch from my own body as you cut me up, dismember me."

Softly, the girl laughed. So cute. He loved her laugh, oh,

her laughter made his dick hard. Everything about her made his dick hard. At last her jeans were free of her legs. After tossing them aside, he straightened up and looked down on her, agonized, one hand tangling in his short hair to see Dottie naked except for her appropriately polka-dotted underwear. "I wish you could watch it, too," she whispered, one hand resting upon the pillow beside her cheek, one leg bending at the knee in invitation to his gaze. "I wish all kinds of things…but I'm so fucking glad you found me. So glad I drew that stupid girl."

"Don't say that…I love that girl. Dottie…" His focus was entirely devoted to those bikini cut undies: even with her as she was, he couldn't make himself remove them. Sensing his weakness, Dottie smiled up at him.

"You want to watch me take off my panties, huh, Harold?" His eyes lifted to hers again and she giggled. "Okay, I'll take them off…but you can't watch. You make me feel too dirty, you lewd old predator. Close your eyes."

"Dottie!"

"I'll let you see my pussy eventually…but you're so scared of me. I think you should get used to touching me before you look at me. Here." Dottie beckoned him with a languid arm. As he knelt at her side, she sat up to slide his tie from around his neck. "Are you going to let me choke you with one of these ties sometime?" A bashful glance up from beneath her lashes—oh, he was an absolute sucker.

"You could do it now if you wanted."

She looked tempted, eyeing it even as she freed the fabric from his shirt collar. "I think I'll save that for when you've been a really bad boy…not that you're a good boy now, but you've been so sweet and honest with me. I think it's reasonable for me to do something nice for you in exchange. Close your eyes."

He did, sighing as her cool little hand trailed over his face. Once she had caressed his cheek and teased around the shell of his ear, her other hand smoothed the silk of the tie over his eyes. She leaned toward him, the floral scent of her body overwhelming to his senses while her hands coordinated in the back of his head to secure the impromptu blindfold.

"Okay, Harold. Almost there…almost time for me to take off my cute little panties for you. Maybe if you do a good job fucking me I'll let you take them home with you, as long as you promise to send me some really pathetic videos of you jerking off on them."

"Christ, Dottie—"

The tinkling sound of her laugh was, when paired with no visual, more frightening than ever. "But first," she continued, "you have to take off *your* clothes, Harold. Go on…stand up."

He obeyed, swaying uneasily to his feet with a soft gasp when her hand landed on his thigh. That dangerous paw of hers trailed up, up, and they both groaned at the same time. "Are you kidding me?" The girl gasped, hand lingering there, leaving him all the harder for her experimental, appreciative, really quite demanding fondling through his trousers. "Oh, Harold, is this thing *real*? Fuck, fuck—it's so big!"

"All the better to please you with," he replied without thinking, smiling faintly at the sound of her giggle while he unbuttoned his shirt. All the while Dottie caressed him through his trousers and every stroke pulsed down to the very tips of his toes, the edges of his fingers.

"Have you ever jerked off to the thought of me, Harold? Me as your secretary—before you knew who I was, I mean… after all, I know you were jerking off when we were chatting."

"Yes." In the darkness of the tie he felt somehow liberated to say anything. It was the same sort of dissociation that made it easy for him to share whatever perverse fantasy came into his head while on the Internet. Ah, Dottie! She had a way with him, an incredible way. "Yes, Dottie. Even before I knew who you were, I was jerking off to you all the time…you're so beautiful, you've bewitched me since we met."

"What a gross pervert you are…I can't believe you'd admit something so sad and disgusting."

"I'm sorry, Dottie." His shirt hit the floor and he drew his undershirt over his head while the girl's inquisitive fingers, ceasing their inspection, unbuckled his belt.

"You should be…very, very sorry. Do you remember what I told you to say earlier?"

Fuck, of course he did. It was all he had been able to think about until standing in front of apartment 306. "I'm a dirty pig, Dottie."

"That's right, you are…real filthy swine. Take off your pants for me."

He obeyed.

"Do I have to tell you to take off your stupid socks, too?"

"God, Dottie, I'm sorry—I'm distracted, I'm an idiot—ah!"

When he bent to obey, his own belt—evidently doubled over in Dottie's hand—struck hard against the back of his boxers. "Yeah you are, you fucking moron. Some things are just obvious…it's okay. Lucky for you, IQ has nothing to do with how good a piggie tastes when it's time for him to be slaughtered, or how cute he is while he's alive. Okay…sit down."

"The boxers—"

"I'm still wearing panties, so you have to keep your underwear on, too…you can take yours off when I say, so—good boy." He had sat and now gasped as Dottie leaned in to press a lingering kiss against his desperate mouth. While his chest heaved, the girl ran the strap of the leather belt down his torso, over his stomach, and at last slapped its flat side a few brisk times against his thigh. He cried out softly while she moaned and exclaimed, "You're so much fucking fun to hurt, oh, Harold, I love being mean to you…and you love it, too! Look at that big cock in there, I'm so excited to look at it! I wonder if it'll be able to tell I'm naked even if you're blindfolded…let's see…"

Harold, afraid to so much as breathe lest he curse her or somehow cause her flight, strained to listen while the girl stepped away. The sound of flesh, soft as a whisper, akin to the caress of silk on silk—her thighs, he'd wager, brushing one another. The subtle, almost nonexistent sound of her tiny cotton panties hitting the floor. Her throaty, open-mouthed gasp and the wet tap of fluid as (sweet Mary, Mother of God—) she touched herself.

"Oh, Harold…Harold, Harold, you've made me so wet! Mr. Fleetwood…" His belt jingled as she placed it aside to enfold his hand in her cool grasp. Somehow, frightened as he was of her before the blindfold, after its application he found himself completely docile. Accepting every touch like a blinded horse, a hooded hawk. That touch guided his up, up toward her, the warmth of her body palpable before he made good his caress, then—

They both gasped. Harold profaned the name of God while the little Whore of Babylon guiding him along her soaking pussy shuddered, moaned, adjusted the spread of her legs to permit the blinded man's more thorough investigation. "Harold," she cried, hands resting in his hair, knocking the blindfold askew not near enough. Now instead of nothing he saw only a flash, a great stripe of pale flesh, an exquisite ivory tower in a snippet of periphery. The non-vision spurred his fingers and, more audacious than ever, his digits glided over her little flower's satin surface.

"Harold, oh, fuck! That's so good—oh wow, oh, most men can't find the clitoris *without* a blindfold on—"

"Oh! It's so small, oh…Dottie, you beautiful creature—I can't believe how wet you are."

"I know, I know…it's because you did it to me, you dirty, dirty old man. Making me bad like you are, oh, you've turned me into a slut already…oh, how does my pussy feel, Harold? Is my tight little cunt as nice as the whores you pay to fuck and whip and eat? God! I wish you really ate them, Harold— Harold, I want to kill and eat other sexy girls with you, yes, and then—and then when we've done it all, oh! Oh, all the different ways, then you can eat *me*, Harold, oh, fuck—oh, Harold"—the futon depressed beside him as the girl, still standing, propped one foot to spread her legs while remaining upright—"Harold, eat me now, eat my pussy, please, I bet you're just a fucking king at it—"

What was this woman? Where had she come from? How did a girl get like this—like someone he had never dreamed could exist in the same world as him? Maybe it was all the years of secretive fantasizing that had drawn them together, their mutual sets of perverse mental images harmonizing them. Magnetizing them. Harold slid to his knees and removed his exploring finger from between those ultra-soft lips, replacing it with a mouth that kissed around her thighs and pelvis until, at her frustrated whining, it planted over her dripping little cunt to yield an immediate cry.

"Harold! Oh, shit! Shit, I was right—oh, Christ, I've never fucked an older man, a dirty old man like you before…you're so good, so good. I'll never date a boy my age again!"

Low in his chest, Harold groaned, staving off protests that if she did he hoped he'd get to watch. Instead he ground his nose against her to her satisfying yelp of pleasure, his well-trained tongue flickering into her sopping hole to find it gasp-inducingly tight. "Surely you're not a virgin," he remarked, leaving her to laugh amid her moans.

"No, no, but you make me feel like one—oh! I get that fucking song now…yes, I get it, the beginning of *Reservoir Dogs* was right, it is, it's because you're so good, I've never known it could be this good—Harold! Oh, Harold, I—fuck, hurry, faster, Harry, faster—"

He had never felt a woman become so aroused so fast before. Groaning, he wrapped his arms up around her hips, forced her down upon his face while her nubile body thrashed. The fingers in his hair tightened, kept him in place while she ground against the tongue that fucked her almost as rapidly as his cock soon would. When finally her cries reached a fever pitch her hands released his hair, and, to his sublime thrill, Dottie yanked the blindfold from his eyes. There she was all at once, an extreme angle at first—but soon, almost sobbing his name with the power of her orgasm, she cringed away and gave him a good look at every last inch of her worshipful flesh. The lips of her shaved pussy glistened bright pink in the apartment's light and a dangling strand of her fragrant pleasure, evidently having been stuck to his mouth, dripped away to leave his lust irresistible. It was as if her body summoned his: he could no longer deny their urges to come together.

The girl, panting, seemed about to say something else but gasped as he tore her down from where she stood to hold her in his arms. "You're so fucking hot." She stared up into his face, hers ruby with love's youthful afterglow. "And so romantic."

"Should I be ready to pull out?"

She laughed gaily at his crass question on the heels of such a compliment and said, "It doesn't matter."

Taking that to mean she was on birth control, Harold drew the girl upright with him and, disguising the effort required (an effort in and of itself), he picked her up and carried her squealing body to the bedroom. A charming room—fragrant like her, full of drapes and scarves and fabrics that left the environment alluring as the folds crying out to him while he lay her on the star-dotted bed cover.

"I still can't believe this," she said, her tone a dreamy murmur. Taking a brief interlude from the ferocity of their passion to mutually enjoy the effects of the post-orgasmic state upon her body, Harold lay petting her in her bed. "You're the sexiest man I've ever known…and you're Mr. Fleetwood."

"Pretty Dottie…how are we ever going to make it through another day at work?"

"By thinking lots and lot of dirty thoughts and waiting for it to be over…oh, Harold." Pawing at his chest, the girl begged sweetly, "I want to see it—please? Please, can I see your cock? I bet it's so pretty."

Exhaling, Harold kissed that addictive mouth and sought to please her. When the boxers were away he lifted his head from the kiss and she glanced down with a sharp, high gasp, a little pre-agonized moan that furrowed her brow and left her eyes bright when they raised back to his face. "Oh, Harold! Jesus, you're so big, oh…is there anything about you that's not sexy?"

"Most women wouldn't exactly call my interests "sexy."" She pushed on his chest; he gave into the pressure and let her roll him upon his back, his head landing on a pillow that filled his lungs with Dottie-scent. "Most would think me abhorrent…a latent criminal, if not an active one."

"Mm, well, your interests are sexy to me…you're sexy to me, the sexiest man I've ever known." Her kisses were so insensibly wonderful, left him so high—he sighed into every one until she drew away, and even after found more than a few helpless moans rising from his lips while she kissed her way down his throat, his clavicle, his chest. At his navel, she regarded the throbbing member whose twitching had brushed her ear. "It's so hard, oh, poor Harold…does it hurt?"

"Oh, it's agony…the accumulation of all the agony you've caused me. All the times it's hurt me to look at you."

Those precious dimples, oh, those innocent little angel kisses in her cheeks—he would never be able to see them again without remembering that moment, the first time she took his straining cock in her soft hand, her grin ear-to-ear as she did. "You dirty old man…trying to blame me for this… oh, it's so hard—it couldn't possibly be my fault that this big thing is so hard, is it?"

"It is, oh…Christ, you cocktease"—if he'd had any hesitance about returning to her all the name-calling she delivered so freely, it vanished at the sound of her gasp and a look of dreamy lust—"ever since you've figured out I'm into Dolcett you've pranced around that office sexier than ever, and now today—ah!" He cried out as her lips pursed against his hyper-sensitized glans, a dot of precum hanging to her lips to be swept up by that wicked tongue. "Oh, Dottie…yes, you're to blame, you're absolutely to blame, you hot little slut."

"How can I help being a slut for you when you've got a thing like this hidden in your pants?" Her cheek rested against his shaft, smile widening as that engorged desire pulsed against her face. "All this time you've had this! You never needed money…you could have just found yourself a sugar momma and called it good. I'm so glad you didn't, though…because you're here with me instead."

Her lips parted. That red tongue, a ribbon of wet velvet, trailed out over his prick. Harold, nearly stung by the intensity of the pleasure and the surrealness of it all, cried out against the soft anguish of a chemistry like he'd never felt. Not a gentle chemical reaction: a combustion. When her tongue again vanished, she made up for it by nuzzling sweetly against his manhood, eyes turning toward him in a winsome girlish plea. "Will you tell me some more ways you'll cook me someday while I go down on you?"

"Dottie, Dottie…oh, of course. Ah—" He exhaled, shuddering as that smiling mouth overtook him in an instant, a snake swallowing a mouse—no, a rat. A filthy, dirty rat. He had no business profaning such a gorgeous young girl, and that notion made him all the harder. While Dottie moaned at the sensation, Harold caught his breath and confessed:

"Ah—you know, ah, oh, maybe December (yes, yes it was December, it was, oh, fuck—), I asked—Christ—Christ, Dottie, oh, I asked you online to—to draw that girl being spit-roasted over the Christmas fire—"

"I remember." She spoke with a wet pop, lifting her grinning head to speak, her legs kicking in the air behind her like a teenager talking on the telephone instead of a dirty cannibal slut sucking her insane boss's prick. "It was fun!"

"It was inspired by you."

"No way!" Laughing, Dottie worked her hand over him, tugging gently at the base of his shaft while he suffocated. "Really, is that true?"

"Yes, yes—ah, Jesus, I heard you"—she was back at it again and he paused to cry her name, to lay a hand upon her bobbing head and keep the hair drawn back from her perfect, perfect, perfect-perfect little face—"heard you complain to the janitor about the heating system, oh, God, Dottie, do you remember what you said?" Her head shook 'no' around his dick. While she worked to force it deeper in her throat, wincing with her own effort, he choked out the words, "Oh, Dottie, I'll always remember. You didn't even think about it, just said, "I feel like I'm being roasted alive," and—Dottie, Dottie, I couldn't think of anything else for the rest of the day, the week. The only way to get you out of my head was to—to have the commission done. God, what a cold December."

Again, her head popped up, her jade eyes bright with true delight. "I wish I'd known I was drawing *myself!* I would have done a much better, more specific job. Harold…oh, my pussy is so wet. I can't wait any longer, please—"

"Yes Dottie, yes, oh, yes, yes—"

His arms extended. The girl straightened up before falling into his embrace, her mouth landing upon his, her tongue plunging in to re-explore the territory it was already learning well. He gasped as her groping hand reached between them, caressed his stomach, lifted his cock to guide him into the wet embrace of her naked cunt. Those soulful eyes found his, remained there: her brow knit and the two shared a single moan as she lowered.

Oh, Dottie. Dottie, Dottie. Harold loved women, and he loved women's pussies, but oh, of all the women and all the pussies, Dottie's was just so tight, so incredibly wet. That was the problem with fucking people you weren't really connected to, or vice versa—everybody was just trying to make the experience happen, to get through it, get it done. Dottie, oh… Dottie was the first time in years, years and years and years, quite possibly ever, that Harold had forged an emotional connection to beget such a flaming physical one.

She cried out, shocked, pained by the size of him, easing herself down farther and bracing her hands on either side of his head to manage it. "Harold, Harold! You're so big, almost too big—oh, my pussy's too small—"

"No, God, oh, darling, it's just right, just right—here, let me make it up to you, let me kiss you, kiss me, Dottie, Jesus, Dottie—how are you so beautiful to me?"

At last, at last! The pressure of her body fully enrobed him and the pair shuddered in time. He wrapped her up in his arms, holding her slight weight down against his chest while those hips fell into work that was, while not completely naïve, far from the professional experience to which he was used. And oh, he loved it. She was so natural—so focused, absolutely focused on enjoying her own pleasure while nurturing his. Trying this angle and that angle, emitting this or that sultry whisper into his eager ear. Nobody wanted to get anything over with. By God, if he could have basked in the pleasure of their first congress forever, he would have.

Alas—no relationship is without its small snafus, its occasional bumps in the road. In retrospect he rather wished she would have warned him, and spared him a bit of trauma... but if she had warned him, he wouldn't have believed her. He might even have been turned off by a perceived inability to distinguish reality and imagination. So it was better it happened the way it did, Harold did have to admit. While her hips worked, her pace increasing, Dottie bit her lip and ran her hands over his chest. "Will you do me a favor?"

"Anything, Christ, anything—I'd give you my money, my company, the flesh of my body, the head of John the Baptist on a silver platter, Dottie—"

Laughing, eyes bright, enchanted with him as he was by her, the girl drew a shoulder coyly to her cheek and sent a few disheveled strands of hair across her eyes and his. "Would you strangle me? Please? Really, really hard—I want to feel you on top of me, ch— oh!"

No need to ask twice. Harold grasped one of Dottie's powerful thighs against his body and, supporting her waist with his other arm, rolled them over. Now sweetly giggling she lay beneath him, and Harold rearranged her legs around him, found a better angle, worked himself deeper by the very stroke.

Kissing her a few times more, Harold lifted his lips to murmur, "How am I going to know when to stop?"

"I'll tap out!" She demonstrate by reaching above her head to tap a few brisk times on the rails of the wrought iron headboard. "I'll tap out, Harold, so please—oh, there's a belt I use in the nightstand there, go on—"

What a sadomasochistic man wouldn't do with his dick in a woman! Harold yanked open the drawer, rifled around, knuckled aside a dildo and found the old belt: softer than his, worn not by a waist but by a wide variety of recreational uses. "Wrap it around the rail here," she gasped, indicating the headboard. "Then you can just—just pull and it's super easy to really fucking cut off everything, blood and oxygen both, black me out—"

"Oh, Dottie, I'll hurt you—"

"Don't be scared! Please? I'll help you!" Her feral look increasing in intensity, Dottie snatched the belt from his hands and looped it through its own buckle. Then, with an arch that deepened his position inside her and made them both gasp with pleasure, she contorted her back to slide the strap around the rail of the headboard. "Okay—okay, oh, Harold, you already feel so good, oh, it almost couldn't get better but—oh, put this side around my neck like—like a collar, oh, yes—yes, your cute little pet girl, your little fuck-slave—"

That tongue of hers was dangerous. She could make him do anything. He eagerly obeyed, his cock throbbing with her every word, his body reaching a peak of pleasure for the simple act of sliding the makeshift leather noose around her neck. Dottie moaned to feel it tense around her. She lifted her head and looked up into his eyes, lips parted, that crooked cuspid bright white against the glistening tissue of her tongue.

"Go on—go on, Harold, choke me, choke me—hrngh—!"

Archimedes knew better than any of the ancients the power of the pulley, but in the throes of passion, Harold struggled to stay in touch with the dangers of the situation. This was what he knew would happen. He knew it—knew it well before even reaching her fatal hallway that things would be disastrous when he had Dottie in his hands. He knew it and did as she demanded, yanking hard on the belt while the girl gagged at the unexpected force. While her cunt clenched hard around him and he cried out, a hint of concern managed to make its way through the almost impenetrable thicket of merciless arousal. Arousal that hinged on suffering. The part of him that she had called gentle was panicking already, however. Seeing how her hands clutched at the belt, he eased his pull, plucked it loose around her neck, began to ask, "Are you—"

"Don't stop, no, don't stop, keep—urk!"

As long as she was okay. As long as she was okay and she liked it, then it was okay. Right? Fuck, ah—he liked it much too much for it to be okay. "What if I killed you, Dottie?" His words were soft, concern turning to fantasy as he pondered aloud into the beautiful green orbs bulging from her purpling face. Slowly they reddened under the pressure of his throttle, filled with lustrous tears. Her mouth, already open uselessly for air, twitched a degree wider at the question. That perfect tongue darkened, thickened, as he'd imagined it would.

"What if I killed you"—he asked it again not with concern but lascivious pleasure and marveled to feel it actually made her wetter—"and this was your last memory, Dottie, eh? Your last moment on Earth—getting fucked by a dirty, evil old man, your wicked old boss."

Her eyelids were beginning to slit shut beneath the blood pressure in her head; though her pussy was hot and tight, the rest of her was going limp. Gaining dangerous confidence, he released his grip on the belt and plucked it loose again, throbbing in her wet confines, feeling like God as she gasped to life for him.

"Ha—Harold, oh—" The girl coughed violently, the cough of a whore gagging on a dick far too big for her, and the association made his strokes within her harder while she moaned. "Keep going, Harold, keep going longer, I didn't tap out—"

"You'll pass out at this rate, oh Dottie—"

"Please, please! I want—I want—I want to share myself with you! Help me—" She reached up and now pulled the belt herself. He groaned, imagining her getting up to this, strangling herself while using that dildo every night after work. Naughty girl. He angled her hips up to pound her that much harder, then gripped her hand upon the leather strap. They pulled together, her obscene tongue lolling out of her mouth like some alien sex organ. The veins in the temples of her forehead bulged in splendid relief—her eyes rolled up in her head, a glorious replication of St. Teresa penetrated by her angel, knowing God, learning the mystical secrets of the divine. It was beautiful—so beautiful oh, Christ, yes, he wanted to fuck her to metaphysical pieces, wished he could have crammed his cock so hard into her that it touched her very soul. The harder he thrust into the pressure the more her swollen cheeks twitched, eyelids fluttered, long legs thrashed and tightened beneath him.

The belt also was tightening, tight, tighter, and she wasn't asking him to stop even though it was tight as the gorgeous pussy that fluttered, fluttered, suddenly seized with an explosive orgasm like none he'd felt a woman have. Her head slammed back into the pillow, that beautiful sex organ gripped rapidly at his; with a cry, Harold succumbed to the internal pressure. Fireworks, oh! Release. A rush of chemicals more potent than in years. Like a young man again, good God, oh, what an orgasm. Her name fell from his lips in a low groan: the last sound of an explosive skirmish before a terrible ringing of ears.

Five seconds, Harold panted through his pleasure: seconds six through seven he became aware that Dottie had gone limp. Swearing, he slid the belt loose from around her neck. Just blacked out. Wake up, Dottie—he touched her face and—

And his panic grew. Harold jerked his cock out of her and lowered his ear to her mouth. No air—no sound. He listened to her chest, pressed his fingers to her throat. His pleasure turned into a screaming nightmare.

"Oh, Jesus—Jesus, Jesus—"

He knew this was a bad idea. He knew it, knew it without question and still he did it. Still he came to her apartment. Still he fucked her. Still he agreed to share their fantasies in real life, in the same room, and even act a few of them out and now—now look what had happened. Oh, fuck. Fuck! She was really dead. He pressed his mouth to hers and blew in hurried air and pushed her chest and still—still, he was but kissing a corpse.

Harold had never killed anyone before. Ever, never. He'd thought about it many, many times in many different ways, mostly sexual—but he'd never done it, never dreamed he would really do it whether on purpose or accident. But— oh, God, not only had he killed someone, but he had killed Dottie! Young, sexy, dulcet Dottie, a lover like he'd never had, an enthusiastic proponent of erotic anthropophagy.

Beneath the panic, beneath the refrain in his head of *What do I do now*, a morbid thrill shot through him to consider Dottie's body. Dottie, naked, dead on the bed in front of him. Dead, dead. Really, truly dead. Her words in his ear, promising he could eat her someday.

Harold shuddered, covered his eyes, turned away. Fantasy was fantasy, reality was reality. He had done something abominable. Christ, what an animal he was. Really, an absolute pig: a dog, an abhorrent piece of shit. He'd killed a girl and all he could think about was how scrumptious she would taste, how hard it would make him to eat and prepare her, how he only wished she could have some way to know so her pretty pussy could get wet all over again. Ah! Damn, damn these intrusive thoughts. How could anyone be a good person—how could there be the slightest chance for anyone to be a good person—when their own mind was so constant with these wicked fantasies? He was a slave to his sinful urges. He was ashamed for not being ashamed enough over having just killed a woman and more ashamed still to find that his only thought was now how he, a wealthy man of privilege and esteem, was going to avoid paying the piper.

Not so ashamed, though, that he did not immediately leap into action. Heart pounding, unable to look at the swollen face of the corpse, Harold drew the nearest free piece of fabric over its face and grimaced to realize he'd just shrouded his victim with his own coat. Blast it—have to burn the thing. Might as well throw a few thousand in the fire. All right, think. Had to know somebody who knew a way out of this situation. Money could do anything. There had to be somebody who would take money to keep their mouth shut without making the amount unreasonable or the period of extortion too long.

After shutting the bedroom door behind him, Harold passed the closed bathroom, reclaimed his pants, and got them on while ringing his oven girl, Simonetta. "Hi sweetie," she began, "can I—"

"I need to talk to you right now, I'm afraid. It's urgent. Please—ah, you're not alone are you?"

"Uh-oh…for a tone like that, I can be."

"I may need you to come out and—consult for me."

"What the fuck does that mean? Hold on." The line filled with rustling. Simonetta's voice in the distance, interspersed with indiscernible male protest: "Sorry baby, it's a real emergency…I'll give you twenty minutes for free later, but I gotta take this. Why don't you wait in your—hey, fuck you! Some people have lives, asshole. Yeah, well—yeah, why don't you suck your *own* dick, then! "Unprofessional" my ass, what the fuck kind of thing is that to say to—get the fuck out of here! For all you know this is my pimp calling, I'll tell him to come break your fucking nose…yeah, I'll bet. See you, fuckface, call somebody else next time."

A door slammed in the background. Harold, trying not to be frustrated, sat staring out the window beside the fish with one hand on his forehead. "Okay," said Simonetta into the phone as if he hadn't just heard her throw out her current John. "What's the problem?"

"I can't—I think it's easier to talk about in person, Simonetta."

"I'm like an hour away from the city right now, baby… maybe two if traffic's bad."

Squeezing shut his eyes, Harold said, "I don't care. I understand. Please, Simonetta, just—get here. I need your advisement in a…situation at a friend's house. There's…an… item that needs to be—removed." The line was absolutely still and he prayed he had not made a mistake by entrusting his freedom to this shrewd young businesswoman. "I've never dealt with…one of these…things, and…I think you may know someone who is able to help, possibly."

"Possibly," agreed Simonetta. The line went quiet again for another long, painful five seconds until she heaved a long sigh. "Jesus, I—I don't know, Harold."

"Please, please. I don't know if there's anyone else I could call, I—" Oh, he was truly pathetic. "I'm afraid. I feel like I'm in a nightmare, please. I need your help."

"Christ. Okay. Why don't you let me come over and—if I get sent up the river for helping you—"

"I promise I'll protect you, Simonetta, but I need"—a bolt of panic whizzed through him as a knock reverberated through the apartment, oh, Jesus, he looked at the front door—"I need your advice in this matter. I need your network and—" Another brisk knock. His stomach twisted. "I need to go."

"Okay. Text me the address and call me if anything changes."

They hung up, he typed Dottie's address, and, at the third repetition of knocks, Harold made his uneasy way through the living room and picked up his lost undershirt on the way. This, he pulled over his head while reciting the conversation he'd have to have with someone he assumed to be the cops. Yes, he was braced. He would look through that peephole, out into the hallway, see the black hats, hear the reports of a disturbance, oh, goodness, officer, how strange. He made sure he had his wallet on him before even approaching the door.

Yet—looking through the peephole, there was no one. Nothing. Had there not just been three bursts of knocking? With a frown, Harold unlocked the door, peered cautiously into the hall. Empty up and down. Not even anybody going in or coming out of their apartment. Crickets.

Another burst of knocking jolted through Harold's body. White terror rose up in a vile ocean—terror and relief. The knocking came from elsewhere in the apartment. Dottie! Dottie! Dottie was still alive? Thank God! Harold shut the door and hurried, throwing open the bedroom with relief. "Dottie, I—"

A corpse on a bed. No, no, he was going mad. Oh, he was mad—these knocks, like Macbeth's voice screaming "Sleep no more!" A hallucination. A persistent one that now, he realized, emanated not from the front door, or the bedroom door…but the bathroom door.

No. Had there been someone listening in all the time? Now terror was augmented by fury. Had Dottie been playing a practical joke by seducing him? Hiding some boyfriend to listen and jeer and maybe even blackmail? No, no, their chemistry had been too real. It couldn't be faked, couldn't—

The bathroom doorknob rattled. Another knock. Oh, God, God, help him. What was this? A bad dream? Had she drugged him? Just his guilty conscience…it certainly wasn't a ghost. There was no such thing. No: there was only madness in this world. And, by God, Harold was many things, but he was not mad.

Resolve set, Harold assured himself he was an adult, a grown man. There was some plausible explanation for these noises, this banging. No more substantial than a spiritualist's knockings during a séance. In fact, yes! Perhaps it was only a pipe. He would open that bathroom door, and everything would be fine. A woman would still be dead, but there would be no boyfriend, no ghosts, no madness. Just bathroom.

Instead…instead, he threw open the door and found Dottie wrapped in a robe, post-coitally flushed, hands on her hips as she huffed a sigh of relief. That beautiful face, mole at the corner of her eye and all, glowed with her glorious smile.

"There we go—thanks! Sorry about that, this door gets stuck all the—oh, Harold—!"

5.

WHERE WAS HE? What time was it? Harold grimaced, reflexively touching his skull, briefly squeezing shut his eyes again at the throbbing of his headache. He tried to sit up but a hand cool as the lunar surface stayed him, brought him leaping back to the present with a startled gasp from his wincing lips.

"Hey! Don't sit up so fast, be careful—are you okay?"

That voice. "Dottie—" Weakly, Harold tried to turn his head but instead exhaled as the girl's furrowed brow leaned into his field of vision. "Am I in your bed?"

"Good thing it didn't get spoiled! I didn't eat all day hoping to keep it nice…it paid off! I'm sure famished now, though."

He had no idea what she was talking about. Try something else. "What happened?"

"You passed out by the bathroom! I had to carry you in here…you don't look like you're that heavy." A worried frown contorting her lips to make them even more attractive, Dottie gently petted his face and hair. "How do you feel? Can I get you some water?"

He could not make sense of it—of her, of this, of anything. He managed now to tilt his head and found only himself and Dottie in the bed, but…but there was the belt, sitting on the nightstand. The girl followed his gaze and bit her lip, one hand coyly fitting against his own to pet his palm and tickle his forearm.

"I'm sorry…I should have warned you, but I just—I've never told anybody before, and I didn't know how to do it. You wouldn't have believed me, anyway. Just better to demonstrate."

"I'm not sure I understand."

"I barely do, myself!" Her grin widened cheekily, that mischief sparkling in her eyes to leave her all the more charming. All the more terrifying. "You should be glad…I thought about really messing with you there for a minute. Like, letting you go home thinking I was dead forever, then showing up at work like normal. But that just seemed too mean. And I want to be mean to you, but not that mean. You might not forgive me! So I just said to myself, you know… get it over with. Then let him decide what he wants to do. Besides…" She bashfully looked at the fingers he wove into hers while he listened. "You were honest with me about some hard things, so it's only fair I'm honest with you."

Nothing was connecting in his brain. He floated on words—on ceaseless gratitude to God like a man waking from a dream in which he had found himself a senseless murderer. With a long exhalation of relief to think consciously of his panic from before and its living resolution now, Harold pressed the pillow-flesh of her palm to his lips tried not to weep. He failed, at least for a few appreciative sobs.

"I thought you were dead! Dottie, I thought—I just don't understand."

"I know." Her tone was gentle and soothing as that of a mother to her sick child. With the same tenderness, Dottie slipped her hand out of his to pet his aching forehead. He sighed and pressed his face into her cool, cool palms as she went on. "I still don't really understand, myself…Dad thought I was some kind of demon the first time it happened."

"But *what* happened?"

"I died." Dottie said this with a laugh and the shrug of a shoulder that emerged from the robe sagging robe. "I was eight. It was terrible. I didn't realize, though. My dad came home and found me." She laughed again. It was the most humorless laugh he had ever heard—an affront to laughter, to joy itself. "He killed himself a couple days later. He couldn't stand it, couldn't handle it."

"Oh, Dottie!"

"I've never let anybody else find out." Those beautiful eyes of hers looked too old. Barely understanding still, feeling now more than ever as though he were in a dream, Harold sat up to marvel at his unexpected lover. "I just thought, you know, like you did: live life and go about your business and hide who you are, you'll be fine…nobody has to know. It's not that important for somebody to be known by somebody else, right? People live their whole lives sometimes without ever having spent a day as themselves…what did it matter if I hid who I was? But…"

She drummed her fingertips against her jaw, then covered her smile to hide it from Harold—a schoolgirl overwhelmed by a first crush. "But I found Dolcett. And that was a good outlet at first. I was just in it for the strangling for a long time but, well, you know how these things escalate. Crossbreed. I don't know how to explain it. But the community art wasn't up to my standards and I was like, great, here's an artistic niche I can improve…and then I met you. And now I've really met you. And…you've really met me."

God, yes.

Yes, he had met Dottie.

Without the slightest idea what to say, Harold looked at the belt, then down at the bedside where the body once lay. "How—how do you…come back?"

"I don't really know! It seems like it's always through the last big mirror I looked into…when I was a little kid I used to think of it, like, a videogame save point. *Alice in Wonderland.* My vision fades out, and I fade back in staring at myself in a mirror, and then it's like, oh, yes, here I am, alive again, over here now instead of where I just was. It's like becoming conscious of myself, I guess. My new body."

"And the old body?"

Jesus, those dimples. Those dimples, those dimples. He wanted to gnaw them off her pretty fucking face. "It's in the bathroom," she said, her tone one mastered by only the grandest coquettes. "Wanna see my corpse?"

Dick hard as a rock, Harold stood between meat-Dottie lying naked in the bathtub and person-Dottie behind him, wrapped in her robe, pressing against his back to wind her arms around his waist. "I've never had anybody I can show this to before," she said softly, cheek pressed to his back while, stunned, he looked in slow-to-grow belief (astonishment, inspiration, adoration) at the carcass of the same girl who swayed against him, caressed his chest, kissed his shoulders through his shirt. "Usually when this kind of thing happens to me, well, it's inconvenient to say the least…I've had to run away to start again a few times and just kind of hope. It's worked out, but…"

"What a waste."

"That's what I thought, too…" Her hand trailed over the front of his trousers and, breath hitching, Harold studied the purple face and saffron skin of their exquisite corpse. Yes, theirs, like a child—a body engendered by their passion. She continued. "But what was I going to do with it, all by myself? And if I got caught…what a nightmare. Prosecuted for my own murder!"

At the sliding away of her hands and her tug on the back of his waistband, Harold turned to stare down into Dottie's face. Her low eyelids, her tousled hair, her appealing lip-bite, oh! Everything about her calculated to incite his lust. Oh, Dottie…Dottie was perfect as Harold was pathetic. Dottie was beautiful as a neon sign in the night, that bright beacon indicating the vacancy of an unexpected inn.

Dottie was everything Harold had never even dreamed he could have wanted, because he had never even imagined she could exist.

"So"—she stared hopefully up into his eyes—"here I am. The real me." Anxious, (the lamb!), she took his hands in hers, swung them back and forth, pressed them to her warm little bosom. Beneath beat the heart: her heart, sustaining the life that he had not long before himself ended.

"Now that you know me…still want to be friends?"

EPISODE 2
DOTTIE CAN'T DIE

1.

HAROLD'S PHYSICIAN SLID back upon the rolling wheels of his stool and once again studied the MRI information. "Fit as a fiddle," said Dr. Ernst while his patient tuned back into reality, away from intrusive thoughts of sensual Dottie and the agonizing nearness of the weekend. "Definitely nothing to be worried about…though it might help me if you gave me a better idea of what I'm looking for."

"You're the doctor, aren't you? You could be looking for anything, I don't know what's what when it comes to the structure of the brain—I fell and hit my head. It's reasonable for me to want your opinion."

"Yes, but—" Clearly aggrieved to be put through this blind ordeal by a patient too wealthy to fire from the practice, the handsome young doctor drummed his pen on the desk, ran a hand over his square jaw, said, "I guess I'm confused because, well—even my most frivolous patients don't generally come in asking to pay out-of-pocket for an MRI when they're not showing symptoms like, I don't know…blinding headaches or sudden vision failure."

"Hallucinations?"

One black brow arched high upon the doctor's forehead. "*Are* you hallucinating?"

Harold leaned back in his cramped exam room chair, already regretting this futile exercise of multiple annoying steps that had started Monday when he arranged the MRI. "That would be the easier explanation, but I don't think I'm hallucinating. This would be quite a complex hallucination. Possibly a shared hallucination of some form."

"Been doing any drugs?"

"Just the ones you prescribe, and only about once every other weekend. Actually, I haven't done anything recreational with chemicals since, oh, maybe a couple of weeks ago."

"Were you doing them heavily around then? You could be hallucinating as a result of withdrawal…" Feeling this theory didn't resonate with his patient, the doctor folded his arms. "What senses are being impacted by the potential hallucinations? Sight? Sound?"

Harold wanted to say "all of them," but any discussion of any sense now evoked Dottie. His body seized with desire and, running a hand over his face, blocking out the vision of his imagination with a well-angled palm against his forehead, Harold said, "Maybe it's just a mid-life crisis."

"Little late for that, buddy."

"Well thank you"—Harold shot a hard look at the grinning medical "professional," as some would call Robert Ernst before getting to know him—"but I'd like to think I've already been through the brunt of that…although—I don't know. God, I'm losing my mind."

"I can tell!"

"It's this younger woman," confided the miserable CEO at last, shifting in his seat, smoothing the fabric of his shirt, wishing Dottie stood before him so he could touch her, kiss her, crush all the bird-bones of her delicate body until she begged him to—ah, stop! Blasted brain! "She makes me feel diseased! I can't think of anything else—I can't even sleep."

"Sleep interruptions! What time?"

Every day right around the same time, as if measured by a perfect internal clock. At 2:15am, two hours before early rising-Harold was slated to wake up with his external alarm clock, he'd catapult out of sleep and awaken to find his body almost vibrating with the intensity of his desire for Dottie. Christ! Her name was the very first conscious thought he'd had that day, in fact. Oh, he was miserable, more miserable still while explaining it to the doctor. "It's as if the lack of her—my empty bed—primes me to want her, to find her. At the very least to be eager to see her."

"Where'd you two meet?"

"That's not important—but it can't be healthy, this feeling. This awful feeling…perhaps it's my heart."

"Oh," said the doctor with a wryly patronizing smile, "I'd say it's your heart, all right…sounds to me like you're in love, Harold."

"But that's what's so frustrating. It's not *like* the love I've felt. I've loved women and men before. It's never woken me up at two in the morning, oh, just yearning to—I've almost called her at that early hour three times now."

"Maybe you've loved people as in "cared about them in a general, human way,"" suggested Ernst still with that irritating little smile, looking like a charmed parent despite the doctor being some years younger than his patient, "but you haven't really been *in* love as in the "chemical reaction, oxytocin-dopamine-endorphin cycle" part. I've seen you in action, brother. You keep up an elegant and thoughtful aesthetic that makes you seem sensitive but inside you're a calculating logician. It doesn't surprise me that your previous romances have been, uh…maybe more on the pragmatic side."

Harold became aware of the fact that his own hand had settled upon his heart to stroke lightly back and forth. After turning away to make a few notes on the computer, the doctor said, "I'm going to make a note to keep an eye on your blood pressure and we'll give you a script for something to help you sleep, but I don't really advise you take it if you can go without. Just feel your feelings! It's great to be in love."

"Humbug," responded Harold without delay. "My God, Bobby, it feels like my skin is burning off. It feels like—like if I don't have her now, have her right now, I'm going to die in your lobby."

"God damn," was the doctor's useless response, his grin widening across his boyish face. "This girl must be out of this world."

That was one way of putting it. That was certainly Harold's impression while standing in Dottie's bathroom a week before his doctor's appointment. The petite girl gazed nervously up at him from within the shelter of her robe, hands in his, her flushed expression as hopeful as if she had shown her new lover some exotic form of niche sex toy. Given the dark depths of their proclivities, well, he was forced to admit the corpse—Dottie's old body—was something akin to that.

Oh, Dottie, Dottie. "Still want to be friends?" That question on her pert little mouth. The only proper response was to tear his hands out of hers, grasp her face and kiss her, inhale her, swallow her. She moaned in shock and fell back against the cluttered bathroom sink before returning his embrace. As his tongue plundered the depths of her gasping mouth, Harold tore open the fabric of that shapeless robe, lifted his head from the passion of their kiss, then caught her clutching hand to guide it from his white undershirt to the front of his trousers. How long had he been out with his head injury? Long enough to recover from their previous acrobatics, apparently. With an eager moan, Dottie responded to his demonstration by hurrying to open his pants; Harold resumed his savage kisses while his palms devoured the soft curves of her tight body—oh, that worshiped landscape!

"You lied to me before," he murmured in her ear. With a sad gasp, the girl protested, but he only nipped the lobe and throbbed at the sound of her pleasurable cry while he went on. "You did, Dottie—lied to me about being a virgin. You were one, weren't you? That body was one, anyway… Oh, Christ, no wonder you were so tight, a fresh little body all the time—Dottie, Dottie, Dottie, what *are* you?"

"I don't know." Spreading her legs and sighing as he caressed beneath her thighs, Dottie lay back against her bedroom mirror and bit her lip down at the erection she'd freed. "I don't know, I've never known, oh, Harold…maybe we could find out together, oh—you really don't mind? You're really not afraid?"

"No, no, Dottie, fuck—oh, Christ." She was already so wet to the touch that he spared no time, reduced from a refined and powerful CEO to a desperate animal by the welcoming sensation of the girl's tender body. While she gasped as he buried himself deep in that moist (Yes! Virginally tight, oh, Mary!) channel, he grasped her face, squeezed her feline cheekbones beneath his thumbs until she yelped. "You're incredible, Dottie—Dottie, you're a gift. Not a demon at all! A little goddess! Thank God your daddy killed himself. Thank God he's not around to protect you from me." While the mad girl threw her head back to laugh, a sound jolting and broken amid the rhythm of Harold's hard pounding, he went on, teeth gritted by the self-control it required to look Dottie in the face without biting off a piece of her soft white flesh to chew and swallow raw. "Any father worth his salt would tell you to stay far, far away from me, Dottie…oh, knowing what you can do…Dottie—Dottie, what are you?"

"I'm a cute little fucktoy for you." She gasped at the shudder she provoked in herself with the words, those limber legs tightening around his ass. Her hand, normally so cool but now hot with the pumping blood of their mutual arousal, rested upon his cheek to turn his face toward the naked corpse displayed in the bathtub. "Look, look, oh, Harold, fuck! You get so hard from looking at my dead body—holy Jesus, you're such a fucking psycho, oh, God! Fuck me, fuck me the way you want to fuck that dead body before we eat it all up—"

He could have wept for as deeply as he desired her, craved her. Oh, God! There would never be enough, would there? Fucking her would never be enough. Dismembering and eating her would never be enough: no, not even that. There could be no relief for his craving, his intense desire to not just have Dottie, but to absorb her—to assimilate her, as if taking her into himself in some permanent way might finally soothe him, fulfill him. Christ, oh, Christ, he wanted to liquefy her body and inject her into his fucking frontal lobe and still it would never be enough to satisfy him. He saw it in an instant. If his sick desires were a road he followed, Dottie was a brick wall in which it terminated; against which he wanted to bash his head forever, forever, forever, the way her head slammed back into the same mirror that had, like a cosmic cunt, birthed this sexy new body of hers back into the world while the old one lay dead. How was such a thing possible? What were the mechanics, what did it say about consciousness?

"Harold, Harold, you're such a disgusting, evil bastard, oh, I can't believe you're not freaked out—oh, God, I'm so happy—"

"Dottie, oh Christ, all the things we can do together, Dottie, Dottie—"

Somewhere in the distance, far removed from the sound of makeup rattling upon the counter and the mirror banging uneasily upon the wall, a knock at the door had the audacity to usurp Harold's attention. A door? Hm. A door. Front door, probably. Salespeople. Cops. Didn't care. Oh, Christ, he couldn't stop—she felt too good, pulled him in, her limbs tightening around him.

"Probably just one of my fucking neighbors, oh—the mirror banging on the wall—fuck me, Harold, Harold, Harold, oh, don't stop, oh, you're right, I'm a bad little girl, I fibbed to you, you'll have to spank me for it sometime—ah! You like that, too! Oh, oh, Harold, yes—"

Down in the trousers gathered at his feet, the cellphone in the pocket buzzed a generic classical music ringtone. Harold swore. Memory at last pierced the fog of his arousal long enough for him to remember with an agonized groan, "Oh, that's right—it's Simonetta, it must be Simonetta. I called a friend when I thought—when I thought I was going to have to hide your body." While saying this, he laughed, and so did she, and by God, he hadn't laughed—really, really laughed— in years. Their thrusting stopped and he leaned his forehead against hers, almost hysterical with the comedy of the circumstances. To go from thinking he had killed a woman to—this! What a transition. What a marvelous life. God, God, he was so happy to be alive, so happy to experience this feeling he could not name. Kissing her tenderly, exhaling low to be forced to stop the mechanics of fulfilling his own desire, Harold studied Dottie's dreamy face and was sorely tempted to ignore both the knocking and the phone call.

The phone rang again, though. Simonetta's time was valuable and, sighing, Harold drew himself out of Dottie while murmuring, "We'll have to tell her something…God, how are we going to explain this?"

Even through her flush-faced haze, Dottie bit her lip in anxiety at the open bathroom door. "I'm scared—I've never told anybody except you before. Can't we send her away?"

"Much as I'd like to, I'm going to need her logistical help… it takes a certain level of networking to get a body out of an apartment building undetected. Rest assured, she is discreet with my affairs; I'm sure we can trust her with this. Come up with a tale for her pimp, but be open with her."

"Listen to you working out the problem," said the girl, her tone lascivious as he pulled up his pants. "You're a natural, you dirty fucking murderer…oh, Harold, will you remember to tell me what it was like to kill me?"

"I'll tell you all about it the next time I have you alone. Ah…" He hesitated, unable to leave her, pressing one more hungry kiss to her mouth as his phone gave the perfunctory buzz to indicate a new voicemail. "Better let her in…she's got a temper."

While Dottie put on her robe, Harold picked his dress shirt up from the futon and was still pulling it on when he leaned out into the hall. The irritated woman was already tromping back to the elevator: he whistled low, not daring to speak her name in the shared space. Simonetta paused with one hand on her hip, her mahogany face contorting into an expression of barely contained disgust as she returned to study Harold.

"Baby," said Simonetta with a sigh, permitting him to kiss her cheek before resuming her petulant scowl, "you really gotta answer your phone the first time. And after giving somebody a call like that…come on, let me in, let's see—"

A hand on his chest, Simonetta pushed past him and in a flurry of sweet-smelling motion looked around the living room into which she'd just barged. "Damn, whose apartment is this, some college student? Cute though. So what happened, Harold?"

"Well…" While shutting the door behind him, Harold could only think that the one verifiable and efficient way to explain the situation was to kill Dottie in front of the prostitute and let her come back out of the mirror. Then there would be two Dottie cadavers and a third living one…and maybe a prostitute dead of a heart attack. Talk about a party! Ah, Jesus, he was so horny. Focus your thoughts, old boy. "Well—my friend and I have had rather a situation, you see, and—"

Bright and breathless, Dottie sprang from her bathroom and shut the door behind her, hair brushed back from her face and robe tightened respectably around her. "Hi," she called, the motion and greeting combining to make Simonetta jump in a rattle of bracelets and necklaces and glittering earrings. "I'm Dottie! It's so nice to meet you, uh—"

"Ah, this is Simonetta, Dottie"—Harold smiled as Simonetta, recovered, glanced curiously into his face before extending her manicured hand to shake Dottie's—"and Simonetta, this is Dottie…Dottie is a secretary at my office," he explained, eliciting a crooked smirk from the prostitute and a sly look his way. He pretended not to notice and continued, looking significantly at his very own little dreamboat, "Simonetta is my oven girl, Dottie."

"Oh," said the secretary, a sparkle of recognition immediately blossoming in her eyes. A new, far lewder quirk to her leering expression, Dottie said, "Well hi. It's really nice to meet you! Harold was just telling me a little about you tonight."

"That's nice," said the woman before turning to look at Harold. "And I don't mean to be rude, but I lost a client tonight—maybe forever!—because of this, so can you please tell me what I'm here for? The way you were talking on the phone I thought you killed somebody or—"

"He did," Dottie said, picking up the explanatory burden much to Harold's relief.

With a scoff puffing from her plump mouth, Simonetta looked between the two of them and particularly assessed the front of Harold's trousers. "You guys are bullshitting me— seems pretty fucking casual in here for that!"

Laughing, Dottie insisted, "No, it's really true," and Simonetta tapped her leopard print high heel impatiently upon the floor.

"Then where's the body?"

"In my bathroom." Simonetta started to move past but

Dottie extended a quick hand to her shoulder, staying her in place. "Um—I feel like I should warn you before you look, it, uh—it might be a little surprising."

"Lord have mercy on my soul…like a dead body isn't bad enough!" Throwing down her purse in outrage, Simonetta turned on Harold and waved an annoyed hand. "I can't believe this—I defended you, you know! You know what the girls say about you? That you're a fucking psycho! That you've got it under control now but someday you're going to snap, and whoever has the hot potato that weekend is fucked—and I always say 'Nah, Harold's cool, I trust Harold, I think he's actually a pretty decent dude, that's fine if you don't want to work with him because it's more money for me,' you know? And now I look like a fucking asshole!"

"Simonetta—"

"I can't believe you've let this happen," she continued, "and I can't believe I agreed to come over here and help you— *Help* you!"

"Perhaps," Harold said, neither wounded nor even particularly surprised to hear the prostitutes warned one another about him, "you had ought to take a look at the body before you leap to a conclusion."

"Yeah," Dottie agreed, looking more affected by Simonetta's insults against Harold than Harold was himself. To his surprise the robed girl slid into his swiftly responsive arm and, hand upon his chest, gazed into his face. "Harold didn't snap—I made him do it."

"What the fuck," said Simonetta to herself, looking at the front door.

"No, for real! I did. It wasn't his fault at all."

No doubt trying to push her emotions out of it and go into professional survival mode in case the alleged murderers before her decided to resume their Dionysian festivities, Simonetta shut her eyes. "All right," she said, eyes still shut. "Whatever. Whatever, whatever. I'm just glad it wasn't me. So who was it, then?" Opening those big dark eyes again, Simonetta stared into Harold's very soul and demanded, "Nobody I know, was it?"

"Well, now it is." Dottie laughed up at Harold and, when his arm tightened around her waist, she said to Simonetta, "It was me."

"You," repeated Simonetta, brow furrowing. "What the hell are you talking about? You two have really gone off the deep end—girl, are you listening to yourself?"

"It's true," Harold said. Simonetta glanced sharply up into his face while, smiling, nodding, Dottie said, "Yeah! Come on!" She released Harold, slipped from his grasp, caught the prostitute by the hand to lead her to the bathroom. "I'll show you! You can match up all my birthmarks, here, it's fun—"

Three minutes later the women emerged from the bathroom. Harold did not realize it was possible for a melanistic woman to pale at all, let alone so intensely as had Simonetta. Perhaps it was only him projecting his own reaction to the corpse upon her, but a certain gray caste had settled over her normally lively skin.

"What the fuck," she said softly, her eyes huge as they made desperate contact with Harold's in pursuit of some, any, explanation. "You guys…"

She seemed like she had a thought there, but in the end the prostitute let it drop away and stood with her hand on her mouth, looking into the bathroom from her position at the edge of the living room. After contemplating for a long time the corpse within, the woman pressed her knuckles to her cheek, shook her head and looked, mystified, over at Harold. As if this was any fault of his!

"Jesus Christ," Simonetta managed, sighing and extending both her empty hands in bafflement. "Jesus—is there anything to drink in this apartment?"

3.

IT WAS CHARMING, really. Dottie and Simonetta got along very well, although that was perhaps testament as much to Simonetta's acting skills as it was to Dottie's personality. Harold could not blame the working woman for having to force herself into the role of sociable guest while they decided what to do: he himself was not particularly settled, but his physiological state of arousal had nothing to do with fight or flight and everything to do with the morbid black desire transfixing his mind, so frequently guiding his stare back to the bathroom door that his neck began to ache. After a time he interrupted a gleeful conversation in which the girls found kinship in both being Harold's sex workers (Simonetta in the more traditional sense, Dottie by bringing his fantasies to life in her drawings) by setting down his glass and asking point-blank, "How do we get the body out of here and into my country house, Simonetta?"

Simonetta emptied her wineglass and sighed heavily. "Shit, Harold."

"Well—what else are we going to do with it?"

"Shit," said Simonetta again, shaking her head, then with some consideration looking between her two hosts. "You two are seriously fucked up."

Dottie grinned, her tongue teasingly jutting from between her teeth. "Why, whatever do you mean?"

"Don't give me that shit…and don't act like I don't know *your* ass, Harold Fleetwood. This is the fucked up opportunity of your fucked up lifetime…ugh, Christ."

The noble-winged seraphs did not appear more saintly than did Harold at that moment. He looked at Simonetta through an expression of sheer innocent confusion. "I'm quite sure I have no idea what you mean."

Dottie laughed while Simonetta rolled her eyes. "All right, you fucking lunatic…and I don't mean that in a fun way, you really are a lunatic. I'd tell you I'm thinking twice about playing your damn kitchen games with you, but it looks to me like you won't need me to do that shit anymore."

"But if you wanted to," said Harold while Simonetta, with a look of dry distaste, finally shook her head as though he were an incorrigible child and leaned back in the futon to dig her phone out of her purse.

"If I wanted to then I'd be crazy as *your* crazy ass, and I don't have the kind of money to be that fucking crazy…"

After a little discussion, another person was in the small apartment: this one a tall, sallow-faced thirty-something wearing an ugly patterned suit. Harold had met this fellow once or twice before—he was, shall we call him politely, Simonetta's manager, and a distant third-hand acquaintance who had been necessary to interact with only once.

"Of course I know somebody," said the sleezy fellow whose name Harold tried quite deliberately to never absorb under any circumstances. Plausible deniability, very important. Folding his ringed hands before him, the pimp studied Harold, then Dottie. "But what's the story?"

With a little coaching and a pinch of method acting, Dottie

had managed to whip herself into tearful hysterics before the pimp's arrival. Now she hiccuped, "I— I— my—my—"

"Her sister," explained Harold, draping an arm around her shoulder. Oh God! Imagine, imagine him—Harold, touching Dottie casually. Touching Dottie like they were lovers. They *were* lovers, by God. The thought struck him with such an explosive burst of joy that he had to repress a grin and felt that Dottie, having turned her tear-dampened face against his chest, did not feel the need to repress hers while it was hidden. As the girl nuzzled into his chest and he tried to stay on the point, he continued in businesslike fashion to the pimp, "A domestic dispute. I don't know if I should really get into it here."

"I understand." Simonetta's manager studied the back of Dottie's head before looking up again at Harold and beginning to casually say, "Well, the average price for a disposal in this city is—"

"Ah," began Harold, as Dottie glanced toward the pimp in admirable imitation of a woman wounded by the notion of her sister's 'disposal.' "Actually—well, this really was an accident, you see, but the problem is we just can't prove it. We want it taken care of but we'd like her to have a proper burial, and it happens that my country property has quite a bit of space. It's very isolated." He felt Dottie hold her breath and his grip on her tightened as he went on, striving nobly to keep the hunger from his voice. "Hardly anyone knows where it is or who lives there; the nearest house is miles away. An impromptu grave would not be noticed there, I think."

"Oh! Well, if that's all you want, I can throw in a burial for—"

"I have a few connections in the funeral industry"— Harold spoke perhaps too quickly but was too annoyed, blast it, these bastard salesmen, just let him have the body, move it and be done, transaction ended—"it will be nothing to have her properly but privately seen to."

Scoffing, the pimp glanced over at Simonetta, waved a hand, then laughed up at Harold. "Gonna have her embalmed or some shit? If only all our, uh…emergency services clients got treated so good. Okay, well…"

The pimp named a price. Vaguely, somewhere beneath his annoyance with the negotiation and the erotic slide of Dottie's frigid hand up his spine, Harold felt the price low compared to what he'd been prepared to pay. After a sidelong glance at Simonetta, (scrolling petulantly through her phone while wiggling the heel of her shoe against her foot, ah, he loved the shapes of her tight ankles and all the flesh on her calves, she was a thrill to look at when disdainfully bored), Harold recognized that she may have been shielding her pimp from her most reliable client's proclivities. Goodness, what a sweetheart she was. Heart of gold, as they said. "That's just fine," said Harold, trying to sound more relieved about getting the situation over with than he to know Simonetta's true discretion, "I'll pay whatever it takes. I'm so overwhelmed, but ultimately we just can't go to the police with this due to the nature of my career."

"Uh-huh," said the pimp, already getting his phone out of his pocket, "you seem real broken up about it…none of my business."

There ensued a quick phone conversation during which the pimp turned away. Dottie seized her opportunity and lifted a smoldering gaze toward Harold, that stare a match lighting the fuse of his blood and setting off all the gunpowder of lust latent within him. They lunged upon one another in the same second, a ferocious, almost angry kiss as if chastising one another for being so delayed in their entrance to each others' lives; when he drew away, quickly before the pimp turned around, he caught Simonetta watching from the corner of her eye. Harold smiled at her while Dottie nuzzled back into his chest. He had expected the sex worker to scowl but instead she studied on: Harold felt curiously assessed by her as he never had until the pimp ended his call, interrupted the train of thought and said, "Okay—I'm going to need a key to the apartment and the rest of the night to work in it. You guys got someplace to go? How about you hit up that fancy country house of yours." While Dottie slipped off to fetch her spare key, bare feet miraculously silent upon the wood floor of her apartment, the pimp continued, "This the place where Sisi parties with you? I got the address in my rolodex"—an annoying wink, ugh, Harold wished to poke the man's eyeball out—"so I'll send somebody by with the delivery once we're through. Then you can settle the balance less the deposit."

Ah—cash up-front, of course. He fished out his wallet as Dottie came back to hand the pimp her key. The businessman made it disappear like a magician: Harold needed to sever Dottie's lease and move her out of that apartment as soon as possible. Goodness, where to put her? His mind was a million places at once. Focus on the money. Yes, ground yourself.

While he thumbed through the bills within the leather confines of his wallet, everyone in the room strained not to watch—everyone except Dottie, who stared brazenly into the contents, thrilling his blood with an open interest in his money even Simonetta and her fellow sex workers tried to hide. He silently counted out $2000 there in front of them, asked if that was enough once he had put the wallet safely away, and made the transaction with a handshake and a gentleman's nod. "Very good," he said while the pimp counted the bills with a poorly repressed grin. "Your…delivery people will receive the balance when they come to the drop off location. D— darling"—he had almost called her by her name in front of the pimp and his elegant solution to the slip of the lip made her flush with such obvious delight that he could not help himself but take her into his arms—"why don't you bring enough clothes to stay the weekend out of town, get dressed…oh, and a funeral dress, perhaps, for your sister's service. A little black dress."

Face straining against her grin, Dottie slipped into her bedroom and shut the door behind her. At the sound of the latch, Simonetta sprang to her feet and said, "I want to talk to her," while hurrying past the men. After a quick knock she was permitted into Dottie's boudoir. The pimp shrugged back at Harold.

"Women, they're sure something else…all right, well, you really sure you don't want me to throw in disposal services? It'd be nothing, I'd give you a sweetheart deal—"

After he had finally gotten the pimp to leave the room, Harold turned his attention to the soft conversation (and occasional burst of laughter from Dottie, his favorite sound from the office and still so surreal to hear outside that environment) emanating from the bedroom. Goodness, now here was a pair capable of getting up to trouble. Ever the libertine voyeur, Harold edged to the door and strained to listen to the bedroom on the other side.

Paper rustled; zippers whisked about; Simonetta said, "God damn girl! This shit is unreal—oh, wow, this one's actually hot as fuck."

"Thank you! I was pretty proud of that one, I liked the way her thighs came out. Do you draw or anything?"

"Me? Nah—I wrote all kinds of fan fiction in middle school, though." While Simonetta laughed at her own confession, she asked Dottie, "Do you still read manga? What's your favorite?"

Perverse sensibilities disappointed (the ego on him to think that the only thing women discussed was men and sex— probably between their lingerie pillow fights), Harold decided the conversation was going nowhere erotic and knocked upon the door. "Almost packed?" He asked the question while leaning in, unable to arrange his expression into anything approaching solemnity—particularly when he saw the very naturalizing effect Dottie seemed to have on Simonetta, who was caught mid-smile and too late transitioned to a scowl to hide her pleasure from him. Nonetheless, the woman glowered, put down the drawing she'd been admiring, and shifted her purse's strap up her shoulder.

"I have half a mind to take her home with me instead of letting you whisk her off—who knows what the fuck you'll convince her to do."

With a shudder and a devilish grin, Dottie turned her doe eyes toward Harold, batting them behind the frames of her cat-eye glasses. "Yeah, gosh…maybe she's right, you could get all kinds of bad ideas when you have me to yourself."

Christ! He couldn't think. His brain burned like a fire, a terrible inflammation of passion having afflicted him. Anything he could think to say would only have given Simonetta true cause for concern. Instead, clearing his throat, Harold pleasantly asked the woman, "Perhaps you'd like to hunker down with us for the weekend?"

"Uh, nuh-uh. No, no way. Not this weekend, Harold, no— shit, no." Shaking her head rapidly, then glancing over her shoulder for a few of the drawings on the table behind her, Simonetta said, "You guys are really nuts…but don't *you*"— she crossed over to address Dottie directly, prodding the girl in the shoulder to make her point—"let him talk you into any crazy shit, okay? Nothing you don't want to do, girl."

"Scout's honor! Anyway"—those eyes burned into him another few seconds before she turned to close her bag—"I think Harold's the one more likely to get pushed into stuff by me."

No kidding. He was reduced once more to a mess of a man when, to avoid the three of them being seen together, Simonetta exchanged phone numbers with Dottie ("You call me if he gets on some kind of crazy shit, okay? It doesn't matter what time, I'll pick up.") and exited. The apartment was once again left populated only by Harold, Dottie, and Dottie's lovely corpse.

His fingers trembled. There was too much adrenaline in his body: he could have run three marathons and still had energy, ah, what did this girl do to him? Upon seeing Simonetta out Dottie lingered with her hand upon the knob, then leaned back against the door to stare down hapless Harold. She had taken his hint and changed into a thin, plain black dress that fell to her knees but was lightly beaded around the bust. The whole effect resembled a negligee, even more when one of the thin straps drooped down her shoulder. Oh…her pale, perfect, mouth-watering shoulder.

"Did you hear that?" The girl, as affected to be alone with him now as he was to be alone with her, stared through eyes whose pupils grew just as her face and throat and décolletage were spotted red with wanton lust. "Simonetta thinks you're a bad man…a scary man. She doesn't think I should go with you."

How swiftly upon being left alone did their temperaments devolve to depravity! In the cannibal chatroom, before he had realized she was one of his own secretaries and only knew her from her screen name as a guro artist specializing in Dolcett, things were much the same—but that was what those sorts of communities were made for. Digital mutual fantasizing and masturbating, essentially. It was easy to slip into fantasizing, into a sort of character, in the space of a few seconds.

But that was online. In real life, Harold had never met someone with whom to play his perverse games—had never met such a tantalizing, truly tailor-made individual whose very existence was a sexual fantasy come to life. Dottie, Dottie. Dottie made Harold feel different than he ever had. Frighteningly different. And after this strange night, especially, well…what was the line between fantasy and reality anymore?

"Maybe you shouldn't go with me." His gaze back into her eyes was for once unflinching. "Simonetta would know. She's an experienced woman…not just with me but many other strange and specialized men. She knows a dangerous situation when she sees it."

Dottie bit her lip, her hand lifting to permit the drift of

her fingertips over her collarbone. What Dottie needed was some fine jewelry to accent that wonderful white sternum. "Are you going to hurt me, Harold?"

"That depends…are you going to do what I tell you to do, Dottie? Help me clean and butcher your old body"—her ruby lips parted and his cock absolutely ached to be slammed between them—"and have a nice weekend together with me? Or are you going to be a bad girl and change your mind? Get upset, try to run?"

Her hand slid down over her left breast and he felt that wretchedness, that unworthiness to be so intimate with such a girl (no—a staggeringly powerful being in disguise as a girl) rising up inside him. Such unworthiness sharpened his pleasure as she said in an almost breathless voice, "No, no, I promise, I promise…I'll be a good girl for you, Harold. I'll do whatever you tell me to do. But—" Her teeth bit that lower lip hard enough to leave a crinkled impression. "But…will you please promise to hurt me even if I'm a good girl?"

"Oh yes, Dottie. Yes, I promise. I will." Her smile widened into that of a coy little girl and, as was evidently her custom when she was feeling shy, the hand upon her breast lifted to shield that smile with her hair. He ached; his trousers seemed to be cutting off his entire blood supply and the throb made him remember he hadn't climaxed the second time he fucked her, interrupted as they'd been by Simonetta. Small wonder Dottie had such immediate effect on him when they were once again alone. He leaned back, received another burst of pleasure as her eyes fell to that effect's most visible piece of evidence.

"Should I give you that spanking now, Dottie? Or would you rather we wait until we're home? Fibbing to me, shocking me like this—you're such a naughty girl, no, I don't think I should wait. Come here."

Either the apartment was cold or she was very enthusiastic about the idea. Her pert nipples indicated how thin the cotton of her black dress truly was while, attempting to assume an expression of solemnity, the girl twisted a few locks of hair around her finger and slid back into the corner. "Oh, why, I've never been spanked before—"

"I can tell. You act like a spoiled brat. Don't make Daddy come get you, Dottie—you'll have a much harder punishment if you do."

It was a gamble. The intimacy shouldering such a role even in a jesting context was high—and they were, in a way, intimate after several years of chatting online about this or that fantasy. But it was very forward nonetheless for him to call himself her daddy on their first true meeting. He only dared to because she had in a sense invited him earlier: and when the word dropped from his mouth, his boldness was rewarded. The girl gasped in shocked delight. A delightful, giddy noise that gratified his very soul. Ah, he loved to please her as much as hurt her…Harold was in terrible trouble, wrapped dreadfully around her finger. Who could blame him! "Yes, Daddy," she said, her eagerness undisguised until she was within a few feet of him, every pretty facet of her face aglow with the kind of unabashed hope he felt whenever he looked at her. Then, near to him, she remembered herself and hesitated in mock fear. "Are you *mad* at me for being naughty?"

"No, princess, of course not…Daddy just has to teach you a little lesson." He lunged forward in his seat and laughed while she, squawking like a bird, flailed in his grasp. Only when he jerked her forward did she relax into her own giggles, and the giggling soon dissolved into low moans as, without delay, Harold bent her over his knee and gave wicked Dottie a well-earned spanking.

"Ow-ee! Oh, jeez!" The girl's legs kicked while he landed the first brisk burst of swats against her round ass—that fine, soft ass into which he wanted to sink his animal teeth. After a gasp for a fairly hard spank Dottie bucked in his grip and, with an attractive whine, said, "You're so mean Harold! Ooh, oh—ah! Your hand's so heavy—!"

"Yes, well, it's what a naughty girl needs, isn't it, Dottie…" He couldn't help himself; he yanked high the hem of her dress over her wonderful ass and—

"Dottie!" Gasping with ecstasy, Harold landed a harsh spank on her bare bottom and chided, "No underwear? What a bad girl you are…naked under that little dress, oh, God—"

"Harold, Harold—oh, Daddy—" Her abbreviated shrieks of pain gradually reduced to a different series of noises altogether. Beneath his brisk assault her bottom had begun to pinken and now it arched against him, welcoming him, inclining as though to encourage a few lower blows. He obliged as she gasped, "I just want you to look at me, that's all—oh, I want to tease you—"

"Because you're a very bad little girl, Dottie, Dottie, I know…ah, God, Dottie, take off that dress."

"What? But we have to—"

"Take it off." He repeated it with a harder spank on her perky ass and she wiggled while obeying, panting as the fabric was yanked free from her head. Then, oh—God.

Then Dottie was naked again, and all his power (assuming he had any in her presence to begin with) was stolen away. His spanking hand, developing a sting of its own, slowed, slowed, commenced to pet. While she sighed, he marveled over the heat emanating from her sweet pink ass, the dimples poised above its red flesh, the indiscernible fade of the valley between those two delectable globes into the pale rod of spinal column leading to her neck. Strangling that neck, the belt wrapped around it. With the girl still splayed over his lap Harold doubled over, first planting his lips in a fond kiss against the flesh of her ass, then following his way up that curve. The muscles of her back were so beautiful he wanted nothing more than to peel off her flesh and practice anatomical drawing. He'd never been good at drawing. Dottie could teach him when she returned from death. While he shifted to kiss her soft shoulder blades, Dottie moaned.

"Oh…Harold…you're nice to me…it's hard to believe you're such a fucked up devil of a man…"

He dared not speak. His kisses continued against the soft curve of her throat, lips seeking in vain for the impression of a belt never wound around this neck. This virgin neck. And *he* was the devil, was he! Harold shuddered and the girl, smiling, turned over in his lap. His shudder climaxed in a soft cry to see her so beautiful, so naked—oh, God, he couldn't stand to behold her naked body without having his cock in her. Having his cock in her made him feel like he somehow had some control over her, or at least some say in her behavior: a means of taming her.

But, separate from this naked body displayed across his yearning lap, Harold's terror grew again. At once unable to touch her, he lifted one hand to his mouth and let the other hang in midair until her delicate palms caught it. With a smile, her smooth hand fitting against his, (Oh, she was so small! His throat tightened with the mad sorrow of perfect love— depraved, consuming love.), Dottie examined his aged fingers, compared them to her porcelain ones, then drew his burning nerves down to her supple mouth. Every soft kiss might as well have been planted upon his throbbing prick: he gasped, almost hurt by the potency of the pleasure at these whispered dots of affection pressed to the edge of his palm, the tip of his thumb, the row of his knuckles. The focus of her eyes slid up from his hand to his face and, mouth relaxing, she extended the cherry tip of her deadly tongue to tease along his ring finger.

"Don't you think we should go, Daddy?" Harold felt close to immolation at the naked girl's whisper. Oh, Christ—it wasn't enough to kill her, to eat her, no! No, there would never be a close enough intimacy! God, she made him want to strip off his skin and scream down the city streets—she made him want to commit himself.

"I suppose we'd ought to." One last time his gaze dared to streak down the pale slope of her body to the tips of her kissable toes. Jaw pained by the impulse to apply pressure to that perfect flesh, he turned to kiss her and found her already leaning up. Harold gasped on the contact: as their lips worked, his hands made one last affectionate sweep over her cool limbs, the soft skin taut over the feminine muscles of her back. "What do you say…feeling contrite enough now, princess?"

Her dimples! He could write whole volumes of poetry devoted to those dimples. Spellbinding Dottie nodded, still in his lap as she turned to pick up her dress and tug it over her head. "I promise, I'll be good…you could take me anywhere, anywhere, and I swear I won't try to run away, or fight with you, or anything. Unless"—her smile widened when he reflexively commenced to smooth her dress, to pull it over her pale knees and pet her lap to work the wrinkles out—"you want me to, of course."

"Maybe sometime soon…but tonight—tonight, oh—!"

What was it about her? What was it? It was so much worse than with other women. Oh, other beautiful women, Simonetta, for example, yes, he felt those compulsive urges rising up in him. But with Dottie it was truly unbearable. What he felt was a burning, yearning, explosive desire to hurt her—worse than hurt her. Perhaps it was because she felt the corresponding urge to yield her sweet girl-flesh to his heinous desires. Much as their bodies desperately sought one another, their perverse psyches had sniffed each other out and were now potentiated by one another's mere existence. His mind rushed to catalog all their fantasies shared as strangers in a chatroom—and Harold pushed them all away. That was Dottie's online persona. Internet Dottie, the artist and (from his perception) cutthroat entrepreneur willing to hustle her art while also working fulltime in exchange for a higher quality of life.

But Dottie the girl—Dottie the lover, the victim, the friend who could be touched and called and whispered to. Kissed. He knew nothing of this Dottie or her fantasies. He kissed her twice more before sliding her out of his lap and into the futon cushion beside him. Then, with a sigh and a long study of her transfixing image, he rose.

"Yes, we'd ought to go…it's quite a drive…would you feel more comfortable if you followed me in your own car?"

"I don't drive! I just use the subway…and anyway"—her grin widened and that crooked little fang glinted in the light—"I like the thought of being whisked away by you, Harold. Helpless. Yes—I want to feel helpless. Like a little bird trapped in a house with a cat."

Shuddering, Harold extended his hand. When she took it he drew her to her feet and into one more ferocious kiss. Then, somehow (only by very deliberately not looking at her, Orpheus and his little Eurydice fresh from Hades' cuckolding embrace), Harold led the way down Dottie's hallway. Her grin reflected at him in the shining elevator doors. He averted his eyes while they descended, slid an arm around her, and waited for the chime announcing they'd hit the bottom floor.

4.

WHAT WERE THEY going to do? Strike that. What was he going to do? Good God, he'd fucked her to completion once and already his brain slipped in these insidious alterations of pronoun. "They, we, us," not "He, him, me"—the mind was a snake!

But that was because his mind knew that what had happened between them wasn't just a fuck. No. It was a murder—he had murdered her, or at the very least committed manslaughter against her person. Dottie had been killed that night but sat alive with him as they drove through the neon city and beyond. Out to where it was dark and quiet. To where they were alone. He thought of deluded Humbert Humbert steering his vehicle of sin from town to town while contemplating the change in Dolores after the first sexual assault. "It was something quite special, that feeling: an oppressive, hideous constraint as if I were sitting with the small ghost of somebody I had just killed."

But Harold's own dolorous Dottie was no ghost—not at all. Flesh and blood, this nymph, although she plagued him like a phantom. Oh, haunted him. Her presence in the car forced him to wonder what damage had been done to make him this way: to receive such an overflowing thrill at the mere fantasy of killing such a girl. Yet—what a rush. By God, his fantasies somehow were no longer fantasies. They were memories now.

And maybe these fantastic desires never needed to be relegated to fantasy again.

"How many times have you died before tonight, Dottie?" He asked the question softly, as if asking a lover if she'd fallen asleep. Dottie's pretty head animated away from the window, rolling against the black leather seat while one bare foot propped up against the dash to flash her leg up to the white of her thigh.

"Mm…four. But I've never been killed by anybody before." Her grin widened. "You really did deflower me, Harold."

Oh, what a girl—what things she said. His hands tightened around the wheel as he resisted the urge to speed. "Have you—I'm not sure how to ask this—when did you start to think about…"

"Being killed by somebody in a sexual way? High school, I guess…but I was always a really weird kid." She threw back her head in a gay laugh that lit his soul like a pinball machine. "My first celebrity crush was Bela Lugosi in *Dracula*, so I don't know if that was an explanation or an indication, but—"

"Mine was Julie Newmar."

"No shit! Catwoman? I love her. That probably explains some things for you, too." Dottie wiggled in her seat to stick the other foot upon the dash beside its cohort. He struggled to watch the road, God, even her feet were absolutely perfect. She was like a Degas—no, no! A Balthus. Oh, a Balthus painting, the way she threw herself around. Angel! "Anyway, I don't know what happened in my brain to make me this way.

Things just kind of escalated, you know? I know you know. Bela Lugosi turned into the typical teenage girl vampire fascination, and that turned into, like, the still-pretty-typical and stupidly edgy serial killer fascination. And serial killers led to erotic asphyxiation, and erotic asphyxiation led to Dolcett…and Dolcett led to your car." Her hand pressed to her ruby mouth in a futile attempt to shield her smile. "I haven't left the city in years…you really could be taking me anywhere, huh."

"I could."

A quiver of anticipation rolling through her, Dottie stared hard into Harold's profile until, when looking over his shoulder during a lane change, he had little choice but be caught however briefly by the harsh scrutiny of those eyes. "You're a murderer now," she said, her tone soft as his had been. His stomach tightened—though, shamefully, not with displeasure.

"You're right, Dottie." On the highway, the traffic light at such a late hour, he was able to ease up his control of the car enough to slide his hand from the wheel to her nearby thigh. She gasped, her foot sliding from the dash to rest upon the floor and give him a place to properly lay his hand. Harold ignored his own screaming terror of the perfection of that body of hers and sank his fingers into her flesh. Oh—so soft, so giving. How easily tender Dottie must have bruised, an overripe fruit. "Yes, you're right. I'm a murderer now—I've killed you once. It would be nothing for me to do it again. Stop the car and strangle you on the side of the road."

"Oh, Harold…" Her hand lay over her throat, the rapidity of her breath evident above even the rumble of the car. "Harold, you're scaring me."

"Good, you should be scared. You know nothing about me really, Dottie—nothing except that I've got enough money to make a body disappear. Why, if I really wanted to—"

His breath hitched and he stared out upon the road, sorely tempted by his own utterance of the idea aloud: "If I really wanted to, I could lock you up in my country house—steal you. Scrub your employee record, tell everyone you quit, pay off the coworkers who cared enough to ask after you. It would be like you didn't exist. Do you have any friends, Dottie?"

"Work friends." She spoke as if enchanted, her thigh splaying a touch wider in an invitation he somehow resisted. "Only work friends. Most people I used to know think I'm dead."

"What a dangerous way to live…and no family since your daddy killed himself, I suppose."

"A couple of people, but they think I'm dead, too."

"What's your real name, Dottie?"

Smiling at that, at his brisk glance over her, Dottie lifted his hand from her thigh and draped it around her shoulders. Harold could not help his sharp sigh; could not contain his urge to draw the girl in and risk a quick peck against the top of her head, God, she smelled so familiar somehow. The scent of women, that musty, almost humid aroma of female flesh— oh, his eager mind ran rapidly through fantasies as the girl, closing her eyes, said against his shoulder, "This is my real name—it's the name I gave myself. The name I got when I was born doesn't matter, does it?"

"I suppose not."

"Sometime I'll tell you," she said. "When I'm sure you're not going to get bored of me, then I'll tell you my old name."

Oh…Dottie, Dottie. Harold was never going to get bored of Dottie. Saying such a thing to her there, then, in the car, their first night together, would have been much too forward. He dared not. He dared not speak nor breathe nor move and instead, still as a birdwatcher, kept her close against his chest, under his arm, overwhelmed by her. A treasure.

Harold was a wealthy man, talented with money its making. He knew a good investment when it appeared. Dottie was the single best investment he had ever set eyes on. The fact that she had made it even twenty-four years without being snatched up by some lab, some research firm, was a testament to her tenacity and intelligence. Most children who discovered an ability to return from the dead in a new body no doubt would have quickly outed themselves in the process of trying to live out some young adult novel fantasy, some coming-of-age adventure that would make them a victim of cold scientific experimentation for all eternity.

But Dottie—she kept it quiet. Hid away her own potential until she met someone to whom it would matter for personal reasons. What would most people do with an immortal girl, after all? He hadn't the creativity to imagine and could only think himself in circles: anyone else would see Dottie donated to military science, ergo Harold had to protect her, and thereby Harold would keep her for himself. For his own pleasure. Harold couldn't let anyone else have her. No, never ever. Not the way he wanted to have her, anyway. *Hanc nisi mors mihi adimet nemo!* At last, he understood.

What a sick bastard Harold was. She wasn't a commodity or an experiment; she wasn't something to be taken or retained. She was a girl. A living girl with emotions and hopes and dreams. A girl who dozed off in his arm, drained from their earlier sexual encounters and whatever process she endured to find herself in an entirely new body. It was not up to him to protect her or keep her safe from anything—she'd done that herself for twenty-four years, after all—but suddenly, perhaps because of the murder, he felt a kind of possessive streak. He had never been a very jealous man (what was the point of being jealous of anything Molly did when he himself was spending so much money on fucking working girls with carrots?) but Dottie was different. Dottie was so different.

Oh…and Dottie was so beautiful. Two hours from the city, by then in the true thick of well-starred country night, Harold turned off his car and glanced down at the girl dreaming in his arm. Her head lolled back against his bicep and as a result her mouth hung open a centimeter, enough to reveal the gloss of pink tongue hidden behind her white teeth. In the glow of a security light that activated to flood the parking area on the car's approach to the property gate, the opalescent veneer of her rapidly flickering eyelids revealed thin blue veins—an elaborate roadmap of life. Tenderly, wishing to suck the very eyeball from beneath, he kissed one lid; by the time his lips had alighted upon its twitching partner, she stirred against him, nuzzling into his jaw with a girlish coo that tore his heart out through his mouth.

"We're here, Dottie…Daddy's secret house." Her back arched up with a stretch that flowed through her feline body and, repressing a groan, Harold kissed her sighing mouth, that delicate chin pinched between his fingers. God, her tongue! It thrashed against his, teased the appetites of his sex and stomach, and slid away before he could scrape his teeth along its sleep-sweetened surface. "Have a good rest?"

"Mmhm."

"That's good. You'll need it."

Flush-faced now, Dottie grinned so wide her lower lip disappeared between her teeth. "How come? What are you going to do to me?"

With a gaunt look of appalling desire down into her agonizing visage, Harold kissed her again, used his free hand to push open his car door, then slipped free to make good his escape under the pretense of getting her bag for her. As she stumbled out behind him, her yawning stretched transformed into a gasp.

"What *is* this place!"

"Just my country house," he answered while tapping the button to shut the trunk of his car.

"It's like a freaking Architectural Digest house!"

"The September 2014 issue, I think…it had been renovated a couple of years before that, but you can imagine they've quite a backlog of exciting places to photograph."

Her laughter was one of shock. "I didn't mean literally!

Holy shit." Dottie shook her head, a mare shaking her mane, a look of delirium crossing her face as she gazed up at the building. "It looks almost like—like a house and a barn crossed over." Then, laughing, she pointed with the enthusiasm of a girl. "Say! Is that creek running through the house?"

While kicking the crooked wheels of her case into motion and making a mental note to buy her new luggage, he explained, "It is—this building was a slaughterhouse." At her sound, almost a gag of delight, he fished out the keys he'd reflexively pocketed and led the way to the yawning plantation-style porch. "I drove past it rather frequently as a young man and it always caught my eye…you can only imagine the torrid fantasies it inspired. The family that owned the farm lived in the front and did their slaughtering in an area in the back, but of course industry standards and factory farming put them out of business in this cruel and calculating modern world of ours. Someone else bought it and was intending to tear it down for a golf course, and, well—I think we have enough golf courses in this state. One moment."

As the door flung open, the security alarm screeched to life. Harold left the girl's suitcase to tend to the keypad. A few beeps later and the siren stopped; automatic lights flooded the white marble floor of the foyer; Dottie gasped as humble Harold absorbed her appreciation for his Versailles aesthetic. "It was a very cute, quaint little farmhouse when I acquired it, and I like to think I've kept that spirit in a few of the rooms, at least…but I was going for something a bit more aristocratic French than rural American, and I think I achieved it."

"No kidding!" Wheeling her suitcase in to park it by the front door where she at once (to his thrill) slipped out of the flat-heeled shoes she'd donned only to pass from car to *maison*, Dottie ran her toes over the oriental carpet sprawling toward the stairs and smiled about at the dark wood wainscoting, the maximalist red and pink damask wall coverings, the abundance of bright green plants whose blessed fronds stole kisses from her face as she leaned in to investigate. "Are these real? Who waters them when you're not here?"

"I pay a housekeeper to come once a week…Thursdays, so I don't have to see anyone. They keep the kitchen stocked and the place clean and maintained. Occasionally I suspend their services for a few weeks at a time, when I'm in the mood for isolation and can't afford to be interrupted."

"Interrupted doing what?"

He locked the front door and the atmosphere changed at once. The alteration afflicted them both—Dottie's posture had changed when he turned around. She was now alert, upright, hands folded in the small of her back, ready for anything. Dottie Dottie—Dottie. Here. Here in his country house. He could not answer her question and she worried her foot back and forth across the floor.

"Did you change the slaughterhouse part in the back, too," Dottie asked, that same insidious dress strap from before sagging with the position of her arms, "or is it still the same?"

"I've made it nicer, but yes—it's the same."

"A nice playhouse."

"Yes," he said, hoarse. Her grin widened.

"A nice place to cut a dirty pig's throat—that's what the stream's for, huh? Carry away all the blood and viscera. Better be careful, you perverted old man…or nobody will ever find you." Her face was flushed. One hand reappeared to trail over her cheek, down her neck. Harold's body burned, wishing to be so caressed by her; he leaned back, braced against the handle of her suitcase, overwhelmed by her sudden snapping from compliant little-girl Dottie to the dangerous and commanding woman Dottie who had cowed him in his own office. "But I wouldn't want to waste any part of my sweet piggie…I could make sausages out of your entrails and soup out of your blood, I'd save it all…Harold." Those shy fingertips pressed her tumbling hair to her smiling lips again. "Are you still afraid of me, Harold?"

"Yes!" The word rose from him in a cry and she laughed—

oh, what a mean little laugh, a witch's laugh. It sent a shiver of pleasure through him, the vibration of his body transmuting into a sharp gasp as she took a step toward him. His hand slapped across his eyes and he almost sobbed while saying, "Yes, oh, God, Dottie—I can't look at you. When I look at you I feel so weak, so foul. I feel these base urges, these cravings to violence! You're right, oh, Dottie, I'm a pig, sweet Christ—"

"You sure are—a fucking deplorable pervert who murdered a girl while your dick was inside her. Oh, you dirty man, you disgusting, dirty man, only animals fuck dead things, you dirty, dirty man—"

The taps of her fast-moving feet on the floor so alarmed him he gave into his urge to look, gasping to find her already so close. Her cool hands pressed to his cheeks: he cried out, unsuccessfully cringing back at the contact. "Don't ever forget to be scared of me deep, deep down inside."

"I won't. God, oh, Dottie, I won't. I promise."

"That's good…I don't want you getting a big head over being able to kill me. It's a reward…a nice thing I want to do for you. But every time you do it, I think you need to be punished for it, just to keep you sensible…oh, you dirty old man." Dottie's pupils were as wild with desire as was her breathless voice, as was the heaving bosom within the fabric of her dress. "Since I'm sure you like being punished, and because I don't want you to get confused about who's in charge even though you're my daddy now"—saying the words deepened the flush of both their faces, caused her hard expression to soften into a sensual, devilish smile—"I'll have to take you in-hand very firmly when I finally get a chance to whip you tonight. Okay?"

"Okay, Dottie. Oh, Dottie—" Somehow in all his life he'd never been whipped by a woman he hadn't paid to whip him: once more the uncertainty and terror rose—but most of all, the gratitude. Her existence! Her very existence, it was just such a gift. Filled with hope, crushed by the power of her,

Harold sank to his knees at Dottie's feet, out of the clutch of those frigid hands, and there he buried his face in her waist with a series of gasps. "Dottie! Dottie I'm sorry—I really am sorry, oh—God, I didn't mean—"

"Sh—Harold." Her fingers carding through his graying hair, the girl whispered fondly, "I wanted you to…I meant for you to. As soon as I realized that you were eattherich— oh, it's the only thought that gets me off now. Making love to you. being murdered and eaten by you. Being turned into your little quadruple amputee fuck-slave"—he moaned and collapsed farther, kissing her feet, kissing the marble lucky enough to support those beautiful feet, those demure ankles on which his teeth craved to ceaselessly gnaw—"hidden away in some spooky old house like this…but I didn't think you'd *really* have a spooky old house. And I never dreamed it would be a *slaughter*house, oh, Harold…Harold. Ah…" At her keen of pleasure, her foot lifted and permitted his kisses to round into her arch. There he was suffused with the heady musk of soft flesh and gasped to hear her say, "Oh, I love the way you kiss my feet…I don't even like feet but I guess you do, huh, you disgusting, pathetic old pig…oh…but I love animals. I love pigs…and not just to eat. Come on."

Nudging him, then bending over to tug on his hair, Dottie said sternly, "You have to get yourself together, you dirty old creep—practice for work. You can't just drool all over me at the office all day." Her lunar hand extended to him—he hesitated to grip it, expecting some electric shock, yes, a thunderbolt from Jove for the mortal audacity to set hands upon such a being as this. When at last he touched her he could not help but press those knuckles against his mouth, to squeeze shut his eyes and beg her to understand, "I try so hard to be a good man, Dottie."

"Poor Harry! I know."

"I want to be—I want to be a good man because that's what God wants for me but, oh, that's not want I want inside,

Dottie. Oh, Dottie—Dottie I'm so weak, so overwhelmed by this rotten core. I'm afraid. I'm truly afraid I'll mistreat you."

"Then just don't…but I want you to mistreat me a little bit. Be rotten and cruel to me sometimes. As mean and snotty as I get to you, the cruelest I ever am—it's okay for you to be a thousand times crueler than that. Just as cruel and wicked as you can think to be. Thinking of you being mean makes me so wet, Harold—oh, Mr. Fleetwood." She laughed, tickling those wonderful fingers over his scalp to make him close his eyes and groan. "Like I said to you before…when you and I are together, it should always be like a beautiful dream. A fantasy. No consequences, no stupid fucking drama or anything boring like that. Let's just both be free and honest with each other, okay? When you want to be mean to me, just be mean to me—oh, Harold—"

Her brow furrowed to see the fire in his eyes—she gasped, legs trembling, her affect again yielding that uncertain fear. Wordless, Harold yanked her down to the cold floor with him, throbbed to hear her cry out, submitted to the urge to tear away her dress. He could not stand it, oh—not a second longer. She was right. She was right! He had spent so long being regretful and cringing; so long crippled by the horror of his own suprasensual nature, because the only alternative to his complete repression was a state of orgiastic ultraviolence. All he wanted was this: was Dottie, this woman, this woman who could truly indulge him. This pure perennial forever fated to be corrupted, crushed, cut off and renewed with the next resurrection. Ready to please the gardener all over again.

His lovely flower gasped to be exposed and cried out, leaning up to bruise his mouth with kisses as his hands roved over her elegant form. He found the flesh of a thigh and slapped it, the noise ringing through the hall and yielding an arch, a gasp, a quaking of her body. The memory of her spanking before leaving her apartment emerged in new reality, a collaged replication amid his caresses: a phantasmagoria of harsh grasps and pats and sharp pinches lain against rapidly over her splaying legs, her tender breasts, the maddening rear he revealed by rolling her over. Everything had to be touched, experimented with, murmuringly commented upon; but oh, that sweet temple of Sodom most especially. The sight alone made him gasp. "Ah, my God! What a side of beef you are, what a precious little heifer! Such a pretty ass—"

"Oh, God, Harold, will you fuck it? Please? Oh, I've never been fucked in the ass!"

"Never? Not in any body? Dottie, Dottie—oh, I'd love to take it. Eat it and fuck it—then eat it in a new way."

"My bag," she gasped, indicating her suitcase. "My bag, Harold, I brought lube—"

"Did you think I wouldn't have any?" Despite his teasing tone he was nonetheless delighted by her prudence—and by the somehow cute image of the girl fretting over the details while hastily packing her bag. He dragged the case his way, never able to leave the vision of that new body of hers writhing on the floor. There was something impossible about it, oh, yes—she was truly a dream-girl, some figment from his head. Or perhaps everything in his life had only depraved him enough that Dottie could someday accept him as her mate.

"Mate," yes, that was somehow the word. She was like a little animal, so eagerly heated for his attention that his own ape body could not help itself but respond. He was unable to wait a second; he did not take off his clothes. He only unbuttoned his trousers, freed his cock and grasped it with a pained cry while applying the lubricant to its surface. At the same time the source of her thrashing grew apparent. Her hand, those delicate fingers, worked between her thighs, and he might have wept for the privilege—the exquisite, unbearable privilege—of watching Dottie pleasure herself. God! God, God. He could have watched her all day. He would pay her to take off her clothes and masturbate for him if that was what it took. She was beautiful, so beautiful, oh, too good for him and all his repellent desires. Even that beautiful little asshole, that quivering pink pucker of love between the globular cheeks he carefully spread, yes! Even that was too good for him to violate—and that only increased the urgency of his need to violate her. Why, strictly speaking, her little ass was mint condition in more ways than one. This brand new body hadn't excreted any waste, had it? Eaten nothing, processed nothing. He gasped at this realization, this opportunity no man on Earth had ever had, and dove down to make her gasp with the audacious explorations of his tongue.

"Oh! Oh my God, Harold! Oh, Harold, that feels so dirty, so gross—oh, God, you're a disgusting man, what an old pervert, what an old creep, oh, oh my God, you're so good—"

Her flesh was so soft, the raw earthy scent of her hindquarters so pristine, that his moan against her resembled a sob. As he worked himself over, throbbing in his own hand, he shut his eyes to drown in the scent of her, the sound of her: not just the sound of her voice, gasping, moaning, chastising (and each appalled little remonstration of the pleasure he provided tripled his own pleasure, rest assured) but the wet sound of her delicate fingers sliding in and out, in and out, working through the slick lips of a cunt he daren't neglect.

"Spread your ass for me, Dottie." The grunted command came from him as if from somewhere or someone else— from whatever black spirit inside him directed the depraved patchwork of fantasies that inspired his sexual drive. Panting, she lifted her hands away from herself to obey; Harold knelt behind her, between those widespread thighs, to tend to the body that begged for his attention as he never knew was possible. While pressing the lubed head of his prick against that tight little rosebud between her splayed cheeks to receive a surge of already overwhelming pleasure, Harold's other hand slipped around her hip—not to grip, but to grope down to massage that wonderful, wet, almost virgin pussy of hers. Moaning sharply to be penetrated fore and aft by fingers and cock, Dottie braced herself upon all fours, his little bitch, and arched back against him to urge his penetration of her ass.

"Harold! Oh! Fuck, Harold—you're so big! You're so big, oh, you feel so good—"

Christ, fuck! He couldn't speak. He couldn't tell her how good she felt because he rather lost the capacity for words somewhere around inch three. The marvelous embrace of her tight channel was absolutely untrained and almost shockingly powerful. At the same time, to finger her brand new cunt was such a pleasure that each wet clench around his digits made him feel as if he had a second prick. Oh, she was a little succubus—yes, a demonic thief of his pleasure, rousing his desire to drain the energy from him until he was not a man, but an animal.

As he filled her to the top with his cock, Dottie groaned, then gasped to feel him draw back and begin to fuck her properly. "Harold, Harold—oh, you better be careful, you'll kill me again, how would you like to fuck me to death?"

"Jesus Christ—oh, it's all I want to do—yes, yes, oh, I might almost be satisfied for just a moment if I fucked you to death, Dottie." He clenched his teeth and gripped the back of her neck with his free hand, satisfied by the sound of her desirous yelp as he was by very few things in life. As his fingers sank into her neck (that neck, that perfect soft neck, a perfect duplicate of the one marred by postmortem lividity) she moaned, leaned up into his hand and back against his prick. Gasping at this new pressure, she rocked in time with the fingers that curled into her tight feminine orifice. "Oh, Dottie, I want to hurt you with my cock, I want to strangle you with my hands, I want to stomp your perfect little face to a pulp beneath my feet! Dottie!"

"Oh, Harold, Harold—Harold, nobody's ever made me feel like this, oh! Hurt me, Harold, Harold, please—"

Moaning, he shifted his grip from her neck to her hair. There he tightened his fist, yanking to expose her throat and shoulders to the savagery of his oral fixation. The girl cried out, sobbed attractively against the grip of his teeth: it would have been wonderful to make her cry. Oh, to truly make her cry—and then to dote on her, console her, beg her for forgiveness until she was so sick of him she could only spit in his face and send him away!

"Harold," gasped Dottie, straining against him as the copper taste of her blood caused another intense throb through his tightly embraced cock. He realized she was cumming when her asshole twitched so impossibly tight that he had to release his mouthful to cry out. Then, seeing the array of developing bruises his teeth had left in her shoulders and neck, he cried out a second time and ran his fingers over the one that had broken the superficial layers of her skin. A red print of his own teeth, there on Dottie's flesh! This pretty body, it would scar for him. Yes, he could mark her up most foully, cut her up and brand her with his initials like a side of beef, and then she would be fresh as a spring daisy whenever he finally decided to slaughter her.

Oh! Oh, fuck—God, to slaughter her—to think so casually of killing her. Yes, to kill her without consequence, as he had already killed her that night. His pleasure reached a pulsing crescendo and as Dottie emerged from her orgasm he achieved his own long-delayed one, spilling into her greedy little sphincter while weeping her name, holding her close, collapsing utterly beneath the unreal weight of—he had to admit within the confines of his depraved, dark mind—what was clearly what they talked about when they talked about true love.

He came to atop her on the floor, still inside her, their bodies collapsed together as if he had thrown himself over her to shield her from an explosion. Would that it had been an atomic bomb! A mushroom cloud whose inhuman fury could fuse their fleshes into one literal lump of abject lust.

"Oh," she sighed at last, a noise as welcome for the pleasure of it as it was unwelcome for its reminder that they were not, in fact, united in physical singularity. "Oh...Harold."

"Sorry that was so quick, darling."

"No, it's okay…oh…I like it when you call me that."

"Then I'll call you that all the time, Dottie. Whatever you want to be called." He turned his head to nuzzle the feather-light strands of hair in disarray against her cheek, pushing them aside with his nose and lips so as to permit him to kiss the curve of her fragile ear. "I—"

Oh, no—no, no, what was wrong with him? He came to his senses before completing his thought, choking back the words 'love you,' humiliated to have even had them arise. Instead he redirected course, finishing, "I'm so glad you let me steal you away, Dottie."

"I'm glad, too."

"I don't think I ever want to bring you back to the city…I don't ever want to let you leave me."

"You're so funny, Harold…I really like you."

His chest heaved with relief to hear a gentler, more cautious variant of his own narrowly avoided slip-up. "I think I like you more than anyone I've met," he said, lips parted against the lobe of her ear as though in awe as he drew himself out of her gasping body. While he tucked himself away, naked Dottie rolled over beneath him. Harold was incredulous to find her no less desirable in the usually placid aftermath of his orgasm than she had been at the peak of his lust. It was as if he could look at her for a few minutes and get it back up again. Like he was a teenager! She thrilled him so that he couldn't help but touch her—but pet her waist with his cleaner hand and laugh with her at the faint rumble of her stomach.

"Why don't we take a quick shower." He marveled at the statuesque features of her charmingly flushed face, bending to brush his nose against hers. "Then we'll have a little bite to eat…hopefully by then our delivery will have arrived."

He could have kissed those smiling lips until they fell off her perfect face. Dottie!

5.

HAROLD VIEWED DOTTIE as bees must have viewed flowers. From no angle was she not beautiful, not perfect—but from some she was simply irresistible. After they got cleaned up (and she had flattered his ego with her enthusiastic praise of his slate-themed master bathroom along with the brooding burgundy aesthetics of the primary bedroom), Harold left her wrapped in one of his robes yet was still somehow stunned to walk back in with the impromptu charcuterie tray and find her there, one arm pillowing her dreamer's head while she fantasized off in the direction of the closed balcony. When her head lifted to shower him with a smile, oh—she might as well have shot him with an arrow. He shut the door after him as if leaving it open might only encourage her to escape, then sat beside her to ease the tray down upon the bed. While she wiggled upright, she exclaimed, "Gosh, this looks delicious! Thank you so much, Harold—I'm always starving when I come back."

"I'm sure you are." Her nimble fingertips caught up a few grapes, juicy purple orbs with no idea how good they had it to be passed between those plump lips and eagerly chewed to pieces. Eat his heart, Dottie! "The amount of energy required to create a new body from absolutely nothing—a new adult body, no less—why, it must be astonishing. I wonder where you get it."

"I don't know! Not from eating, that's for sure…I feel like I could eat a freaking horse. Or a man." Her grin widened until she popped a piece of fig behind her lips. "Man, I still feel like I'm tripping out."

"Oh! *You* feel that way, do you, Dottie?"

Giggling, she rolled her eyes and said, "We can both feel that way for different reasons, it's not a contest…this is my life, I'm used to it. But what I'm not used to is—having somebody to share it with." Her grin widened and, now bashful, Dottie ducked her head toward the chest peeking out from the dark blue fabric of the borrowed robe. "You make me feel almost normal. That seems super dangerous somehow."

"It does to me, too. Escalation is a treacherous thing… who knows where we're liable to end up. We—at least, I—will have to work very hard to stay in touch with reality." Harold extended a grape between thumb and forefinger for Dottie to take. With a sultry quirk to that smile, the girl leaned forward and permitted him to press it between her lips. The brush of his fingertip against her teeth interrupted the very rhythm of his heart. To be that grape! To be masticated within those delectable jaws. He shuddered as, half-chewed grape visible in the crass open mouth he longed to kiss just then, she said, "You're one of those weirdos who likes to watch people eat, too? Dirty old man…my dirty old man." She swallowed the grape, her tongue lifting to make it vanish like a street performer disappearing a watch with sleight of hand. Then as she bit her lip, the dreamy concern of her eyes somehow only emphasized by the glasses reshaping them.

"Are you sure you really don't mind me calling you 'Daddy?' And so soon—"

"It's you who should mind. We've been talking long enough…talked about that long enough, and many other things. I don't see any reason why we should hold back just because we've only now realized one another's disguises."

The girl laughed as he guided her down to lie against his chest. Her head nuzzled through the fabric of his robe until she could lay her head against his naked heart. "But you were only just saying we should be careful about escalation, Daddy…careful about the difference between fantasy and reality."

He selected a few nuts, slipping one in his own mouth before pressing the others behind her waiting lips. "Of course, we should, but why…that is the reality. I'm your daddy now, aren't I, princess? The father of this beautiful body." His invasive hand, one of the same hands that had taken her perfect life that very night, slid within the confines of her robe to caress her breast and waist and yield a wanton gasp that would haunt him once the perfect bubble of their weekend was broken by the responsibility of the week. "I had been thinking before we left that the corpse was a kind of child of ours, but having thought on that since, I revise the notion now…your old body is the fertile material with which my hands engendered this body, your new body. Ah, Dottie"— she sighed as he drew open the robe and left her exposed, some lovely faerie queen embraced by the opened petals of a supple blue rose—"my gorgeous girl, my nymphet…I love to look at you but can hardly stand to. When I do it reminds me of all the things I must look at in the world that aren't you. Oh"—he moaned to stain her lips red with pomegranate seeds, the fruit with which she'd so often unknowingly teased him in the office—"it's a cruel world, yes, that reveals to me your existence and burdens me with duties outside serving you around the clock."

"You goof." She laughed at his romance, her grin as pleased as the blush of her face while she turned away to shun the eyes that drank in the fertile slopes and narrow curves of her athletic body. "Nymphets are, like, twelve."

"If I recall, Humbert lists the age range of nymphets as eight to fifteen…but he did not comprehend his own premise, being as he was a child-tormenting fool who would have told the reader anything to justify his illness. I love young women, I admit, but adult women…but now, having met you, I can't help but think Humbert comes closer to the truth of nymphet magic in that moment early on when he describes the necessary age gap required for a wretched old man such as myself to come under the nymphet's spell. And, oh, Dottie—I am humiliated to confess you've ensorcelled me. Slain me. Sweet Christ, one second I want to crush you in my hands and the next minute I wish to be your slave, your wretched slave worth little more than to kiss the dust off your boot."

What he liked about Dottie was that even when she teased him the light of joy was so visible in her face—so clear. When the women he paid to insult him did it you could see true disdain, hear the honesty in their disgusted insults. With Dottie, her delight to playfully jeer at and chastise him was barely-contained. The thrill she got to belittle him oozed out of her condescension even now as, sitting up and assailing him with her nakedness in a way that hadn't affrighted him quite so much when she was supine in his arms, she said, "Aw, but you'd be such a good slave to me, wouldn't you? Not totally unworthy. I know you'd do a good job keeping my boots clean, for instance…I wouldn't be able to help myself but praise you. Especially for being such a big sexy bull for me—ugh, Harold." Face flushed, she glanced down into his lap, shuddered, stared back up into his eyes from beneath the veils of heavy lids.

"Harold," she began, faltering, then looking at him in fear he understood better than he had ever understood any expression in any woman. Her hand lifted against his cheek;

he squeezed shut his eyes, pushed a long chain of kisses into her palm.

"Dottie," he said, tone almost miserable. "Oh, Dottie, Dottie…you can't make me feel like this."

"I think it's good to feel like this."

The country roads were so quiet he could pick up the sound of a car in the far distance and felt with an anticipatory stab deep in his gut that it was the delivery they'd been waiting for, or something related to it. So long as it wasn't the police. "Of course it's good," he told her in whisper as, removing her glasses and setting them upon the pillow beside him, Dottie drew his own away and leaned against his chest to kiss him. "Oh, God, Dottie—yes, of course it's good. Yes, but—"

As predicted, the car pulled into the gravel of the renovated slaughterhouse's driveway. An interruption in paradise; only brief, and necessary, but he was so loathe to even leave his bed now with her here in it. Ah, his soft and kissable little pet! "But oh, Dottie—where else is there to go from here? My feelings will only intensify—we will immolate each other—"

"Most people fall out of love after awhile…maybe you'll get bored with me."

Imagine that! He quite literally laughed, then glanced with reluctance toward the balcony. "Some loves are doomed to fade, but a few are doomed to deepen, and after tonight I can't help but for the first time feel a difference in the traj—"

"Do mean to say"—burst the barely contained girl, face glowing—"that you love me?"

Oh, Christ. Where was his gun? Somewhere in this house, fuck. He wanted to blow his brains out right there. Dying of embarrassment, Harold lurched away, swept up his glasses, cleared his throat. "Ah—ah, well, I—I'm very fond of—"

"I love you! I love you, too—Harold, Harold!" The girl laughed in delight, either oblivious to or overjoyed by the heart-wrenching agony such words from her could cause. As he gasped, aching, the intercom on the property's gate buzzed through the house's inbuilt speakers. Harold scrambled to the phone, answering, "Hello," as, in the background, Dottie said to herself with a giddy tone of delight, "Oh, I've never loved anybody before—you bad old man, making me feel this way so soon…"

"Hey baby"—Harold was meanwhile surprised to find Simonetta on the line but supposed she'd had to navigate to the obscure location—"we got a van coming in something in a few minutes. How you feeling?"

"Great," was his automatic answer while Dottie, giggling girlishly to herself, nibbled on a few pieces of cheese. Only belatedly did he realize it a good idea to amend that assessment. "Ah—all things considered, that is, goodness, what a surreal night."

"Mmhm."

"I'll buzz you in," he continued, merrily ignoring Simonetta's wry tone as he hung up the phone. Then, caught up in the act of watching the girl, he stood in appreciative silence until her attention forced him into action.

"Is my "sister" here?" She tried to keep the tone dry and casual, but the anticipation burning in her voice was more than evident. Maybe because he was so keenly in touch with his own explosive anticipation, his own rapid-racing heart.

"Almost." He divested himself of his robe to enjoy the lascivious burn of her brazen gaze into his anatomy. Lingering at the bedside, he crawled upon it once more, took the nude girl in his arms and kissed her sweetly flavored mouth. His tongue was unable to resist its slow dive into the pool of those lips. "Almost here, princess, oh, that old body of yours…my God, I'm so excited! I'm not sure I'll even know where to start."

Her grin was wild as she leaned out of the kiss, her eyes slowly opening. "Lucky thing this place used to be a slaughterhouse…I'm sure there's some useful stuff somewhere."

The intercom buzzed a second impatient time and Harold, smiling, stole one last smack of a kiss from her mouth, then slid out of bed. In the walk-in closet adjacent to the room he engaged in his usual country house custom of ignoring Molly's spare clothes (When was the blasted woman going to pick these up? Had to box them and ship them off to her—) while obtaining his own. This time the task of such willful blindness was much easier—easier than it had ever been since even before the divorce. Better yet, there was no shame attached to the mere thought of Molly's existence. Rather than a normal woman who'd mistakenly married an unacceptably depraved monster of a man, they were now just two people who hadn't been right for one another. Oh…how truly dangerous it was for Harold Fleetwood to feel even close to normal!

Especially given the circumstances. The power of the human mind to protect itself with cognitive dissonance was never more amazing to Harold than when he left naked Dottie alone to fetch the remainder of the money from a safe a few rooms away. *The* safe, in case you wondered. Yes, the same safe overflowing with his homemade faux snuff films, these videos of over-acting prostitutes pretending to be afraid of being eaten. Went back as far as 1999. After putting the money in a black leather bag and resisting the urge to go even slower at the third agitated buzz of the intercom through the house, he decided for fun to leave the safe open. Just to see. Would Dottie snoop? She'd find more than cannibal porn if she did. The idea of little Dottie taking to criminal impulses and robbing him blind was something of a queer thrill, but one of those many queer thrills unlikely to make it to reality. Just as well—he'd prefer to fear and trust her rather than fear and mistrust her.

At last, the money in the bag and the bag in-hand, Harold buzzed Simonetta and her pimp in on one of the many intercoms located throughout the house. He thought about that gun again, this time for self-defense purposes rather than histrionic over-reactions to his own inescapable emotions, but ultimately he decided such a thing was only asking for trouble. Better not have a gun on one's person if one didn't want to use it.

By the time he was down in the front hall, his guests were on the porch and the pimp looked infinitely more patient than Simonetta. Her expression was tight to see her client when at last he answered. "Took you long enough," she said with an annoyed wave of her crossed arms. Then, with a sharp glance to the empty space behind him: "Where's the girl? I want to talk to her."

"My goodness, Simonetta, I didn't realize you had such sisterly instincts. She's in the master bedroom"—the woman shoved past him to tromp off in the direction she knew well as her own house—"but please knock first, I left her in bed. Help yourself to a few bites of the cheese plate, if you're hungry."

Muttering something inaudible, Simonetta continued up the stairs and left Harold alone with the pimp. "Harry, baby," said the gregarious pimp, forcing a rapid handshake while stepping into the hall. "This is some house! You got a real sense of style."

Hard to take that compliment from a man whose profession was roundly known for its absurd tastes in fashion and jewelry. Nonetheless Harold forced a polite smile, expressed his thanks, and said, "Here's the rest," while passing the bag over. "I take it we can expect my—companion's sister any minute?"

"Yeah, they should be right behind us." Unceremoniously unzipping the bag to count the money then and there, the pimp went on casually, "They just had to finish cleaning the tub from the dismemberment, and—"

Harold's stomach sank a few inches, cruel, uncontrollable reality intruding on the dulcet tones of his fantasy life. "Excuse me? You dismembered her?"

"I didn't dismember her, the people I hired on your behalf dismembered her...some gratitude! You rich people are so entitled."

Now he was really glad he hadn't brought the gun, or he'd have considered holding the pimp up to get a partial refund back. "Perhaps I wasn't clear," said the CEO, trying to remain calm, praying they had done nothing else to hasten the decay of the body and ruin the meat or in any way interfere with the process he had envisioned. "I wanted—"

"It doesn't matter what you wanted. How the hell else are you supposed to get a grown woman's body out of the third floor of a fucking city apartment building?" While Harold, still reeling from being told that what he wanted didn't matter (only a pimp would have the audacity to say such a thing to a man like him), the pimp started counting from the top again and said with a shake of his head, "Be realistic. You or she or somebody killed a girl tonight. You don't get to be picky with the disposal details. Already weird enough that you're so concerned about doing the burial yourselves." Now the pimp glanced sharply up at him, stared into his face for a contemplative pair of seconds, returned his attention back to the money he counted on silently moving lips.

"Pretty interesting Simonetta won't tell me nothing about you," the pimp continued after satisfying himself and folding the bills over to tuck into the lining of his sportscoat. "She usually tells me everything. You must be into some real weird shit."

"Aren't we all." Another car in the distance, this one heavier, traveling faster. Even disappointed as he was to have had half the fun done for him, anticipation rocked Harold to his core. An ad hoc funeral procession for the cadaver he himself had made. Meat, delivered from the butcher. He supposed from that perspective he should try to be grateful for the dismemberment included in the deal…why, having never so much as butchered a cow on his own before, he might have done a sub-competent job even with Dottie's help. At least these fellows had experience in the task of dismembering this particular breed of dead animal. "Well"—Harold affected a sigh permitting him to stare away from the pimp of whose presence he'd long-since tired—"I apologize for being rather shocked to hear of the—method of transport, but I appreciate you organizing all this."

"Hey, no problem. But, uh, between you and me—a couple of professionals, men of business as we are—I don't know if I can continue sending Simonetta to you in good conscience. You understand, don't you?"

Harold glanced back sharply at that, keeping his face a perfect boardroom mask. "Accidents happen."

"And of course, I understand…but, like I said: *my* girls?" The pimp touched his own chest with one hand while gesturing broadly with the other. "They tell me *everything*. And I don't like this—this secretive shit. Usually, you know, Simonetta comes home from work with a funny story. A thing that happened, that the guy said or did. Something that made her laugh, whether it was on purpose or just something fuckin' stupid."

The pimp regarded Harold's face quite hard now. "But I don't hear none of that shit with you," he said softly. "And I figure…okay, he's a rich boy. He's private. I get it. But now…a thing like this happens…and you don't want the problem taken care of, but delivered to you, and apparently in one piece—I don't know," said the pimp at last. "I don't know."

"What don't you know?"

"I don't know what I don't know," was the vague, vapid response. "But what I do know is that I don't like it."

"Then I suppose we haven't much else to say to one another, have we?"

"No. I suppose we haven't."

"Very good." The intercom buzzed again as the van rumbled to a stop outside the gate. Without looking away from the pimp, Harold reached over to hit the red button of the intercom. "Who is it, please?"

6.

AFTER ACCEPTING BACK Dottie's spare key and engaging in a few minutes of discussion, Harold saw that the dismembered pieces of Dottie's old body—wrapped in plastic wrap like sides of beef and, to Harold's relief, undoctored by horror movie nonsense like lye or bleach or hydrochloric acid—were taken to the walk-in freezer in the back of the home. The loading area where trucks once pulled up to receive orders was still in-tact because it lent an aesthetic that Harold had enjoyed, but now he was very glad of it for far more practical reasons.

And all the while, as the men who had driven the black van unloaded the parts from within, the pimp watched. And watched. And watched.

"Some place to store a body," said the pimp, studying the parts arranged on a shelf bearing packages of other staple meats. Harold worked as hard as he possibly could to not gawk at the arrangement, much as most men struggled to avert their eyes from a sexy woman on the beach in the presence of their wives. "Don't see why you don't just want us to bury it for you."

"I don't see why it concerns you," said Harold, short with the fellow after all his incessant hovering. "Our transaction is over and you've already made it clear you've no intent to work with me further. Perhaps you'd ought to collect your employee and make yourself scarce."

"Touchy, touchy…I'll leave you two alone." With a glance in the direction of the starting van, the pimp studied Harold one more time and said with a tip of an invisible hat, "Adios, muchacho—pleasure doing business with you. Well…taking your money, at least."

Thank God! He left through the loading dock doors. Harold waited until the man had rounded the corner of the house before shutting those doors after him and, in the fulfillment of a long-held dream, sealing himself in with Dottie's dismembered corpse.

Dead or alive, in one piece or seven, Dottie had the same effect on him. Time slowed to a grinding halt and all space warped around her, it, them, these pieces of meat arranged on the shelf. Oh—God. One package in particular, big and round, called to him. Fluttered his heart. He edged near the shelf, past the empty beef hooks that had once been for display only but now would come to serve real purpose in his life. In Dottie's life—and, of course, Dottie's death.

With true reverence, he reached up and—oh, could he touch it? Could he? God! This was a human head—Dottie's head! An impossible dream: a nightmare for most but for Harold Fleetwood a most foul and ecstatic fantasy of romance. Divine love. Yes! Like Pygmalion saved by Aphrodite from the hopeless madness of loving a statue, Harold had been granted this grace by Love, by God, by the Devil. He had been rescued from emptiness, whisked into a fulfillment he'd so long and so piously resisted. He had every resource and inspiration to give into his temptations and indulge his perverse proclivities— and he had not. He had accepted he would not.

And the world had rewarded him with Dottie.

No. He couldn't touch it, her, the head, just yet. His hands recoiled, eyes misting with tears. "Oh, Dottie"—speaking to her corpse as if she were really dead! But wasn't she, in a sense? Wasn't this body irrefutable proof of the death of the woman yet living upstairs? Oh, he was going mad! What was consciousness, what was life, what was the soul?—"Dottie, Dottie, I love you, oh—I didn't mean to kill you, but I loved it, God, forgive me. God, have patience with me. This girl, this girl—"

He never wanted to be so far gone that he did not worship this girl. Whatever else happened in his life—however dissociated he became from consequence, from reality, from remorse—Harold prayed he would never fail to appreciate Dottie. That he would never truly hurt, betray her, while drowning in the sea of his own arrogance. Such things were steps to losing Dottie.

And having seen already what his life would be with Dottie, oh—Harold could never afford to live without her. Never, ever again.

After shutting off the lights to leave Dottie's corpse yet unmolested, Harold determined the pimp had not yet left but was nowhere to be seen in the foyer. At the house's top landing, a burst of feminine laughter emanated from the bedroom. The pimp, having apparently just found his way in (in his defense, it was quite a large home), leaned against the door while flirting with the women within. Harold loomed up behind him, satisfied to produce a slight jolt of panic response through the man.

"Jesus! You're one spooky fuck, you know that—all right, well, come on, Simonetta." With a little whistle and jerk of his head out to the hall, the pimp said, "Let's hit the road, our work here is done."

Dottie, wrapped safely in her robe while proving a natural hostess from where she sparkled upon the bed, grinned up at the prostitute. "Sure you don't want to stay the night with us?"

"Some other time, baby," said Simonetta, bending to familiarly kiss Dottie's cheekbone. Oh, she had a way of charming even the most guarded individuals, that was certain. Striding up to her (Former? Who could say.) client, Simonetta sighed, looked hard into Harold's face, then relented into patting him on the chest and leaning up to kiss his cheek. "Will you call me sometime and let me know how—how you're doing after all this?"

"Of course…if your employer will permit it."

"Let's talk in the car," was the pimp's response to Simonetta's fast look. She slapped away the hand he began to ease into the small of her back.

"I've told you not to talk to me like I'm a fucking child, Joe"—blast, well, at least he'd evaded learning the man's last name—"especially in front of clients."

"Ah, baby, you know I don't mean it like that—"

"Don't you 'baby' my ass right now—yeah, we'll be talking in the fucking car, all right." At the bottom of the stairs Simonetta stopped to point aggressively up at watching Harold. "You will call me," was all the woman said before yanking her purse high up her shoulder and storming out with the embarrassed pimp slinking after. They shut the door behind them and Harold waited for the sound of their car's engine before strolling down to bar the gates of Paradise once more.

Yes—to leave himself alone at last with Dottie. Dottie living, and Dottie dead. So much potential here. Oh…it was like another planet. The idea that real life could ever dare intrude was so offensive a notion to him that he banished it outright. He felt as if he could will the weekend to never end: could, by sheer force of his intense destructive desires, convince time to stop like Faust losing his bargain with Mephistopheles. "Stop, time," he whispered, his disappointment at his failure to control the very laws of physics diverted by the most attractive interruption possible.

"Are they gone?" Dottie leaned over the rail of the open second-floor foyer, her arms folded and chin resting upon them.

"Gone, gone." Oh…her beauty was so alarming to him. He was relieved he hadn't opened the package with her old head while alone in the freezer—that beauty might have compelled him to stay and miss out on this beauty, animated with life and bashful, girlish vigor. While she hid her smiling mouth behind her arms, Harold lifted a hand to her. "Would you like to come see yourself with me?"

That eager child's nod slew him. His extended hand folded in support of his heart while she, gay as a bird, scrambled down the stairs to fling herself into his arms with a cry of delight that he echoed. "Oh," he said, while Dottie gasped into his chest, "We're alone! Oh, really alone…Harold."

"Yes, darling…not entirely alone, though. Come on." Taking her delicate hand into his, Harold smiled and guided her through the hall. "I'll give you a little tour of the house while I still have the frame of mind to…"

For oh, that frame of mind was not to last and disintegrated every step they took through the house. Every room he showed her—the game room, the sitting room, the workout room, the cinema room—was but a torturous delaying of both their gratifications, a kind of sexual tease in which he was able to savor the tension of the girl's energy-packed body. Amazing that after all she'd been through, all the ways he'd used her, she was still so vibrant with activity and desire. Soon their held hands became an arm secured around her waist, lifting to pet her shoulder or reaching around to occasionally fondle through her robe (and bra, he couldn't help but notice she'd slipped into) a soft breast that heaved with interest while he showed her the family kitchen, the vast pantry, the sprawling wine cellar. "You're like Bluebeard, huh, Daddy…"

"Oh, don't flatter me so much…but do." He chuckled a bit while she laughed. "I love when you flatter me…and this hall"—he turned the knob of a custom-fit door adorned with Florentine frescos on one side and fearful, unbroken red paint upon the other—"is one of the ways to the slaughterhouse. See this, Dottie"—he opened a door in the hall to a spare bedroom, long and broad and mirrored along three walls and the ceiling for obscene accentuation of the sexual act—"it used to be a locker room, essentially…I had the showers partitioned off to make it a little less stark, but I had to keep that white tile behind the headboard wall up there, though…lends it such a fun butcher shop aesthetic, don't you think?"

As the girl slipped from his grip to hasten, grinning eagerly, into the echoing chamber, her head whipped from mirror to mirror, walls and ceiling, gasping with pleasure at all these other Dotties beaming back. "Oh, Harold, it's so cool in here—I love these!" With a coy grin back at him, she said, "You can imagine, I love mirrors…they make me feel safe."

"I thought you would love this room for that reason. Well"—he slunk after her to wrap his arms around her delectable frame once more—"don't worry…Daddy will put mirrors in every room of every house where his little angel dwells. Make it easy for you to find your way home again if you're ever lost."

His lips pressed into the top of her head and lifted away only to permit his appreciative study of their paired reflections, their images sharing the same mirror's space. Dottie too seemed captivated by the sight and clutched the forearm draped around her sternum, flushed to gaze into his face. "You're really good-looking, you know."

"You flirt…you do have a way of imbuing a man with perhaps unjustified confidence. I feel obligated now to look into laser eye surgery and start using my workrooms more avidly, I must admit."

"Aw, why? You're handsome with your glasses! All scholarly and quiet-looking…that makes it all the sexier when you turn out to be such a fucking psycho."

"What a tongue you have." He gave her one good whip of his hand against her soul-crushingly perfect rear and watched a multitude of Dotties gasp in pin-up response. While falling into the pattern of rubbing that same rump roast he'd stung, Harold studied her fluttering features and asked, "Would you ever consider losing the glasses, Dottie? Not that they're not exceptionally cute, but if you've ever thought of anything like LASIK or anything at all of that nature, I'd be happy to take care of you."

It had pained him to make the suggestion because he really did love the steely-eyed secretarial look the frames imparted to her glamorous green eyes. Luckily, she only laughed and wiggled against his body. "Trying to bimbo me up? Give me the old 177013 treatment?"

"No, no, just extending an offer. I want you to know—I want to be there for you, Dottie."

"That's very nice, Harold." Tilting her face back to part her lips in silent request for a kiss, Dottie let him smother her in love and knock both their spectacles askew in the process. She laughed softly, thrilled him with those dimples as he rectified the frames on her little nose, then told the riveted man, "I don't know if I've ever really thought about laser eye surgery… the idea freaks me out."

"Having seen the things you draw, that's astonishing."

"Well! It's eye stuff…ugh." She shuddered and then, going on with a little glance back into the mirror, said, "And anyway…I'm so shy. I have an easier time looking at people when I don't have to really look at them. I can take my glasses off and I'm blind. And men don't look at you as much when you have glasses…most men," she added with a bashful glance away, slipping from his arms to investigate the bathroom still completely lined with its original tiling and fit with very public shower stalls just made for disturbing acts of sexual depravity. While she leaned into the room with a little grin Harold was plagued by genuine shame to have heard her say such a thing, especially as she continued, "It really made me uncomfortable when I was, like, starting to develop and men started to catcall me—or just look at me, or whatever. But I found out when I finally got my eyes taken care of that they didn't pay me as much attention, so it was like a shield, or something…"

"I'm sorry for staring at you, Dottie—God, I tried so hard not to—"

"It's fine, Harold—"

"—you've just always been so beautiful to me, and you know—"

"Harold," she said more firmly, leaning her cheek against the door frame, "it's okay. Okay? I forgive you. You're a rancid pervert and we both know it…but now that I know who you are, the thought of you staring at me all the time back then—it turns me on. The memories are different now that I know who you are and what you were thinking. That's what's so disturbing about being a woman looked at by a man—you never know what's going on in his head. But I know just a little of what's going on in your head, Harold."

Her hand ran up the frame as if she desired to touch him instead; the robe shifted open and he caught a glimpse of the girlish peach lace of a bra matched to the floral fabric of her panties. "And I want to know more…I want you to stare at me. I want to look up from my desk at work and see you, door open, trying to catch glimpses of me from across the heads of all your other employees. I want to look at you"—she followed his gaze and her hand stroked back down the door frame, traced her shoulder, opened the quilted fabric of the robe that soon fell at her feet—"and see you remembering what it's like to fuck me…and to kill me…and to eat me."

Above the sound of blood rushing through his nervous system, Harold managed to make out the words, "Where's my dead body, you murdering piece of shit?"

"This way," he said, almost trembling with desire—the desire not just to penetrate that beautiful body now contained only in its lingerie, but to do with deliberation and careful enjoyment what was before performed only by accident. Following his gesture, the smiling girl left his robe behind and hurried through the room. He stooped to pick up the abandoned garment and bore it with him, following her on the path to the hallway's end. "Oh," she said with a gasp of delight, throwing open the door, "why, Harold—"

He had compromised with himself in the end. The abattoir had been divided in half as the room, owing to the nature of the enterprise, was just so vast; but the primary chamber was still the same in original design. Still tinted by the blood of so may dead cows, still with the carefully guided creek flowing through a concrete-lined disposal trench intended to carry effluvia off and away from the site with minimal effort. The wing of the room he had destroyed had been elaborately remodeled so that, prior to its flowing through the killing floor, the meekly moving creek irrigated a sumptuous botanical garden. This greenhouse (full of enough of lively variety that Harold could have shut himself into the house with Dottie for months and fed them both amply on a combination of his vegetables and her meat) was visible from the abattoir by way of a great glass wall, and it had a way of making all guests taken for a tour stop in their tracks.

Dottie was no exception. He caught up to her and kissed the feather-soft curve of her neck while draping her in his robe again. Without tearing her eyes away, she asked, "Will you show it to me after?"

"Of course." No need to ask her 'after what.' Such clarification was beyond either of them. After their passion had again receded enough that they could function, perhaps. After he stopped feeling in her presence so much the animal, so much the feral beast presented with prey unlike any other.

Her hand slipped into his. He drew the breath from her lungs with another kiss before guiding her to the cold storage where her old corpse was being kept. While the light flickered on, she took a step toward herself with a noise of displeasure. "They cut me up already!"

"Trust me, I gave our delivery boy a piece of my mind about that…but it occurred to me that they saved us quite a bit of trouble and experimentation on our first time out."

He was unable to follow her and released her to investigate her own dismembered parts. "I guess that's true…just more reason to do it again." With a sultry look back at him for too short a span, Dottie turned to do what he could not. She reached up, hefted her old head down from the shelf, and laughingly said, "Wowee! It's way heavier than I would have expected."

And then—oh, St. John the Baptist, pray for his crippled soul—then that she-devil, that thief of his heart, knelt down upon the floor, lay the parcel in her lap, and began to unwind the blood-obscured saran wrap concealing her own severed head.

"How ugly." Her nose wrinkled as she examined the bloated head, it lips painted with mother nature's own necrotic purple cosmetics. "It doesn't even look like me anymore, really!"

"You only say that because you're so used to seeing yourself in mirrors. Inverted." He dared edge near her; nearer still until, with trembling fingers, he leaned down to draw her hair back from her living face in aid of her assessment of the dead one. "She is all you…look, her little beauty mark. God." He brushed its duplicate on her face to make her sigh, ruminating on her comments about her discomfort with eye torture while his thumb came to rest against that sweet freckle so dangerously high upon her perfect cheekbone. Poor angel. He wished more than anything to sin against her in those ways he was certain she would not enjoy. The girl stoked the fire of his sadistic imagination and made him wish to create new offenses, completely novel indecencies mankind had never had the capacity to summon up before Harold Fleetwood met Dottie Shipman. Ah—Dottie Shipman, who gazed up at him adoringly with her own head in her lap. "Amazing that you should be so beautiful, head severed, blood pooling in your cheeks—"

"I want to keep it and practice doing makeup on it. Like one of those Barbie heads! I always wanted one." Laughing gaily, Dottie hefted the thing to examine in the light. Her hand lifted from its chin to its forehead to smooth some bloodstained hair away. The priceless artifact wobbled on its pedestal: Harold gasped, cringing forward, seeking to hold it upright—

And realized only belatedly that he had dared to touch it. Cold flesh—so cold! Oh, it didn't even feel like flesh somehow. Yes, this was the difference between flesh and meat: this heft, this stillness unsupported by self-aware consciousness. He gasped quietly to touch it, then again to find Dottie watching him closely, her hand still upon the forehead against which she smoothed her thumb.

"Harold." Dottie glanced at his trousers, smiling, the two of them kneeling together to hold aloft her abandoned head. "I like you an awful lot, Harold."

"I like you an awful lot, too, Dottie."

"You want to watch me kiss it, huh, Harold?"

"Yes, Dottie," he said, breath held so tightly he could barely form the words. His eyes, unable to meet hers, settled somewhere around her smiling cheeks. "Yes, I'd like that very much."

"Okay…since you're so nice to me, Mr. Fleetwood, I'll let you watch me kiss my own dead body…oh"—the minx paused mid-lean and seized his heart with frustrated anticipation as her tone grew sheepish—"but you won't tell anyone I'm such a dirty girl, will you?"

"No, no, of course not, Dottie…oh, Dottie, all this is just our little secret. Yes"—he held his breath as she turned to face herself, her smile fading into a flush-faced look of wonder; of lust enough to shame his own—"yes, our secret. Daddy won't tell if you won't, angel."

He couldn't keep himself from crying out to see her press her lips to those of her own decapitated head. It was a sight more resplendent than any he had beheld in his life up to that point in time—like something from an erotic fever dream, but so much better. It was real. She was real. Dottie slipped her tongue into the mouth of the old self Harold had murdered and his cock pulsed with the same incredulity that forced him to remind himself this was happening. It was too easy for him to convince himself all this was some dream.

But it was not. No dream. Time elapsed. Seconds passed. He stroked her hair while she kissed herself, daring to slide his hands beneath the robe's fabric and draw it away to admire how her body dimpled sharply with the intense cold of the freezer. She fell forward all the same, the head in her hands, nursing hot red kisses from its gray lips as she so passionately did from his. Oh, Christ! She made his body hurt, ached his prick for her embrace. Harold reconsidered the cunt he had earlier scorned in favor of her pristine asshole. How he craved her…he bent over her, kissing the curve of her spine, hands running over her body while he admired with a condescending tut the bruises and scabs his savage teeth had scored into her shoulders.

She lifted her face away from her head and chided him with stained lips. "If you start fucking me here, Daddy, how will we get dinner started? I just wanted to give you a little show…I didn't mean to make it all hard again."

"You wicked girl, of course you meant to—lying to me again, are you—"

Giggling, the girl clutched the head to her bosom and rolled away with it until, far enough from Harold, she sprang upright to set it on the shelf. "I can't give it to you all at once! You're already spoiled, you bad man…you don't need to be spoiled more. Here—grab this."

She indicated a longer package set adjacent to the head and, while he erased his own doubts and satisfied himself that clutching her dismembered limb to his body was almost as good as clutching her living ones, Harold took the package and laughed despite himself when she said, "You're pulling my leg!"

"Goodness, you silly girl…"

He had to admit that she had a disarming way about her—ugh, more limb-related puns. Unintentional, rest assured. Regardless, Harold found her levity eased his fear of touching her. Of holding that long hindquarter of meat, his victim's little body. The fear had been in the disgraceful nature of it, but by staying bright and funny and, well, Dottie, she let him relax. Let him take it less seriously and, most importantly, see it not as a desecration, but a celebration. A celebration, yes—of their love. Of their coming together. Finding one another.

Tucking the parcel under his arm, he drew her quivering frame close and lowered a lingering kiss to her mouth. He gasped to taste the copper blood of the corpse upon her; his tongue dove in against the same one that had lashed dead flesh but moments before and the lust of it all was so intoxicating he could only push her away with a gasp. "God, you're right—if we don't cook something now we won't make it back to the blasted kitchen before Monday."

She laughed at him, leaping giddily up and away, saying with a schoolgirl's pure mirth, "I told you, I told you—you dirty old man, you can't keep your hands off me—"

While her feet padded swiftly away and paused only to grab the robe, he found himself weak to the bone with the knowledge that she was right. Oh, never again could he be in her presence and fail to feel the phantom sensations of her body pressed to his, sagging his arms, held in the happy palms of his hands.

When he caught up with her, convinced he was either the most rewarded or the most tortured man on earth, Harold found Dottie's pert little ass poking around the edge of the refrigerator door. "There's so much food in here! Oh my gosh, what'll we start with? I'm so overwhelmed, it's like being a kid in a candy store—"

She stood up at the thump of her leg upon the kitchen island and laughed as she was dragged into a smothering kiss. "Hey"—she giggled into his mouth—"you're supposed to eat my old body, not this new one yet…gosh, Harold—"

"You don't understand—Dottie." He clutched her bare shoulders so hard beneath the robe that she yelped, then gazed at him with fresh desire. "This—what you're doing for me. I couldn't possibly thank you. Not the way you deserve to be thanked. I'm going to take one bite of that flesh and be your slave forever."

"That's my plan," she said softly, that devil light rising up in her bright eyes again. "Yes, that's what I want…for you to be my slave forever, Harold."

"Oh, Dottie…"

"If I were really mean"—she glanced over at her severed limb then back at him, drawing her fingertips down his chest—"I'd cook my leg myself…I'd make you watch me eat it all up, bite by bite, and not give you anything at all."

"Cruel mistress!"

"So you better remember your place and do a good job begging me for my meat." She stared hard into his face, expectant. "Yes, you better beg and plead and give me some good reasons why I should let you become my slave…why you should be lucky enough to get my attention forever, even for the mean treatment slaves deserve."

Oh, it was true! It was a privilege, an absolute privilege, to drop to his knees on the hard tile of the kitchen floor and be stabbed by her laughter as he gripped the robe around her, buried his face in it, demeaned himself upon the ground to kiss her perfect pale feet. "Oh, Dottie, please, you demon! You goddess! I would do anything for you—oh, I've known you, truly known you and all the wonders you contain for just a few hours; yet I'd end my very life for you, Dottie! I'd leap from a window for you! My God, oh, Dottie, I'll buy you cars, jewels, drugs, homes, *people*! I'd cut off my arm for you."

"No you wouldn't," she remonstrated him, laughing and catching his arm as he sprang up. "Okay, so you would—but don't. I don't know if we could get it back to you."

"Dottie, I'm mad for you—Dottie—" He gasped from the inception of the words, unable to help himself as he continued to say through eyes reddened with tears of desperate obsession, "Dottie, I love you—oh, I love you, and it makes me realize I've never loved anyone before. I've never even loved myself."

"Harold…" Her mocking smile having faded to genuine awe, Dottie bit her lip and lay a hand upon his chest. "You're too old to say a thing like that so soon after sleeping with a girl for the first time."

"Then you should know that I mean it—that I am truly mad, truly desperate, if I would dare say a thing that would be so preposterous to me if anyone else said it under any other circumstances. But you, Dottie—I mean it. I meant it before when it was an accident but now, darling, oh, Dottie, now, I'm saying it willfully: I love you."

Eyes sparkling, the girl whispered back into his face, "I love you, too," and his heart screamed with pleasure. Oh, Christ, he could have leapt in place to hear it. It was one thing to hear it while dying of embarrassment as he'd been before, but another thing in a moment like this: a pure moment, a moment where his only shame came from his inability to openly share that love with the world. He wanted it in press releases, written in the sky: DOTTIE LOVES HAROLD. No wonder idiots carved such things in trees.

And, speaking of carving. Looking unable to bear another second of the intense intimacy they shared, the girl slid away to study her hindquarter up-close. He braced himself against the kitchen island, mouth and nose brushing the top of her head as she carefully unwrapped the plastic from what looked like, whether on accident or with Simonetta's subtle guidance, a quarter close to properly butchered—half that cute little ass he loved. Jesus, Jesus. He was really seeing this. Oh, his heart raced in his chest. Yes, a dismembered piece of lovely, lovely young woman meat. He swooned; moreso when the girl grinned and fondled herself, twisting her dismembered limb this way and that, then saying with a laugh of recognition, "Oh, see my birthmark?"

She indicated her attached calf below and he said, "No, no I haven't, let me—" even as she tried to ward him off with, "That's all right, I'll show you—hey!"

He had stooped again, now to lift the robe up and hum and marvel over the same little bruise-like blot on the back of her divine dexterous calf. While he kissed it tenderly, she laughed and shrugged the robe off to permit it drop upon his head. "You dork!"

Overwhelmed by Dottie in her lingerie again, Harold swayed to his feet. A peculiar look crossed her face; her delicate fingertip pressed beside the duplicate birthmark, a deathmark now, stamped upon the meat.

"Your turn," she said.

His mouth watered; his blood rushed. Harold knew very well what she meant and, making eye contact until the very last second, he leaned down to paternally press his lips to the light wine mark forever stained on the flesh of Dottie's body whether old or new. As awareness of what he was doing rose up in him, he felt only an insane thrill, a fantastic achievement: yes, yes. He had done it. He was doing it. He had killed a girl—killed her with her permission.

And now, also with her permission—and with her very help, by God—he was going to eat her.

When he straightened to admire Dottie's enchanted visage, she took a few seconds to appreciate his face before grinning shyly. "I have no idea what to do," said Dottie. "Do you?"

"God no," said Harold. Together they laughed while regarding the leg, then all of five minutes later sat nearby, a spare tablet set up and running helpful Internet videos of butchers breaking down cow legs into all variety of mouth-watering cuts for sale. Harold watched very quietly, fading in and out, his attention drawn so often back to Dottie. Dottie leaning forward in her seat to see the hindquarter of beef hanging from its hook. Dottie with her fast breathing as the flesh was manhandled and slapped to demonstrate this or that muscle worthy of differentiation. Dottie and her shifting in Harold's agonized lap as the proper work began—as fat was carved from muscle and muscle hacked from bone.

"Looks like we'll need a lot of tools," said Dottie, her words a whisper when Harold finally gave up the cause of attention to the task to instead pay it to the nearly naked girl in his lap. While he pressed kisses over the mouthwatering curve of her shoulder, she sighed and rolled back against his touch. "You've probably got a bone saw around here, right? An old slaughterhouse..."

"All kinds of fun antiques, but who knows what shape they're in. We'll have to buy new tools." While Dottie leaned forward to skip the ad before the next video, this of a whole cow being dismembered by a mobile butcher, Harold ran his hands over her ribs, down her waist, over her squeezable hips and thighs. "Assuming you ever feel inclined to indulge me this way in the future...who knows. I may botch the job so badly I offend you. Oh, I'm terrified."

"Don't be...I've never done this before, either." She rocked in his lap, again riveted to the tablet and the dead cow lain on its back in the grass. Harold's body seemed to glow as she said, "Of course I want to do all this again, Harold. This is just practice—tonight, this weekend. It's like a template. We can always do things different or better in the future...it's just a start."

As the carcass on the screen had its tail removed and its hide stripped, Harold planted kisses along the curve of Dottie's ear. "I want to kill you again, Dottie."

With a gasp that sounded far more of delight than of fear, the girl glanced over her shoulder, tilted her head back, offered her mouth to his kiss. His tongue slithered into her mouth, attempting to steal some taste of what her dead body would soon enough offer, and her hips reflexively arched. Those nimble hands slid between them and pawed through his trousers until he pushed her away to free himself. While he did, she pushed aside her panties, and as she surmounted the peak of his pleasure once more, they gasped in time with the recorded snap of a bovine bone. She soon fell into rocking upon his lap again, bathed in his kisses and the caresses of his hands until with a new gasp as the video ended the girl admonished him: "Harold! It's two in the morning—at this rate, we'll never get anywhere. Come on—"

"No, oh, Dottie, please—" He gripped her, kissing her ear and almost sobbing as she escaped his clutch by boxing his ear.

She dismounted him with a laugh. "You pathetic weirdo… I'll let you fuck me all you want later. For now, let's see what we have to work with!"

After some consideration for the relics of the house (and no small amount of clearing his head with a brisk breathing exercise in the bathroom) Harold did manage to come up with a passable bone saw and a wide number of specialized knives, all of which had been relegated to decoration in the slaughterhouse bedroom. Once he returned to Dottie, well… that was where the real fun began.

Oh—but you didn't want to hear the details of the messy first time, did you? It *was* a mess, truly. Harold was embarrassed, especially given the way things would develop later. For him to admit that he was never an expert at the art of butchering dead women for consumption would be tantamount to Dottie admitting that she did not walk out of the womb with a pencil in her hand and an autographed manga by Shintaro Kago under her pudgy cherub arm. There were certain parts of the process an artist kept to themselves.

Certain elements of that first time were worth noting, however. He was not completely inept at the task. Dottie insisted he commit himself to it and permit her to watch that first time, and he found that very quickly he fell into a kind of meditative grace. A personal relationship—solitary, almost religious—with this meat he had made from this girl that he loved. And oh, he did love her! Loved the soft, supple flesh of her rear into which he plunged the ultra-sharp tip of a cruelly curved blade, penetrating her less than a centimeter. Beneath Dottie's studious, often gasping attention, Harold peeled back the flesh from the assortment of white glossy fat and luscious red meat that made him consider how long it had been since his last full meal.

Perhaps it was the years of fantasizing, or the juxtaposition of this meat against the cow butchering video they had just watched; either way, Harold only realized late in the process just how fully dissociated he was from the notion of his cannibalism. He *wanted* to be aware of it—this automated compartmentalization of the taboo act seemed some unconscious mechanism, some act intended to protect the fragile psyches of ill-fated survivors found in the Alps or trapped adrift at sea. But he did not want to be protected by his own mind. He wanted to know. He wanted to be aware, hyper-aware at every second, that he had killed Dottie; and she was now meat; and mankind, an omnivore, was made to eat meat. He was going to eat Dottie. He was going to feed Dottie her own body, her old body. They were going to cook her together.

And all the while, Dottie was riveted. She did not judge him for his missteps, and there were many. Oh, he was embarrassed! It was awful to think about, one of those memories that made a man cringe when it floated up in the middle of the night. That beautiful body, that beautiful leg Dottie had by then carried for some years, he savaged it—and still the girl assured him he did a perfectly fine job carving. He had to admit not all of it was bad. He was pleased with the job he did on the round, cutting deep into the gluteus maximus and watching Dottie's face haunted by hunger and unspeakable desire as he braced himself down against the counter to tear the meat cleanly from the bone. She hurried over as the white joint shone with its exposure and, gasping to do so, held the bone down to aid Harold's task. The round peeled away in one great piece and she admired it with him, prodding her own soft flesh and bending back to kiss him.

"Thank you for working so hard for us," she whispered sweetly.

"A man had ought to provide for the woman he loves… speaking of, you don't eat much, do you, Dottie?" He leaned against her little body, pinned her to the island to make her gasp at the hard prod of his cock. Oh, he was aching to be freed again from his trousers—to at the very least press against her ass. Chin upon her shoulder, Harold demonstrated on the meat, pressing a finger invasively here and there against the tendons. "Not much marbling on you at all, princess…we'll have to fatten you up just a little for next time, won't we?"

The girl laughed at him, nose wrinkled. "You're not going to make me *fat*, Harold."

"Oh, not fat…but I can tell you're not spending your money on food." He lowered his red-stained hand to grab her ass through her peach panties, then slide his bloody fingers inside them. There he stroked and slapped and made her moan, throbbing, dying. As her hand lifted to cradle the top of his head and urge his kisses down her neck, he sank his fingers into her new round cut in the making and massaged the tender muscle. "I mean it. Let me take care of you, Dottie. You'll want for nothing."

"You bad man! Stop teasing me and finish this job. I'm so tired…and hungry!"

So was he. God, he was famished. The task was hard work but his hunger was owing to far more than energy expelled. It was irresistible, this hunger—and more than hunger, too. Oh, there was never a chance his hunger for her could be sated. He knew that for a fact going in. But—well.

He did not expect her flesh to have the precise effect that it did.

7.

A TASK THAT would someday take Harold all of twenty minutes took them roughly an hour the first time they worked together—but the result, though rough, was beautiful. They saved the bones for use in soup and stored the fat for general purpose, debating about what to do with the hide until Harold reluctantly agreed it had ought to be incinerated in the slaughterhouse's old bone waste disposal unit for want of anything better to do with it at that point in time. Again, another painful memory! But first times were for mistakes, it was true.

And the goal of the process was not the hide at all, whatever culinary and fashion uses it had. The goal was the meat, the red and beautiful meat that, once broken down, was wrapped in butcher paper and reverently stored in the refrigerator for their meals over that weekend. By then it was three-thirty in the morning and they had decided their first meal together would be breakfast. Since Harold had done all the labor of breaking down the cuts, Dottie insisted on cooking. It was his great domestic pleasure to sit at the kitchen table, drained from a hard physical task, eagerly anticipating the sights and smells of a meal being cooked for him by a divine girl decked only in bloody underwear. Yes, lord, oh, Harold Fleetwood was a happy man; an eager man.

Was it possible for him to look too eager? He didn't want to scare Dottie off but it was absolutely imperative he keep her. How pitiful—Harold felt he had to trick her into staying with him, nothing beside her even with assets worth billions of dollars. And it was true, wasn't it? He *was* nothing beside her. Money couldn't buy immortality. It couldn't buy you an unlimited supply of girl meat. It couldn't provide you with this, the surreal of experience of having that girl meat cooked by the very same girl. The girl he killed, the girl he killed. It all kept coming back to his new identity as a murderer.

What cause had she to give him time of day—their shared interests? There were plenty of real depraved shitheads into the fantasy of torturing, mutilating and eating women, and Harold had the strong sense that more than one billionaire was among that group. If all she wanted was someone who was obscenely rich and into Dolcett, well, she could have had whomever she wanted. Therefore he feared their love was a matter of circumstance. Of convenience, and novelty. He could already tell that the novelty would never—could never—wear off for him. He wanted to nail shut the doors and keep her hostage until he expired of natural causes or her machinations to escape. He would never tire of Dottie.

But oh, God, he prayed Dottie wouldn't tire of him. When breakfast was ready she wiped sweat from her brow and insisted, "Let's go eat in that garden you showed me," which was quite a walk away but worth it in the end. They took a little picnic of steak and eggs and French toast down to the greenhouse with them and there amid the emerald flora Harold and Dottie huddled together beneath a carefully cultivated mimosa tree. They observed their plates in awe. So innocuous, the little meal! Beautiful coloration on the steak. What a good little cook—vital prerequisite for a wife.

"Go on," whispered the girl, looking up into Harold's face. "You should take the first bite. I want to watch you."

"Oh, I feel the same…let's do it together."

With a short laugh, she said, "Okay," and sank her fork into a rare piece of the pre-sliced steak. Harold did the same and smiled as, perhaps meaning it as a joke, she hooked her arm around his as though they were sharing wine. When her giggling faded they each took their respective bites from within a tunnel of eye contact that failed as the flavor settled on Harold's tongue: then, he shut his eyes beneath a gasp.

Wagyu beef—yes, that was the closest. Carefully seared A5 wagyu steak, specifically his favorite strain from the Hokkaido region of Japan: pampered cows imported at a fortune because their meat was so obscenely delectable that people who had it once would never look at the experience of all steak the same way again. Dottie's flesh had the delicate, melting quality of wagyu, but there was more to it than that: the infamous pork notes were in there, along with an almost literal buttery flavor so intense it pushed the meat out of the savory realm and into a sweet one. Even without a notable amount of fat owing to Dottie's low-budget meal habits, the dense explosion of flavor overwhelmed all Harold's the senses. It was as though everything else disappeared. All that was left was the taste and texture of Dottie's meat—oh, God, Dottie's meat!—as he savored it, chewed it, swallowed it. Her.

Oh, God. He swallowed her.

"Say, this really is—Harold!" The girl laughed as he dove upon her, bruising her mouth with the force of his kiss until she gasped and twisted her head. "Harold, oh—that's very nice, but your breakfast—"

"Ah—" She was right, blast it. Would that he had two mouths. It was so difficult to focus on the sensual experience of the meat when he was also overwhelmed by the notion of what a gift the experience was—of how beyond the very concept of value Dottie stood in his mind. One arm sliding around her lovely waist, Harold committed himself to focusing on the indulgence that was her flavorsome meat before availing himself of the pleasures of her living flesh.

Yet there was almost something living about her dead flesh. Every bite was swallowed with the acute awareness that he was taking Dottie, beautiful Dottie into him—into his body, to be integrated into his system as energy. Dottie, sustaining his very life. Oh, miraculous girl! Strange creature from heaven—for no matter how wicked she was, such a perfect being could never be from hell. Indeed, this life he had lived, it was hell without her whatever his achievements. Oh, he saw that: saw it especially as the flesh's psychedelic effects kicked in.

With experimentation he would learn these effects were controllable; that cooking preparation, more even than amount, had a great deal to do with the degree of effects on Harold's person. Consumed raw or partially cooked as the steak was, for instance, Dottie's flesh had a way of exceeding what he would come to regard as the customary aphrodisiacal quality of her meat in favor of something far more dissociative. A certain tolerance build-up was also notable: therefore, eventually Harold would decide the best way to avoid being overwhelmed by the effects of Dottie's flesh and losing consciousness to another black-out episode of primitive lust was to simply eat a little of her every day. To inoculate himself, as it were, against the overwhelming compulsions and spiritual nature of her meat.

Though oh—what wonderful compulsions they were! Once he learned to recognize a trip's onset—and once he learned how short it was in duration—Harold began to look forward to these marvelous effects and would sometimes force himself (torturously) to go without Dottie's flesh for a few days so he could enjoy a short psychedelic episode. The first time, however…

During his "rich white person tries Shamanism" phase, Harold stumbled across a video of a jaguar that had eaten from the ayahuasca vine. The great beast, thrashing about on the ground—that was what Harold quickly came to resemble, he sensed. One minute he was enjoying the closeness of Dottie's living body while dining on her flesh, the next minute his ribs felt oddly pressurized and his chest tensed in a way he couldn't explain; he lowered the fork, worried that his ecstasy had brought on a heart attack and he would die right on the cusp of true happiness.

"Are you okay, Harold?"

Dottie's question echoed. He turned his head and was startled as the plants around broke into a series of geometric shapes still in the vague color palette of the greenhouse fauna. This surreal but beautiful kaleidescope then reformed into linear spacetime when he stilled to focus on Dottie.

Oh! Oh—Dottie, Dottie. Dottie, Dottie—he couldn't think anymore. His eyes fell upon her and his blood surged. His ability to form a stream of consciousness vanished and everything was reduced to a set of responses to Dottie: that most important stimulus in his life. Harold pushed the plate aside, and hers, and while she cried out he caught her face in his hands and kissed her with bruising force.

"Harold, oh—what's gotten into you, oh, you brute—oh, don't stop—"

He wouldn't. He couldn't. Oh, it was exhilarating as it was terrifying. The rest of reality trembled, whizzing away in some fractal-tunnel of ego space, and in the black void left behind there was Dottie in the center. Dottie, pure as snow. Dottie, more real than anything in his life. Oh! His false and pointless life. What a dream it all was! What a fiction! Yes, it was nothing. The Lord giveth and the Lord taketh away. Someday Harold would be dead and what would his money be to him, then? What, what? Who would even bother to come to his funeral? Those that did would have simply gone on with their lives. And him?

He trembled, feeling as if his muscles were set to burst from his skin while he tore her underwear from her body and moaned with animal desire. "Harold, Harold, oh, your eyes—your pupils are huge!"

In the process of trying to remove her bra with hands that could rely only on muscle memory to accomplish such a task in that moment, he slipped and tumbled forward. Laughing, Dottie scrambled up from beneath him to push him onto his back. "Oh, Harold, your pupils aren't the only thing that's huge…did my meat do that to you? My nice, tasty girl flesh?" Her hand ran over the front of his trousers and much as the sense of taste had overwhelmed him to hold her steak in his mouth, his sense of touch was now all he knew. It blotted out his every other drive, crippled him with its intensity so he could only lay helpless, receptive as her hair tickled his face and her head bent to press a kiss to his obedient mouth.

"You really *are* my slave like this, huh…*my* fuck-slave, Harold. Let's get this out."

"Oh, oh—"

"Gosh, you're so sensitive! Oh"—her pornographic gasp made him moan, made him clutch for her thigh until she climbed aboard and immediately claimed each inch of his cock for her own screaming, greedy pleasure—"oh, fuck, fuck! Harold, your dick is so big!"

"Dottie—"

"You like that, Harry?" Her hands braced upon his chest, Dottie rocked those splendid hips up and down his throbbing length; he gasped low to feel how soaking wet she was and nodded mutely as the perverse little strumpet went on. "I bet you do…oh, gosh, my meat sure does have an effect on you."

The light of pleasure rising in her eyes, Dottie reached out of his field of rosy vision and returned with a piece of meat pinched between the delicate fingers of her hand. "Open your mouth, slave…your mistress has a gift for you…"

His whole body throbbing for more stimulation by the

second, he did, lips parting while his hips thrust up hard into her. While moaning to be assisted in her self-impalement, Dottie lowered the piece of human meat into Harold's mouth and her pussy fluttered around his cock to place it on his tongue.

"A nice treat for my good slave…good slave." While he chewed her up, she stroked his face and fucked herself until she looked ready to cry. "Oh, yes—such a good, good fucking slave, oh, Harold…oh, here—"

The next piece, she delivered from her mouth to his. Her tongue pushed the soft piece of longpig past his teeth and continued the kiss for an unsafe second before she sat up to watch him chew and swallow. She reared back and he recognized she had always been a beautiful, coiling serpent: that she had slithered out of the jungle to teach him how to use her venom as that treasured ayahuasca vine was said to have taught its own ways to the shaman. The shedding of her skin, this skin she pushed and kissed into his mouth until she had fed him every last bite of herself, was the mystery of birth, of transmigration, illuminated for the human being. The mystery of God, demonstrated by this maligned reptile. Beneath all the skins, all the rebirths, what lay inside the snake?

He drew back to reality just a little when her orgasm seized his cock. Groaning, Harold managed to regain enough muscle control to reach up, catch her face in his hands and watch her scream for the intensity of her pleasure. When the quake was reduced to aftershocks he drew her down to his chest and rolled her over, and with her upon her back he drew her hips up high. She braced herself against the tree behind her head while he worked her over good and hard, almost blinded by the intensity of the sensation but beginning to rapidly return to himself. Reality vibrated a little less at least, and he had frame of mind enough to extol to her through clenched teeth, "Christ, oh, ah—Dottie, Dottie, if it was your last supper re-enacted every Sunday, the Church would fill every pew in every cathedral. Dottie! Ah, fuck, my hot little dead girl, my scrumptious little carcass, you liked watching Daddy eat you, didn't you—"

"Yes! Yes! Fuck, Daddy, yes—oh, fuck, fuck me, Harold, oh, Daddy, oh—hrnk—!"

Her legs had wrapped around his hips and he took advantage of his liberated hands to catch her around the throat. While her pussy fluttered with a second wet climax Harold moaned to see her accepting face redden with the pleasure of asphyxiation. "This is how I'll kill you next time, princess—with my own two hands, just like you've always wanted." He tightened a little more then released, her sharp gag of a gasp sending a hot tremor of urgency through him.

"Yes, oh—yes, please, thank you, Daddy! Please, will you do it again—"

"Mm—last time we had an accident, princess…I don't want your death to be an accident again. I want your next murder to be thoughtful. Planned. A nice date before, a candlelit dinner like you deserve."

"Hah—hah—hah—oh, Harold, ah—"

"Dottie, Dottie, keep singing for me, Dottie! Ah, all the hot little noises I fuck out of you—"

"Harold! Harold, oh, shit, you're the best I've ever had! The best cock, the best man—"

"And you're the best meal I've ever had," he told her, gasping to drill his way to their final orgasms of the night. With the well-aimed stroke of a particularly sensitive target within her, Dottie clutched around him, shuddered, almost shrieked his name; Harold sped, tensed, released that tension in a glorious explosion of satisfaction beyond comparison to any of his previous painfully forced orgasms from previous painfully forced relationships. He gasped above her, foreheads pressed together, their panting harmonized while Dottie pulsed around him to squeeze him dry. Could she get pregnant? Maybe that would trap her—oh, a little baby with

Dottie. A happy family he'd never thought he'd deserve. How pathetic he was to already be dreaming of such a thing as that, but good God…how could he help it?

After catching her breath and coming down to Earth, Dottie's brow un-furrowed. She gazed at him, eyes glassy with love, and reached up to pet his chest.

"You big monkey." Her fingers curled against his bloodstained shirt. "You made me forget about the toast."

"Will you forgive me?"

"Okay," she said while he buried his head to plant kisses down the line of her throat. "Just this once…but next time, it's a beating."

Oh, promises!

8.

SHE DID BEAT him that weekend, just a cheerful little flagellation to break up all the fucking, the buggering, the caressing, the kissing, the holding, the gazing—all the sensual love-making that made him feel like a wretched teenager, regressed not just to Dottie's age but somehow even less.

She filled him with such vigor. She was an astonishing discovery—an explanation at last of why Harold had been so alone in the world all this time and why his every moment was oppressed by sexual thoughts too dark to communicate to any human being. All this in spite of his constant efforts to be a good man, a good human, a good Catholic.

Ah, but now he understood. Now he felt as if the answer had been before him all along, like Newton establishing a means to describe gravity or Archimedes grasping how to detect the purity of gold. Here she was, oh, his answer. Beautiful, naked, (almost always either robed or naked that first weekend, one somehow just as good as the other and each for its own reason), that answer slept beside him well into Saturday's noon. He could not sleep, himself. He watched her.

Oh, how sad! What a pathetic compulsion it was to watch someone sleep, but having glimpsed her dreaming visage in the car from the corner of his vision he watched her openly now and savored each second of her gentle breaths, the hypnotic in-and-out of her dreams.

By the time she awoke he had developed an inexplicable love of her shoulder blades. Angel wings. Angels did not truly have wings in scripture: in point of fact, most angels described in scripture were identical to human beings, Ezekiel's reeling nightmare visions and so forth aside. They came and went about the world unnoticed, all the while tending to the sometimes merciful but more often abjectly cruel works of God. And then, when their work was done, they would part.

She let him have Saturday, Saturday night. Sunday came. She let him have that too but he felt queer from the morning and grew sicker by the minute, attributing to exhaustion what he knew was simply the work of cruel, unfeeling time. Hateful time. Time that would rip his darling out of his unready hands. And oh, he strove nobly to ignore it—to stay in the moment, to celebrate her presence there without looking forward to her absence—but then, suddenly, it was Sunday evening. He walked into the bedroom to find her, dressed, (no, no!), bending over the luggage (no, damn it, no!) and smiling sweetly at him (God, no, why?) to say, "I've had a really nice weekend, Harold."

At once, he was old again. Nine times older than he had ever been. Worse—he was dead. Harold sagged back against the door frame, hand on his heart while, oblivious to his pain or striving to ignore it, Dottie returned her attention to the bag. "Do you have, like, a cooler? I'll help you pack some of my meat so you can take—"

"Come home with me." Taken aback, the girl looked up and laughed until she saw the desperation in his eyes. Then she was just shocked; twice so as he hoarsely pleaded, "Live with me. Dottie, live with me forever."

"You can't mean that, Harold...we can't just spend one

weekend together and then move in. You're my boss, and anyway, these things take— Oh, Harold! Poor Harry."

He wheeled out of the room, one hand covering his tear-filling eyes as he said, "No, you're right, of course. Of course you're right—oh, I'm pathetic."

"Yes," she agreed, hurrying after him to catch his free hand. "But not right now. Right now you're just being sweet… you remind me of me with my first boyfriend." While she laughed, she pulled his other hand down from his eyes and forced him to look miserably into her bright white seraph's face, even lifting her glasses up into her hair to push it back like a witch's elaborate mane. "Will you kiss me, Harry?"

God, would he, would he! He cradled her to his breast, laying waste to that beautiful mouth while her gasping lungs stole all the breath from his moaning lips. When he lifted his head it was only for a second—only so he could lower it again, rest it against her shoulder while swaying with her in his arms.

"I can't stand the thought of being apart from you, Dottie—oh, God. Going home to my condo, my empty condo—waking up alone, oh, Dottie! I love sleeping beside you—"

"You've hardly slept at all this weekend!"

"Because! Because I knew that—I knew I would have to take you home. I—"

He really, really for a few hard seconds thought very clearly and in a very detailed way about whether or not he should just drop the games and literally hold her captive. Lock her up in his greenhouse like a lovely bird of paradise, yes, oh, his pretty pet. His grip of her arms tightened and he gasped against her shoulder, saying, "I can't be without you. Now that I've had you, now that I've been with you, I never want to live in this world without you again."

"So I guess this means I'm invited over next weekend?"

Harold laughed just once at her wry comment, lifting his still tearful head to bask in her smile. "I should say so—oh, but darling, please. I mean it. I'm an old man. I haven't time to waste: every second without you is a second I'm closer to death, a second better spent holding you. Besides, you can't keep staying in that little place by yourself after what happened the other day. It isn't safe."

"Well…then why don't you just keep the spare key you've been conveniently forgetting to return to me this weekend? You can check up on me sometimes if you want…but I don't know, Harold." She frowned and stroked his cheek. "I don't want to get you in trouble. What if somebody finds out and you have to quit?"

"Then I'll be able to love you openly. Be free to take you anywhere, do anything."

"But what if *I* have to quit?"

"Darling"—Harold couldn't help another little laugh, this one with a hint of unintended condescension—"Dottie, you don't have to *work* when you're with me, you realize—"

"But maybe I want to." Still petting his face, Dottie ran a thumb over his sideburn, stroked up into his hair and made him sigh. "Maybe I'm glad you've got money in a general way, like a way that means I don't have to take care of you the way I have more than one bum ex-boyfriend…but maybe—maybe I'm worried."

"What are you worried about?"

Whatever it was, she didn't want to say or didn't feel capable then of explaining herself. He respected that decision but God, it ached him. Oh, absolutely drove him mad as she leaned against his heart to gaze up into his face. "Will you give me your phone number, Harry? I'll give you mine…when you're sad and lonely in the middle of the week you can call me. Any time."

That was the terrible thing of it, though. Harold was just a sad and lonely man. All the time. Always. Oh, he hated that about himself. But it was true—it pained him sharply to be apart from Dottie because without her around to command his attention he got back in touch with how sad and empty he was within the confines of his own head. His own condo. Oh…his hateful, empty condo.

He drove her home that baleful Sunday night. They didn't speak during the long drive back to the city. Harold thought the whole time how it might have been preferable to crash the car. Dottie would appear back in the country estate, and Harold, God willing, would die. What was this woman doing to him! He couldn't stand it. Couldn't stand his own emotions. The distant city that usually inspired a kind of banal depression anyway now made him want to set himself on fire rather than broach its limits. Another week at work? Five days? God, he couldn't do it. Five days, five days. Five days, and then—

"You really will see me again on Friday, won't you, Dottie? Let me take you out to dinner and whisk you off again. Please."

"Okay," she said with a dreamy smile. "That sounds nice." He slid the car to a stop along the curb in front of her apartment building and turned to kiss her before she got out, receiving a stab in the heart: her eyes had been reddened by a gloss of secretive tears. "I love you, Harold."

"Oh—Dottie, Dottie, I love you, too! Please, let me take you home with me."

"But I'll never leave again."

"That's the idea."

Laughing, the girl leaned up to kiss his mouth, then threw her arms around his neck to hug him. "I'll see you at work tomorrow, Mr. Fleetwood."

And, dallying only to get her poorly rolling bag out of the back of the car, Dottie disappeared into her apartment. The only reason Harold didn't drop his head against the wheel to weep right there was because city traffic was such a disaster that he was really just asking to be hit. And he was. God. He would have given anything for a little fender bender, the minutiae of miserable paperwork, some good old hellish bureaucracy to jolt him out of these emotions.

At least he had a small consolation prize. Home for Harold was far on the other side of the city, a high rise condo fairly close to the bustling place's economic center. He nodded at the doorman who held the entrance for him, tipping his hat and saying, "Welcome home, Mr. Fleetwood," with a smiling glance at the cooler he bore. "Say! Have a barbeque this weekend? I like a good winter BBQ, myself. What'd you cook up?"

"The most beautiful side of beef you've ever seen…oh, she was delicious."

Upstairs, overwhelmed by the silence as soon as he set foot in his apartment, Harold lay his keys upon the telephone stand that had not been used for a telephone since perhaps 2005. The rattle of their metal reminded him of Dottie's key floating untethered in his pocket. He kept it there, held like a charm against his body while in the kitchen he turned on the light. There he set the cooler upon the black counter. As though opening the Ark of the Covenant, Harold slowly lifted the lid and ruminated on its contents. First he removed the plastic-wrapped arm he'd brought home for practice and stored it carefully in the refrigerator. Then, still almost frightened to profane it with his touch, Harold took a breath to steady himself as he drew Dottie's head out of the cooler.

Not in the best shape. Now forty-eight hours postmortem, the head had been kept in cold storage consistently but being unembalmed and owing partly to the cause of death, Dottie's features were bloated with necrosis and warped by muscles relaxed in death. An orgasmic relaxation, he was sure…oh, Dottie. What was it like? What was it like to die, to be aware, to return? Dottie, Dottie. Dottie, Dottie. Harold slipped his thumb experimentally into the severed head's limp mouth. With his other hand he drew his phone from his pocket, opened his speed dial, and pressed the device to his ear.

Nine seconds later, Dottie picked up. "You really can't stay away from me, huh, Mr. Fleetwood."

"Talk to me, Dottie." Harold gazed down into her perfect dead face. "All I want is to hear you talk to me for the rest of my life."

9.

YOU WANT TO know what Harold did with Dottie's first severed head, do you? You sick fuck. Of course—he should have known. It's never enough to imagine. He learned that very well himself during that initial weekend, the acute experiential difference between mere imagination—even play-acting—and the hard edges of sensory reality. Cold and real as the severed head into whose mouth he slid his thumb while talking with Dottie on the phone.

"All I want is to hear you talk to me for the rest of my life," Harold said, staring into the bloated visage while Dottie laughed softly in his ear.

"What do you want me to talk about?"

"God, anything. Tell me I'm boring, that you can't stand the sight of me. Tell me you love me and you want to spend your whole life just looking at me. Then I could look at you forever, too. God, I love to look at you."

"Are you looking at me right now?"

"Yes."

"Is your cock in it yet?"

"Dottie—" His softly gasped admonishment brought him back to Earth: to the thumb that had penetrated those cold and swollen lips. He jerked away while her laugh filled the phone.

"It's okay…I like the thought. Oh, Harold—it gets me really hot to think of you using my dead body parts as your sex toys when I'm not around to fuck you. Talk about Fleshlights…"

"Oh, Christ, Dottie. Now that you mention it…why didn't we cut out your little cunt for me to bring home?"

Her gay laugh of dark surprise to hear him say such a thing was a pleasure of its own. "Gosh, you're so shy in person…you let me do most of the dirty-talking this weekend. I'm not used to hearing you speak to me that way, Mr. Fleetwood."

"Oh, Miss Shipman, I'd do so much more than talk to you if you were here…no reason to tell you what I'd like to do when I can just demonstrate."

"I guess so…what do you want to do right now?"

"I want to fuck you blind, Dottie Shipman—ah, I want to ram my cock so far down your throat that it chokes you. Touch yourself for me, you little slut."

"Oh! Harold—yes, sir, Mr. Fleetwood, oh—"

Yes, oh yes. Much as with online chatting, it was much easier to talk on the phone than it was to speak when he was overwhelmed by the glorious sight of her resplendent figure. Much easier to talk to the severed head whose mouth he experimentally opened to admirethe fat gray tongue defrosting inside. "That's right, you horny little cocktease— ah, you have no business making me feel this way, then refusing to come stay in my condo with me. Dottie, Dottie. If you were one of my whores this would be very poor customer service."

The giggling minx told him, "But it's your job to please me, Mr. Fleetwood…you're my slave, remember? Now that you've eaten my flesh. And nothing pleases your mistress like the thought of being mean. Meaner than mean to you, Harold."

"Oh, Dottie—"

"How hard is your cock?"

"Oh, it aches—it's dying to fuck you, why didn't you let me bring you home?"

"You're so pathetic! Disgusting…yes, you're disgusting. Take out your cock, you disgusting animal."

With a low shudder of anticipatory pleasure, he set the phone upon the counter and turned on the speaker-phone to talk to her while he obeyed her every command. "I'm sorry to be so repugnant, Dottie," he said into the face of the severed head that every second resembled more closely, in the lens flare of imagination, the living Dottie to whom he spoke. He stroked himself with a low sigh for the poor relief it was compared to any sensation generously delivered by her body, dead or alive. Meanwhile his thumb returned to that mouth, that face, fondling, exploring, two fingers jamming past a rotting uvula as far as they could fit. "Oh, Dottie, Christ, I'm so sorry, so sorry for killing you, darling, oh…"

"You should be…dirty murderer, you evil man, getting your dick all hard over this. Gosh, now I do wish I were there…that's not allowed. The next time I get you to myself at work you're in for a talking-to, Harold."

"Oh yes, Dottie, yes, oh, darling—tell me I'm despicable, tell me I should be ashamed."

"Oh, you are, you should. Yes, yes, be ashame. You're wicked and foul. Looking at my severed head while you stroke your dick, what a nasty pervert you are."

"Christ, oh, Dottie—I'm sorry I'm this way, you deserve a better man."

"Instead I'm in love with a total loser…ugh, I can't believe you made me fall in love with you! You dirty old man." His fingers slid from the chamber of her throat, still surprisingly tight in death, and he experimentally lifted the lid of one thoroughly misted eye with a shudder of pleasure for its repellent empty stare. "You're not allowed to make me feel this way, you creep."

"I know, darling, I'm sorry—"

"Put it in."

"Oh, but it's so cold—"

"I know you're too much a pussy to do what you want to do without me telling you to do it…that's why you called me, deep down inside. You wanted me to give you my permission—my command—to slide that big, hard dick into my dead little mouth." As he moaned, she chuckled, saying, "Yeah…that's what you wanted. So go on, you piece of shit. Go on." Her voice had dropped to a husky murmur of intense desire. Once more, she insisted, "Put it in me, murderer. Fuck the dead girl you made."

How he throbbed to! He couldn't resist it anymore—carefully cupping that perfect face in his hand, he drew it to the edge of the counter, got used to the head's oddweight. Then, with a glance at the phone as if she could see, Harold pressed the cheeks to hold the jaw open and slid his erection into its hanging mouth. "Oh"—he gasped at the cold, cringed away at first in brief horror of what he was doing before the drive to taste sublime ecstasies unknown to mortal men overwrote everything and urged him on, forced him to grow used to the cold tongue as a point of pride while he worked his throbbing prick over it—"oh, God, Dottie—I wish you were here, oh, Miss Shipman—"

"Mr. Fleetwood!" The urgency of her pleasure grewaudible; he gasped to hear a faint wet noise over the line as she begged to know, "Oh, oh, is it in? Oh, Harold! Are you fucking my severed head?"

"Yes, oh, yes, darling I am, ah, Christ—ah, it goes so deep when you don't have to worry about a gag reflex or a little thing like breathing…oh, Dottie, Dottie, I wish it was fresher."

"I know! You disgusting old necrophile, you dirty fucking monster, fucking my old rotten head…next time, oh! Oh! Oh, fuck—"

"Using that cute dildo on yourself, are you? Use it harder, princess, use it like Daddy would—"

"Oh, fuck—hm—" Her poor neighbors! His own were probably getting quite an earful and if he had a hand free he might have turned down his phone, but, well, he was occupied. Dottie gasped on, "Um—um, next time, Daddy, oh, next time, when you want to fuck my severed head, let's start with me living at first, okay?"

"Oh yes, yes Dottie, oh, you've read my mind—maybe it's because I'm almost fucking yours." He rested theweighty sex toy upon the nearby bar chair, an almost perfect height to prop a human skull for a little bit of hard fucking. First he pulled his prick out and rubbed it on the corpse's face, coating the edge of its blood-crusted nose in precum before pressing the throbbing tip of his cock into the glazed sac of her eye. While jerking off against the lifeless orb, he told his one true love, "Yes, next time, darling, oh, I want to have you sucking my cock first, then decapitate you with it still in your mouth… end up coated in blood and have the freshest possible little ball of fuck-meat for me to—oh, Dottie, and you could help me, Dottie—"

"Yes, yes, Harold, oh, Daddy! If I were there I'd help you fuck my severed head, oh, yes, that's what a good little girl does—"

"And my Dottie is a good little girl," agreed Harold, his hunger for depravity reaching an intense height. Once, twice, three times his cock pressed firmly against the eye; the fourth time he pushed hard against the ball of jelly, gasping at the peculiar sensation, then gasping again as it collapsed beneath the pressure of his onslaught. Rancid ocular matter splattered over the tip of his dick like the precum of death while he groaned, saying to the speaker phone, "Oh, Dottie! But maybe it's good you're not here, ah, sweet fuck, your little eye-hole is so tight—"

"Harold! Harold! Fuck, are you fucking my eye?"

"Oh, darling, I know you said you don't care for such things, but—"

"No! Fuck, Harold! I want you to do everything to me! All the things I don't like, everything I don't want, oh, fuck—that's what I want from you most of all. You pervert, oh, Harold, you fucking psycho, I can't believe—Harold! Harold!"

"Oh, Dottie—" He gasped, smoothing dark hair away from the putrefying forehead of the parceled-out sex doll brought home in lieu of his living darling. "Dottie, I love you so much, yes—oh, yes, come on, cum for me, angel, cum for Daddy—"

"I love you! Oh, oh—oh Harold, I love you too much—I can't believe—" She shuddered and gasped and he heard a sudden dearth of noise, realizing that what he'd taken for background static had actually been the sound of her vibrator. "I can't fucking believe you would do this for me…Harold, Harold, you're a dream come true."

"Me! Darling"—he laughed until he moaned as the tip of his cock pressed against a tight little sinus cavity in the back of the orbit, a challenge he throbbed tosurmount—"oh, darling, it's you who's the dream…oh, my God, my little Annabel Lee…oh, Christ, I'm going to cum in your brains, Dottie."

"Do you think we could brain damage me?"The girl gasped in delight heart-wrenching for its purity. "Oh, fuck, you could lobotomize me, Harold! Yes, uh-huh, tickle my nose with an icepick until I'm not good for anything but drooling on your big, hard dick. Then when you get bored you can just cut my miserable throat and voila! Not only will I be back, but then we have more meat."

"Oh, yes, Dottie, Dottie, yes—Christ, I can't wait to kill you again."

"I know! Oh, Harold, I know, do you think we can this weekend?"

"Anything, Dottie—I'll do anything you want me to, anything you don't want me to. Oh, Dottie, Dottie, whatever there is to be done in this world, I want to do to your body. Invent whole new crimes just for us…sweet angel, oh, Dottie! Dottie, I wish you were here."

"I wish I was there, too, Harold…but I love you, and we'll be together again soon enough. You just keep fucking my cute little skull, go on—put those hips to work, Harold, oh yeah, let me feel it. I can hear your breathing from here, oh, you big dirty monkey man…you turn into such a fucking ape when you're horny. I love it. You're so quiet and reserved and thoughtful, but when that dick gets hard it's a totally different story. Just a big savage cave man…I can't wait to give you more of my flesh and see how hard it makes your dick to eat it. Maybe I can revert you to a primitive state forever with enough of my tasty girl-meat! Wouldn't that be fun? Then you could be my big, dumb pet, obsessed with my smell, your dick leaping to attention every time I walk by."

"Dottie, Dottie, it already does, fuck, oh, Christ—"

"Are you going to cum in my eye socket, Harold? Oh, yeah, do it—do it, fuck, I wish I was there to see you stroking that big dick into my skull. That must be how you're doing it, since it's too big to fit…oh, Harold, next time I'll stroke it for you. Just pretend it's my soft little hand, Daddy…oh, I wish it was."

"You awful tease…Dottie, Christ, oh, Dottie, I—"

"Harold! Yes! Oh, Harold, that's right, baby, oh, yes, desecrate my corpse—oh, Daddy, Daddy, your little Dottie loves you."

The chair ground back against the bar as he braced himself, expelling deep enough in the orbit of the skull that he hoped at least a little might drip through the sinus cavity and into the gray matter beyond. Harder to get to than one would think. Not a straight shot. Have to knock out the back of the eye socket next time. Fuck, fuck—oh, next time. Time, yes, time existed. Harold eased back into reality and shudderingly refused to look down at that from which he extricated his cock. Only when he was free did he look down and see what a horrible mess he'd made of it: oh, yes. Desecrated, certainly. God, what was wrong with him? Why was he such a repugnant excuse for a man—worse, one who reveled in his own abhorrent nature?

"Oh, Dottie," he marveled softly, leaning against the bar with a sudden surge of self-pity. "Dottie, I don't deserve you."

"Nobody deserves me," agreed the softly laughinggirl. "But that just makes it all the more significant that I chose to get to know you, don't you think?"

"I love you, Dottie Shipman."

"Oh, Harold…Harold Fleetwood, I love you, too."

"Will you—" He glanced anxiously toward the shut drapes of the window, off in the direction of distant Dottie's abode. "Will you please consider changing the locks in that apartment of yours? If you won't come stay with me—I'm just worried, darling. Those people knowing where you live—"

"You're so sweet, Harold…nobody's going to do anything to me. It's okay."

"I'm scheduling a locksmith tomorrow."

"I love you, Harry. Good night."

"Good night, Dottie. Oh…Dottie, I love you, I love you. Good night."

Alone, reluctant, Harold hung up the phone, then studied again the ruined head sagging dejectedly upon his barstool. Having come to his senses enough to feel genuine shame without taking lascivious pleasure in that shame, Harold fetched a tea towel in which to wrap the head. With it thus shrouded he was able to store it away in the freezer. Then, after rinsing off his hands and briskly mopping bodily fluids from his cock, Harold left the kitchen, was just about to turn off the light for the night, and at that second noticed with a noise of displeasure the rusty stain that had oozed upon the fabric of the stool. Evidence of his horrific inequity, permanently sealed.

He looked away, turned off the light, and went to bed, thinking of Dottie every step of the way.

10.

HAROLD FLEETWOOD WAS a pathetic man. It was true. He told himself so whenever he was unable to even look at a beautiful woman in passing, let alone hold her gaze for more than a few seconds at a time.

But something had happened that weekend. Something had happened to Harold and it took him until the office to realize it. He didn't even realize he was able to watch a cluster of pedestrians cross in front of him and follow with his gaze one pretty bronze Latina until she mounted the curb—he was so busy thinking of Dottie that he did not even realize he accomplished this without constant, compulsive thoughts of undirected gynophagia. Yes, they were directed now.

It was at work that he finally noticed this shift in his thought process—or, rather, when Pearl noticed it. Harold's proper secretary and Dottie's direct supervisor, Pearl had worked for the corporation for going on twelve years and knew Harold better than almost all the other employees. She was a shrewd middle-aged woman, not unattractive in a strict schoolmarm sort of way, and she had gotten used to Harold's habit of gazing out the window or staring off into a corner of the room while discussing business. When she came into his office to discuss the usual Monday business, for some reason she kept stuttering. Finally, Harold noticed and could not help but indicate, "You're a little distracted this morning, Pearl."

"It's just—you don't usually seem so…focused."

It was true. He hadn't even realized he was actually making eye contact with Pearl until she pointed it out with that discreet comment. While off in his own perverse little world of love, Harold was now free to look anywhere without shame or compulsion. Somehow, though she fused fantasy and reality in those off-hours, Dottie accented the importance of reality and Harold's role in it. She brought him down to Earth—and he hadn't been down to Earth in years. Years and years. He exited his office during the workday, greeted his employees by name, poked his unwelcome head cheerily into their business to micromanage as he hadn't in at least a decade and a half. Goodness…it was like he'd been asleep all this time.

And here came Princess Charming, that tender-hearted heroine who roused him with a kiss. Right on time, nine in the morning. Just like always. He had been bending over the work of a female accountant to ask why this line of the budget seemed rather inflated and when he straightened up, he saw over the woman's short cubical Dottie seated at her desk on the distant other side of the office.

And his mind exploded at once, overwhelmed by a bouquet of fantasy, memory, plans, dreams. The one woman he still could not look at for more than a few seconds at a time while within the walls of their mundane workplace, surrounded by all the unwashed and unworthy masses with no idea a goddess worked quietly in their midst. He excused himself from his conversation and, casually rounding the office the long way, passed Dottie's desk with little more than a brisk tap on its corner. "Oh," she said, surprised, then pleased, then forcing it all into boredom as she bent her head over her work again. "Good morning, Mr. Fleetwood."

"Good morning, Ms. Shipman—Happy Monday. Don't you think it'll be a lovely week?"

"Yeah," said the girl, glancing up after him just as he looked over his shoulder to steal one more glimpse of the beautiful lover whose severed head formed the centerpiece of a de facto shrine in his condo's freezer. "But, let's be honest, sir...I'm already looking forward to next weekend."

EPISODE 3
DOTTIE'S BODIES

1.

HOW HARD HAROLD TRIED to rationalize his feelings for Dottie! His mind was in a constant state of problem-solving throughout the first weeks of their relationship. Realism was important. He was too old to permit himself to be hurt by a woman, the woman—the only woman he had shown himself to. And what a dark self it was! Every bit as dark as Dottie was a glimmering, sensual little goddess: a muse of love and sex and the death that made all things possible in life. Though they had many interests in common there was just so much that was different between them, and Harold wondered bleakly if these differences would matter.

What differences? Oh, many. Start with their age. Harold was…oh, might as well have out with it—Harold was fifty-nine, yes, God, he was almost sixty. His hair was far more gray than blonde although the same eyes that stubbornly refused to fully perceive its own wrinkles also somehow made a mental translation of hair color so as to save his pride. He didn't often look at himself in the mirror, although since meeting Dottie he had done it far more often, worried over his appearance like a middle-aged woman whose vanity had been challenged by a recently acquired stepdaughter. How could Dottie continue loving an old man when the novelty wore off?

This led to another issue. Dottie was, in essence, immortal. Harold was not—at least, so far as he was aware. Having never to his knowledge died, he supposed he could have been immortal all this time without realizing it…but he wasn't exactly keen to check. It was obvious enough to him that he was mortal, anyway; he aged. Did Dottie? She looked so young. Trotting around the office in blouses and pencil skirts and prim hairdos she cut the severe figure of a somewhat up-tight office professional, the kind of small woman whose power was derived from her shrewd business sense rather than physical presence. But when the glasses came off and the clothes, too, and her hair tumbled down, and that lovely flushed face overflowed with adoration for his, she became a wild nymph. A chambermaid of Persephone—no, that very deathless Kore herself, forever returning from the underworld to seek the earthly spring.

Oh, she enchanted him. When she walked past, whatever else he was doing became an insignificant blot in spacetime— and this was a problem because of the third, perhaps most stark and frustrating difference between them. Harold was a very rich business owner, and Dottie was a very not-rich business employee. While it relieved him to think that if nothing else his money might be a means with which to keep her close at-hand, it also meant that so long as she stubbornly refused to quit her job and become his adorable little hausfrau, (The sheer audacity! To think that she would not want to drop everything to submit to his constant caresses!), Harold was forced to pretend like he was not absolutely, constantly, painfully obsessed with the woman who was, strictly speaking, one of his many employees.

What did such a thing matter when there were so *many*

employees at the company? For all the board knew Harold never saw Dottie around the office at all, had no idea she existed. For all the board knew Harold met Dottie on the street, they fell in love, and they only later realized after conversation that she worked for the same firm he had founded in his youth. What did it matter, what did it matter? He thought about resigning his position just to save himself the hassle, but then he could not have surreptitiously watched Dottie all day, every day, peering through the open door of his office in the hopes of catching a glimpse of her at her desk. Secretly Harold prayed she would slip up at her job or start behaving like an entitled brat so he could have an excuse to be very strict with her, but it pleased him more to see she worked harder than ever to prove her merit in the office was unconnected to their budding romance.

And it frightened him to see how easy it was for her to pretend like everything was normal. Her mask was so convincing that between the hours of her arrival at nine in the morning and the hour of his lunch around noon it was as if she was a different woman altogether—the woman he had thought she was, the cold and disdainful little bitch who laughed at him behind his back and shuddered in horror at the thought of his interest in her.

But then! Then lunch would roll around, and his heart would slam in his chest because lunch was always different somehow. Lunch, Dottie brought the mail and smiled as she crossed the threshold. "Hello, Mr. Fleetwood, here's some mail for you…what's for lunch today?"

"A tongue sandwich," was his answer on Thursday. With no one between them and the rest of the employees in the exterior of the office, a productive beehive buzzing through the open doorway, he admired Dottie with open abandon until he became overwhelmed with eagerness to fuck her then and there. She had worn smart gray slacks that day and they had an unbearable effect on her ass so that by the time she rounded the desk to toss down his mail and lean in to see the sandwich, he was hard as a diamond and breathless with desire. "Never cared much for tongue growing up, but this one is wonderful."

"Is it? How nice." Dottie leaned back up, face flushed, her ponytail falling upon her shoulder. To reach up, to grip it, to just yank her pretty head right down against the edge of the desk and suck out her fucking brains! Oh, Dottie.

"I saw you had a doctor's appointment this morning"— the girl continued speaking, her faint tone of genuine concern drawing him somewhat out of his compulsive fantasies and into tangible things like errands and doctors and schedules— "is everything all right?"

"No," he told her, able only in his role as her boss to stare so boldly, as he was just then, into her pretty face. "No, no, nothing is all right, I'm dying. The doctor said it's very important I find a young caregiver to look after me."

Her laugh! It stung him, rattled him to the core while she shook his head. "What a goofball you are…what are you dying of?"

"Loneliness. Oxytocin withdrawal. The cold of an empty bed."

"You drama king."

"You're so cruel to me."

She glanced at the open doorway, elegantly ignoring the low tones of pleasure in his desperate voice. "I'm very nice to you, Mr. Fleetwood…professional."

"I don't want to be professional with you, Miss Shipman."

"You bad man…"

"I need you so badly, Dottie."

"You have me—part of me." She grinned at the sandwich.

"The old you, the dead you. I want the"—Pearl walked by the office—"paperwork on my desk by Monday morning, if you could"—the coast was clear again, his voice dropped while Dottie grinned in evil delight—"I want the living you, my hands full of the hot, writhing, screaming you! Oh, Dottie, please, can't I see you tonight?"

Thursday, Thursday! That day was Thursday. So many long days since their weekend, oh, four. He couldn't wait another. Four wasted nights, no Dottie. Just her delicious flesh, the psychedelic effects of which had reduced to nothing more than a pleasantly heated desire for her since he had been eating every day of the arm and head in the freezer. Perfectly naturally to feel a surge of lust for the girl you nibbled… though he had a sense sometimes that even in a very low form the aphrodisiacal qualities of her meat remained perceptible above and beyond the buzz of more standard lusts inspired by her comely features or their shared proclivities. Some mechanism of her mysterious species, designed to attract and keep a depraved mate. It worked.

"If I give you too much attention you'll be bored of me, Mr. Fleetwood."

"Dottie—"

"Have a nice lunch, sir."

And she was off with a grin and a wiggle in her hips. Harold, who had not even been able to sneak in a touch of her thigh or a whiff of her hair, was left to moan in a fury at his seat. Agony! Some women really did know how to make men suffer. She was a little tease, clearly reveled in her ability to torment him. Christ! She needed to be taught a lesson. A good thrashing would have her crawling to his condo no matter what day it was. Surely after enough visits he would wear her down and she would see the value in cohabitation— in being present, the idol of his lust, whenever he needed her to be. What a selfish and scheming man! He had never known himself to be so possessive; but then again, he had never known anyone like Dottie.

Pearl, Dottie's supervisor and Harold's true secretary, was in his office that afternoon going over the details of some things he didn't really give a rat's ass about if he was being honest.

He had been bored of his career for a long, long, *long* time and only maintained such a consistent presence on-site during the workday because it would have been even more boring if he was semi-retired and fooling around at home. That was how a man got into trouble—say, got into elaborate projects like bringing his renovated slaughterhouse into working order and permitting himself to do with it as came natural.

But Dottie made that all okay, didn't she? This was the 21st century. Consent was paramount and all else was piddly private detail. She fully consented—frankly, had already several times induced him—to acts of extraordinary perversity that he had previously known only in vivid imagination. Vivid and constant imagination. That imagination was acting up again as Pearl droned on, but was then tamed when she said something that caught his attention while turning over to the next page in her agenda:

"And then there's the matter of Dorothy Shipman—"

He tuned his mental frequency back to Pearl, at whom he had been placidly staring without really seeing. "I thought this was a payroll mistake when I was signing off on her timecard for the week," the old biddy said while flashing a bit of paperwork, "but someone told me you personally approved this pay-raise for her? Were you aware it's double her current salary?"

"Of course."

With a little scoff, a kind of surprise at his honesty as much as his flat disinterest in explaining himself, Pearl went on. "Does she have a new project assigned to her? Something I should be supervising?"

"Don't you think our starting wages are too low, Pearl? Well—I suppose you might not think so because it's taken you so long to get to where you are, but—"

"She's making more than me now, technically," was Pearl's cool response. "So I suppose I'd agree our wages are too low in general, if I can speak out of school."

Good God! He tried not to look as taken aback as he felt. Really had become a space cadet with the slow onset of time, hadn't he? "How out-of-touch I am." With a very real noise of displeasure, Harold scrounged around his desk in pursuit of a notepad and jotted a to-do for himself. Vital that Pearl be kept disinterested; and if already interested, quiet. "I've spent so long docilely sitting in this office, letting the board do my most important work for me…I think I'm going to talk to them about increasing wages across the company. Miss Shipman and I had a very interesting conversation that led to her wage increase and, frankly, I think it's the right thing…what do you think, Pearl? You've been here over a decade. Is"—the number made her eyes widen—"reasonable, given your job description?"

"Well—well I—" Flabbergasted, the secretary withdrew somewhat in her assault of his motivations and clutched her notebook to her chest. "I—that would be very nice, Harold. I would appreciate that very much—was your doctor's appointment all right?"

"Fine, thank you. Why do you ask?"

"It's just—it's like you've been visited by the Ghost of Christmas Future."

He laughed at that and checked the calendar. "Little late for that. Valentine's Future, maybe…you learn more by listening than by talking, Pearl, and I learned a lot by listening to Miss Shipman. Sometimes"—his eyes bounced across the open door, across the heart-throbbing back of Dottie's head as her ponytail bounced mid-conversation with some suited drone—"sometimes you realize you've lost perspective, spending all this time in this office. Sometimes you realize that your own private world is so…I don't know, so privileged, so isolated, that you've almost forgotten altogether what suffering is. What mortality is. You only live once, Pearl, that's what they say. Shouldn't my employees be paid wages that are not just living wages, but good wages? The support for not just any old life, but a good life?"

"I—I don't know what to say."

"Say 'thank you,' then," said Harold, still watching the conversation across the office. As Pearl belatedly expressed her gratitude, he continued, "Speaking of Miss Shipman, would you ask her to see me this afternoon? I'm planning to leave around four. If she could stop by then, I do have one small matter to discuss with her. Something she left unsigned."

This might have been gilding the lily. Pearl looked suspicious again but, too cowed by her sudden windfall (some might say bribe) to say anything, she chose to keep her comment to herself. "I'll tell her."

"Very good, thank you. Anything else?"

"Not today…really, though, Harold—are you sure about this?"

"If the board doesn't like it, they can fire me…don't worry about my welfare, Pearl, I assure you I'm doing just fine. Ah— and I do have a small errand to run, one last little thing, so if I'm gone before you leave at three, have a good day."

"You, too, Mr. Fleetwood."

Left alone, he pulled on his coat, checked the time, then followed Pearl out of the office. On the main floor, rather than going the short way to the elevator, he looped around the long way just to pass Dottie's desk and study more closely the young man who was taking up her time and attention. This young fellow saw the company CEO coming from a mile away and smilingly wrapped up his conversation, then fell into stride as casually as if he'd been planning to do it all along. "Afternoon, Mr. Fleetwood," said the young man while they crossed paths. "Beautiful day outside."

"It is, isn't it?"

Ah, rats—what was this fellow's name? Dale Carnegie would slap his wrist for not remembering. Handsome sort of lad the ancient Greeks sculpted in bronze. Fuckable, certainly. Harold didn't mind the thought of Dottie fucking anyone to whom he was at least a little attracted—it was the thought of her giving the time of day to someone unworthy that made him flare with the jealousy of a normal human being. Just had to see it all up close and make sure, although there was an added bonus of Dottie's embarrassed, slightly worried stare, caught as he turned around to hit the elevator door buttons. It was reassuring to think that within her confident shell she was just as insecure about the relationship as he was.

Not that he wasn't eager to fix that as soon as possible. He had made the call on Monday and the artisan had promised turnaround by the weekend, which had impressed Harold and in the end earned an exorbitant tip. The final product was infinitely better than he could have imagined, an achievement that filled him with more dread than delight. What if she felt he was coming on too strong? After all, he was. He was coming on very, very strong—but he couldn't help it. It was how he felt; he felt very strongly about Dottie. Like he would have done absolutely anything to put his own mind at ease and guarantee her loyalty and love forever. Gifts, items of jewelry, these were nothing more than trifles. Small vanities: decorations he could look at on her person and use to assure himself that she at the very least considered his love in a conscious way—kept it present in her mind.

Four rolled around. Dottie appeared flush-faced just to lean in to his office. Oh, rare vulnerability! His favorite jewel worn by her. "You wanted to see me, sir?"

"Yes, Miss Shipman…come in. Close the door."

She did and he immediately dropped the routine, setting the hard wood case on the edge of his desk. "I have something for you."

Pearl's surprise earlier had been understandable, but that Dottie should have been surprised by his gift filled him with delight, with thrill. Yes, he wanted to keep her on her toes— to keep her love for him as much a perpetual novelty as his love for her was fated to forever be, so long as she could not die forever. Yes, it was a love of renewal like the coming of spring, and he wanted to watch springtime blossom in her face eternally. Her bright eyes wide behind her glasses, Dottie hurried over to stand behind his desk with him. "What is it? Oh, you shouldn't have—you can't get me gifts so soon, Harold, gosh, I wasn't expecting this—"

"No time like the present…figured I'd ought to start soon and go hard on the gift-giving so you know what to expect from me." He watched her face: she opened the box and cried out at the necklace within, a very simple set of rubies in gold that he thought would look exotic against her pale skin. While she stared wild-eyed into the case and lowered slowly onto his right knee (oh happy, lucky joint, blessed joint, celestial throne) as though no longer able to stand on her own, Harold lay a hand in the small of her back and rubbed her tender flesh through the silk of her blouse. "I'm an unworthy, wretched slave to you, Dottie—all I can do is try to compensate for my repulsive urges to defile you."

"Oh, Harold, you don't have to get me anything—this is so beautiful, nobody's ever given me anything like his before… Harold, oh, are you sure?"

"Surer about you than about anything in my life, Dottie. That's a rock and some metal but I'll bring you more, more and more, as much as you want." She removed it from the box and he took it gently from her hands to drape it around the column of her neck, confident nobody remaining in the office so late in the workday would have attention span enough to notice Dottie's new addition on leaving his office. "Yes, like a desperate bird trying to attract a mate into his nest, oh, darling, I'll bring you all the shiny things I find and line my condo with everything beautiful. Everything it will take to bring you home to me for good. God, oh—Dottie, you look so beautiful wearing my money."

His beaming bird of paradise craned her neck to see the effect of the jewels against her own pale sternum; at the same time, he peeked down the back of her blouse to admire the other ornaments of his passion still lightly discoloring her neck and shoulders. Could still see the imprint of a cuspid. "Harold"—the girl's flesh dimpled attractively as, unable to help himself, he bent forward to press his lips to that lovely livid bruise matched to his teeth—"this is wonderful, but I'm so worried…I'm a much more boring person than you are."

"How can you say that?"

"I am! All I do is sit inside and draw."

"Your fertile imagination is marvelous, the way you look at life is so fresh and vivifying to me. All this to say nothing of your truly unique quality. Don't sell yourself short, Dottie."

The bite of her lip turning into a slightly crooked grin, Dottie turned a bashful look upon him before bending to kiss his mouth. God! Oh, God. He hadn't had a kiss from her since Sunday night and eagerly opened his lips, gasping at the fast-increasing aggression of her kiss. While she shifted to straddle his lap and clutch his face in her cool little hands, Harold ran his palms up under her blouse. A true stab of physical pain struck his heart on contact with her flesh.

"Oh, Dottie—Dottie, I'm begging you, I'm begging you, I can't sleep anymore—"

"Harold—"

"The doctor gave me sleeping pills but I know the only thing that will let me sleep is this, you, oh, Christ, your body— Dottie, please, please, please, never has a woman made a man suffer so!"

With one last little laugh and a shake of her head, Dottie said, "You really are something else, Harold…I love how emotional you are."

"I'm not—oh, God, you make me this way. Can't you see? You're crushing me! I can't take it. I know you have plenty of better things you could be doing—"

"Oh, Harold, it isn't that—"

"—but God, oh, Dottie, it would make me so happy, please, oh, I would be so happy if you would just see me tonight! Just for a few hours, please. You don't have to come to my place if you don't want to—let me come to yours. Just let me be near you and read a book, Dottie."

After studying him for a long few seconds, Dottie sighed, and it was as if he could feel the surge of testosterone the victory imparted him. "Okay," said the girl, "but—"

Harold caught her face in his hands to gasp a kiss out of her mouth while she laughed, pulled away, admonished him, then completed her caveat. "But I have some commissions to work on, and you can't expect me to just drop those, and I'm super boring and quiet when I'm drawing, so—"

He had never been so thrilled by the prospect of sitting around doing nothing. Oh, God, never! He had been on the verge of offering her money for the privilege of watching her work through the night, suspecting that her devotion to her freelance creative work was the real sticking point preventing her from abandoning herself fully to their perverse love. Were he a younger, spryer man, Harold might have been much too busy himself—his own need to work weighed against his passionate desire to have his dick buried as far inside of Dottie as he could get it at every second of the day. She was a young professional. More than that, an artist, which was a category of person he found fascinating and alien. There was a shared quality between the entrepreneur and the artist, an inner drive that determined the success of each.

And that was just one of the qualities Harold and Dottie shared. Because the truth was that there was very much that was different between them—but amid his many fears and rationalizations and grim self-warnings to keep his expectations low, Harold could not stop himself from thinking just as often of all the things he and Dottie had in common. Instincts, needs, senses of humor, sexual fantasies: these foundational aspects of the human psyche bridged the gap so that little issues like age or socioeconomic status or mortality were all revealed as utterly meaningless, artificial divisions between himself and the girl who dominated his every square inch of mental real estate.

To say nothing of his body. His heart raced as he knocked upon the door of apartment 306: when she opened it the very sight of her rippled through him in golden anticipation. He trembled, wasting no time before taking her in his arms and savaging her with kisses until the bookshelf against which he'd pushed her made faint protest. "Harold!" She gasped, laughing, forcing herself to pout up at him and transfigure her demeanor from tender delight to the stern admonishing she knew he adored in excess of even her sweetness. "Close the door, you big mongrel. Gosh, were you raised in a barn?"

"I'm sorry, Dottie, of course—"

"Always apologizing…you sure do love to be pitiful in front of me. I guess it *is* your natural state…" While he shuddered and tried to reach for her again, she slipped away. "I ordered delivery—you can have some if you promise to get the door when it comes."

If he could bear to leave her side for a second. Oh, Jesus. She was so wonderful to look at. He had the sense she had dressed as casually as possible to prove to him that she wasn't worth his time: naturally, the opposite effect had been achieved. Harold was used to his whores and his socialites, two similarly dramatic types of women who went elaborate on make-up and never permitted men to see them in any state of dishevelment. To see Dottie in a baggy t-shirt, her hair messily pulled up and not a trace of make-up on her foxy face, oh, it was like a striptease to him—but her *shorts*.

Oh, Christ, those little blue shorts. Light blue. Baby blue. Periwinkle, powder-soft, corpse-lip blue. Short as underwear, those little shorts—and just a smidge too big for her, so that when she bent over to retrieve a sock abandoned on the floor Harold restrained a gasp. Paradise, glimpsed behind the slightly over-sized leg holes that left the satin shorts' crotch deliciously askew. He throbbed, covered his mouth, tried to moderate his breathing as she straightened up and paused in the doorway of her bedroom.

"Are you staring at me *now*, Harold?"

"Oh, Dottie, I don't mean to—"

"You're such a dirty old creep…well, come on." With a shake of her head and a sigh at his incorrigibility, Dottie coaxed him into her bedroom, hurled the sock into the hamper and resumed her seat at her desk. "You're going to be bored to tears by the time the night is over…I bet I'll never see you outside of work again after this."

"God, Dottie, I love you so much—you can't bore me, oh, you don't understand."

She couldn't. No, she couldn't understand. He wasn't sure if anyone could understand, except perhaps for those few lucky perverts who spent a lifetime alone before finding a soulmate in depravity. Dottie could have done nothing—truly, nothing at all—and Harold would have happily sat there, watching, captivated by her every slightest sigh. He had grown out of television in his twenties and movies in his forties. What he liked to watch was women but he could never bear to do it straight on or for very long because of the terrible shame tainting his thoughts.

But Dottie had come along. Emerged in his life like a rainbow in a dreary, overlong day. And in the same revelation that had liberated him from his compulsive fantasies of murdering other women, Dottie had doomed herself to become the subject of his absolutely obsessive attention. This was the undaunted focus that had made him one of the richest men on the planet. Applied to Dottie, it produced a level of scrutiny that any naturalist would envy for its insane patience, its total absorption in its subject. Yes: the wild nymphet, Dorothea dolcettus, in her natural habitat. Observe her perched upon her desk chair, one bare foot propped upon the seat's edge; watch her falling into the deep tunnel of her work, some strange invisible world to which Harold was destined to be forever blind; thrill at her every tiny graceful gesture, her small twitches and languid shifting as her unconscious body kept itself comfortable and out of focus of her busy mind.

Harold lay across her bed and watched everything. Every beautiful second of her hard work, before and after the Chinese food came. Her final products were astonishing but he now found he loved the process more. The secondhand experience of her creative process was beautiful, not to mention fascinating. How effortless she made it seem! Once or twice, without moving from the bed, he leaned up to catch a glimpse of the work-in-progress which she carefully inked. Pelops served to dinner for the Greek Gods, rendered in her usual style so packed with minuscule details it made Harold's old hands hurt to imagine filling them in. How did a person so young get to being so skilled? She truly must have drawn every single day of her life for many years to already be at such a point of talent. Twenty-four; God. She was so young. Had Harold ever been so young? It astonished him.

"Are you bored yet?"

"Just jealous of your chair…I could only be happier if I had the chance to hold you while you worked."

Though the girl turned away in apparent disgust he swore the edge of one deep dimple appeared in her cheek. With a hefty sigh, she stood and swept up a drawing board leaning against the side of her desk. "You're such an attention whore," she chastised him, affixing the completed upper half of the drawing to the board and carrying the whole thing over along with her pens.

Harold did not have to be asked; he rolled onto his back, sat up slightly, bit back his gasp as she sat in his lap. Christ! Oh, Christ, at last. His hands fit against her hips and his nose buried in her hair's dark bun while she warned him sullenly, "You can't talk to me until it's finished, though."

Oh, never. Never would he interrupt his glorious artist, whose body was too sacred for him to look upon, let him touch this way—oh, to think she permitted him to profane her as she did! To think of the way she had coaxed him into killing her last time…Christ, that tight little ass was just crushing the life out of his cock, all her weight centered directly in his lap.

His instinct was to rock against her, to please himself with that wonderful body, but oh, he daren't disturb her. It was beyond a fear that he might not be invited back. He was unworthy to even exist in the same time period but ah, so blessed, too blessed, that he did! All he deserved was to be her chair, and then again he did not even deserve that. The slight weight of her body, all that ultra-soft skin perfumed by soaps and floral lotions, oh…she was right. He was a mongrel, an absolute disgusting dog. His body screamed to knock the drawing and pens out of her hand: to punish her for failing to devote every single scrap of her waking attention to him. All these sordid impulses to be perpetually resisted. Yes, he supposed he was a bit of an attention whore—but it was so difficult not to crave Dottie's attention. So difficult to ignore this feeling, the feeling that he would wither up and die without her gaze on him.

"Your dick's so hard, Harold…" He shut his eyes, held his breath to avoid falling into the trap of responding as she went on softly, "You're really just dying to fuck me right now, aren't you? I've never met a man who's as horny as I am, but you might almost qualify."

Years of repression, dear. Years and years and years of miserable cringing and hiding and wincing and shielding giving way to this, this walking, talking, laughing mirror who held up his own sins to him and showed him that they could be found elsewhere than in his head. Plaguing other people's heads. Expelled from those lovely heads in the form of drawings, one of which was finished after she had sat there for another forty minutes of diligent work. Almost seven-thirty. Simonetta or any other one of his whores would have taken him in, done what he wanted and had him back out the door—assuming it wasn't a country house weekend. He was so unused to simply holding a woman! Oh, he felt sorry for himself, sure that sometime Dottie would discover how pathetic he truly was. She would awaken to his unworthy nature and reject him fully, just as he deserved.

Then he would just crawl in a hole somewhere and die. Dottie, Dottie. How had he ever lived in the world without little Dorothy Shipman?

"There," she said when it was finished, sighing in relief and shifting in his lap to show him with pride. "What do you think? You're allowed to answer now."

"Oh, darling, it's extraordinary—your illustrations are better every time I see them, Demeter tearing her gown open in agony here is so marvelous, so animated—"

"I'm glad you like it! I have to let the ink dry more before I can erase the pencil lines, but I'll give it to you once it's really done."

With a gasp, Harold asked, "Why, this is for me?"

"Of course! I was so happy about this necklace today"—taken as he'd been with her lovely appearance, he hadn't even noticed the gold chain of the necklace had been just visible beneath the cotton collar of her t-shirt all this time—"but to be honest I was little disappointed…I've been working on this since Monday, hoping to give you the first gift of our relationship!"

"No, no, oh, darling, now I'm doubly glad I took the time to arrange that little piece for you…ah, Dottie, this is wonderful." He caught her delicate face in his hand for a kiss, gasping at those splendid lips. So soft! Oh, softer than anything on Earth, softer than silk, softer than the satin of the shorts toward which his hand slipped. What a pleasure it was to clutch her tight to him until she wiggled and moaned a protest.

"Let me put your drawing down, you dope, don't wrinkle it…"

"Of course…oh, darling, that's so marvelous—I'm overwhelmed."

"It's nice you care so much! I didn't think you'd be near so excited…" With a fond look down at the drawing, Dottie touched the edge of her desk and said in a dreamy way, "I've been thinking since this weekend how I wish things were the other way around with us…like I was the rich one and you were the—well, less-rich one." She turned upon him that adorable cheesy grin he loved so much, that fang of a crooked cuspid hooking into his heart on sight. "I wish I could spoil you, Harold! Take you out to eat every night and ply you with wine. Be your sugar momma."

"You already spoil me with your existence—you needn't do more than be near me."

"You keep saying that…I'm telling you, I don't want you to get bored of me."

"You're only saying that because it's you who's at risk of being bored of me, Dottie." As she lay back with a huff and a big sigh, her head flopping upon the same pink pillow upon which she'd died last Friday, (upon which he'd killed her last Friday, oh, his hand slid up the leg still draped with its cohort across his happy lap), Harold tutted and asked her, "What?"

"I don't want to hear a bunch of stuff about how you're too old for me, okay? That's part of the point." The girl hefted the other pillow and tossed it at his head, her eyes bright with pleasure to see it bounce off. "I think you're beautiful, Harold. You're beautiful to look at. Do you like Balthus?"

"Oh, that's exactly what you remind me of…a Balthus painting animated. I was thinking about it the other day. The way you throw yourself around. Ah"—he bent over her, unable to help himself but to press a kiss to her taut stomach through the baggy t-shirt she'd worn to unsuccessfully dissuade him of her splendor—"yes, I like Balthus, Dottie."

"You remind me of him. I saw a picture of you as a young man on Wikipedia—you look like his painting, *The King of Cats*."

"God, don't tell me *that*…he aged terribly."

"Because he smoked. You're aging nicely, though." She smiled as he grew courageous enough to push up the fabric of that t-shirt and gasp at the sight of her soft, pale belly as if he'd never seen it before in his life. "You don't smoke."

"Clean living, yes, princess, that's the secret to a happy, healthy life…oh…Christ—I had to drive back to the country place on Tuesday night to pick up a slice of your pretty belly. Oh, it was so good on Sunday dinner—your arm was nice, but Christ! This pretty little stomach—"

"What a greedy old pig you are, Harold." Her voice had dropped an octave and she stretched elaborately, a tremor rippling through her tensed limbs. Harold, hunger in his heart and stomach and groin, drew back to see her arch that body up like a hunting bow: she drew her t-shirt up over her head, then did away with the sports bra beneath—then she was trying to get rid of those cute little shorts. With a hitch of breath, he stayed her hands, whispering, "Oh, no, please—Dottie, let me look at you in these a moment longer."

"You like *these* ratty old things? You weirdo!" She laughed, glancing down at herself and then, after consideration, bending one lovely knee to ache his dick with a leg show that went all the way. "Oh, I see…that's why! Because they're so loose, huh. You sure do like to peek, Harold…you dirty, dirty old man…"

Her bent leg shifted to slide her foot over his thigh; her other leg curved around him so now, contained within Dottie's spread limbs, Harold was not only given a good, long look at his favorite Courbet as seen through a pair of girlish shorts, but was also permitted the simultaneous caresses of a dexterous little dancer foot. God, he was so afraid to move! Nothing could be interrupted…but he could not resist himself. He had no choice but to stroke her leg, to massage her calf, to rock his hips up just a bit as that foot worked over his trousers.

"I keep trying to dress down to show you how lazy I can be…instead you keep proving you're hopeless."

"Yes—and you keep proving you're beautiful." He might have said more but, thunderous eyes glittering into his, Dottie ran her hands over her bare breasts and teased her erect nipples with those delicate fingertips he loved to kiss, to nibble, to bite. She sighed to stare luridly into his face and he fell into a brief trance before murmuring, out of breath, "So beautiful, Dottie…I've wanted to fuck you all day, all week, but especially since seeing you like this. My easy-going girl."

"That's what you need, Harry…somebody who doesn't take themselves too seriously…somebody who likes to explore… free-form." One hand slid into her shorts and he groaned as fingertips flashed at him through the cracked window of alluring satin. "Boy, you sure do like these things…I'll wear them all the time now."

"I hope you do, Dottie—look how wet you are, you're as much an exhibitionist as I am a voyeur. What a dirty little slut my Dottie is."

"Oh, Daddy—Daddy, aren't you mad my room's so messy?"

Absolutely hadn't noticed it, been too busy staring at her all night. Suddenly all he could see was the panties scattered across the floor and the t-shirt hanging out of the hamper. Harold twisted her legs around and landed a few smart swats upon the backs of her thighs while a gasp of pleasure leapt from her. "You're right," he said, "stop teasing your father and go pick up your clothes, Dorothy Shipman."

"Oh! Yes, Daddy"—the girl hurried up and he groaned to lose contact with her but was soon quite literally on the edge of his seat for the chance to watch her bend and move and exist in this hot little shorts, oh, he really did love them—"yes, I'm sorry…I didn't mean to make you mad."

"You're not sorry yet, you spoiled brat…oh, Christ, stop— wait."

He couldn't stand it a second longer. She had bent to pick up a pair of underwear sitting by the dresser and the pink lips of her pussy glistened through at him so tantalizingly—

Eros's blindfold, it was just too much! He hurried over to kneel behind her, that beautiful ass and those pale thighs tense with the stretch of her position. Through the loose satin of the shorts, Harold pressed a few long kisses upon that beautiful cunt and had his lust furthered by her gasp.

"Oh! Daddy, that's so naughty—"

"Ah, I know, but you're such a perfect girl, and so wet…and from some angles, in some moments, you are so impossible to resist—"

"Oh, ah! Oh—do you want me to clean my room, or what? You can't spank me for being cluttered if you distract me like this!"

"I can and I will, young lady—"

"Mean man," was her giggling complaint as he was in the middle of knocking her over so he could have his way with her on the floor. Before he could accomplish the act of pulling her down to his level, however, that blasted phone began to buzz in his pocket. Harold groaned and pressed his face against Dottie's precious satin shorts.

"No," he said, but Dottie was more concerned and took a professional tone, nudging his head.

"What if it's somebody from the office? You should answer it."

"It's nobody from the office…what day is today, Thursday? Probably it's just the—"

Just the housekeeper for the country place.

Ah—ah, fuck.

Heart racing, Harold sprang upright, said, "Excuse me," and answered the phone a second before he was fully out of Dottie's room. "Good evening Giorgio—"

"Mr. Fleetwood! Hey, good evening, how are you?" The man's customary upbeat tone left him at greater ease but God, God, what a fool he was! Distracted by Dottie and woefully sleep-deprived. He had barely managed to make the doctor's appointment and call the locksmith for Dottie's apartment;

what he had not remembered to do was ring the country place's housekeeper and tell them to skip this week, and maybe the next several. He was going to have to give up at some point and hire a traditional personal assistant again, but he was stringently opposed to the idea for the same reason that he did not hire a live-in cleaning or maintenance staff at any of his properties. Having housekeepers come through was really just a liability to privacy at the best of times, to say nothing of when one had dismembered human body parts in the freezer…even if those body parts belonged, strictly speaking, to a living woman.

"Sorry to bother you," the housekeeper continued after a rudimentary exchange of greetings that Harold barely noticed amid his panic, "but I just wanted to give you a head's up. It seems like you left your safe open."

Oh! Oh! Oh, oh oh. Oh! Oh, haha, oh, thank God. Was that all? Harold tried not to sound relieved as he said, "Goodness, did I? Must be going senile."

"Yeah, well, I closed it for you, but I just wanted to let you know in case you were—I don't know, leaving it open for a—"

"Yes, yes, no, very good, you did very well, thank you. I appreciate your diligence—oh, but you know, I'm so embarrassed! I meant to call you and tell you to take a couple of weeks off, Giorgio."

"No kidding!"

"Yes, no, I'm so sorry. Don't mean to waste your time— why don't you head on home and consider tonight money in your pocket for the inconvenience. I'll call you when I need you again, maybe in two or three weeks?"

"Gosh, all right, well, why don't I just order some things for the pantry for—"

"Ah, no"—too fast, old boy, slow down, relax, relax—"no, that's quite all right. I've got some orders coming in this weekend, actually. Just thinking about hunkering down for a bit of a staycation…you know how particular I am."

"All right, Mr. Fleetwood, whatever you say. Enjoy your time off, sir!"

"You, too, Giorgio, thank you as always for being so diligent."

And so trustworthy. Harold had a great appreciation for a fellow like Giorgio: a man who followed directions and asked only the questions that mattered. Still, Harold hovered by the fish tank, paranoid, checking via private streams directly to an encrypted app on his phone one of the three security feeds from the country house. Many paranoid billionaires would consider wiring up the whole property, or most of it, but Harold was not nearly as paranoid as he was private. The whole point of the *petite maison* was to serve as a dreamy shelter away from reality and all its prying eyes. It was a lovely place of romance and permissive fantasies and such things could not be indulged beneath a security camera's eye in a genuine way. Another reason he did not watch the films that had compulsively piled up in his safe was because it was all so humdrum, so fake. Another reason he loved Dottie was that everything about her was real.

Well—almost everything. After watching for a few moments the video feed of the outer door to the cold chamber storing Dottie's dismembered body, Harold looked up and noticed with a laugh of surprise that her aquarium was fake. The tropical fish were an illusion, a hologram of some kind; the tank was fraudulent; the base upon which it stood was a record stand. Had to explore that one of these days, see what music she liked and which of his acquaintances might impress her. For now he was edgy, body vibrating with the very real fear of exposure.

No, beyond exposure—of having his life obliterated in an instant. Oh…he ran a hand over his face and, tail between his legs, slunk back to Dottie. She sat against her headboard with one leg attractively propped up, dutifully wearing nothing but her shorts, the edge of one worried thumb pressing to her lips.

Harold groaned at the sight and dropped his face into her lap without delay.

Her hand lowered into his hair as she asked, "Is everything okay?"

"Oh, yes, well, now it's fine…I was stupid, that's all. I've been so excited about you, so absolutely sleepless and obsessed with thoughts of you…it's not your fault, of course, but I need to stay in touch with the depravity of my love for you. The dangers of it. There may be few dangers to *you*, but oh, my…I would hate to be separated from you by any means, and a prison cell is far from my first choice."

The deep fear of her gasp as her fingers tightened in his hair pained his heart. Poor Dottie! "No, I don't want you to ever go away…I would come out and tell everyone about myself if that's what it took, Harold."

"Dottie, darling—no, promise me you'll never do that." He lifted his head and caught up her hands, pressing both to his lips while squeezing shut his eyes. "No, absolutely not. I won't see you in some lab on my account."

"Better than seeing you in prison."

"Maybe we should come up with a contingency plan for if the heat ever turns on…oh…no. Whatever happens, I can't be parted from you."

"Harold…" Frowning, Dottie traced her fingertips under his eye. "You really are sleeping rough this week, aren't you?"

"God, yes. Every day since we've parted I've woken up at two in the morning just—oh, dying for you, Dottie!"

She laughed in shock, her beautiful bare chest speckled with scarlet. "Really?"

"Yes, it's awful…I'm exhausted. I barely slept this weekend, either…I was too busy watching you sleep. Too busy being awake near you. I can't imagine the sleeping pills my doctor gave me will really work."

"If they don't, you could always slip them to me and see if you can make me cum in my sleep…I'm sensitive to pills."

While he moaned and buried his face against those sweet white thighs to avert his gaze away from the face that knew his every depraved thought before he dared vocalize it, Dottie ran her hands down the back of his neck. "You don't need pills, Harold…poor man. Maybe I *am* being cruel…I'm having a hard time sleeping, too."

Hope! Shining, beautiful hope. "Really?"

"Uh-huh…it's funny you should say that, too…I've also been waking up around two in the morning. Just, like, super, outrageously horny…wetter than you'd believe."

"Ah, Dottie"—he groaned and leaned up, catching her face in his hands to kiss her luscious mouth—"Daddy's sensitive little girl! That must be the hour our bodies are most attuned to one another…some harmonic moment in the night when, were we but lying together, any pleasure we might share would be naturally doubled by some natural ebb and flow whose mechanisms we know nothing of."

"You're so dreamy, Harold…metaphysical." He settled back against her headboard and slid the girl into his lap, one hand fitting into the bare small of her back and the other lowering to cradle and pat her biteable ass through those dastardly shorts. "Maybe that's true, but I feel attuned to you all the time…like I've been waiting for you forever, and now I've finally found you."

"Just imagine how I feel." His patting became languid petting. While he restrained a sigh to fondle that wonderful backside and let his long fingers furl just within the boundaries of those loose shorts, Harold stared into her flushed face and murmured, "Such a long time, I've waited…I had given up hope of connecting. And now, you, my little fantasy…so far away from me every day I could scream. It's not natural…my body wants yours, your body wants mine. I know my mind craves everything that fills yours; the same could be said of my soul, and I can only imagine you feel those urges to commune with me as I do with you. Dottie…oh, Dottie"—he gasped as his creeping fingers received a thrill—"why are you so wet, angel?"

"I don't know…because you're teasing me."

His fingers probed a little deeper into the leg of those shorts, plunging between her soaking lips and encouraging her legs to spread. "Am I really?"

"Uh-huh…you can't touch little girls like this, Daddy…oh, you're naughty to put your fingers there…that feels so good…" Her head lolled back when his finger pushed into her against half-formed mock protests. "Oh…Daddy, you're going to make a mess of the little shorts you love so much."

"God, I hope so…I want them wet as this pretty kitty, you little slut…"

Between the kisses he had begun to liberally apply to her gasping mouth, Dottie managed to whisper, "Ah, oh—oh, Daddy, don't tell anyone I'm such a dirty slut for you, please, please—"

"Do you promise to do what Daddy says?"

"Yes, oh, I promise—"

"Then he won't tell, precious, don't worry…go get that dildo of yours."

She gasped as he removed his fingers but hurried to obey, springing from her bed to rifle through her disorganized nightstand and retrieve the hot pink vibrating toy from within. His prick throbbed at the thought of her using it; he coaxed her back into his lap, hands sliding over her breasts while he murmured in her ear, "Let Daddy use it on you and he'll tell you a nice, fun story about the romantic date he has in mind for you this weekend."

With a low moan of excitement, the girl gazed at him with utter adoration. "Really, really? What kind of date?"

Gently removing the dildo from her hand, Harold lay one hand on her thigh to encourage her legs to spread apart. As Dottie obliged him, he tapped a few buttons on the device to get used to the settings, deactivated it again, and commenced to tease the tip up and down the length of her inner thigh. "A lovely dinner date…dancing…do you like to dance, Dottie?"

She nodded eagerly, lip bitten in that coquettish expression that made him want to scream with desire. While he teased the tip of the toy up into the hypnotically loose leg of her shorts, Dottie gasped. Her legs spread a few degrees more and her hips rocked up to welcome every scrap of attention he provided. "I don't know how to dance well or anything though," she whispered, riveted to his face as he teased her with the cool tip of the toy. "But I want to learn."

"Well…I'll teach you…yes, darling, I'll teach you how to dance"—he eased the head of the toy past the obscenely slick lips of her tight little cunt and groaned in time with her to see the dildo disappear into the shorts she wore—"and after that, you can come and cuddle with Daddy in his special bed in that nice, fun room with all the mirrors…and we can play a very special game."

"Oh—oh, what kind of game? Oh, Daddy! That toy—I like it when you play with me—"

"Did you ever use this thing on yourself when we were chatting online?"

"Hm—oh, sometimes, oh, Harold, but it never felt this good, oh—" Her eyes shut and her hips arched up as he worked the dildo out and back into her again. "Yes, yes, oh, Daddy, oh, please, harder?"

"Just a little harder…but now I want to tease you the way you tease me, princess…make you suffer as long as you're making me suffer. Then, come Friday, I'll relieve us both… really relieve us. Won't that be nice." The wet sound of her little pussy taking the toy over and over again made his cock throb so unbearably that he reached down behind her prefect ass to pull it out. Gasping to feel it free, he pushed it up against her pretty nate, rocked it against the crack of her backside and generally thought about replacing that hardworking dildo with his own, long-suffering dick. But it was so fun to watch her with the toy in her. So fun to think about watching her take a dick other than his own.

Her mind was elsewhere. Gasping, Dottie slid her arms around his neck to gaze into his face. "But—oh, oh—Daddy, I'm nervous! If you kill me after dinner, if you strangle my cute little throat until I'm, oh, fucking dead—you like that, huh, you disgusting old creep, oh, dirty old man—oh, oh, but if you do that after dinner then I might piss myself while I'm dying, Daddy—"

"And won't you be such an embarrassed girl when you come back after that…so ashamed." He absolutely had to have her: no, couldn't wait a moment longer. Harold slid the dildo out of her and lay her back upon the bed. She covered her mouth to see his dick, her smile to see it pleasing to his vanity in every sense. As he used the head of his cock to investigate that intoxicating satin hole that concealed like a veil the tantalizing cunt lips beneath, Dottie moaned. Her head rolled back against the pillow and her legs spread to encourage him as she whispered, "I can't believe you're such a dirty, gross pervert to like something like that…"

"All perfectly natural, princess, part of the process… accidents happen all the time, especially in death. Some things are inevitable…we'll clean the meat, won't we? Oh! Oh, Christ, Dottie"—he gritted his teeth and she groaned in time with his slow push into her, her channel slick beyond all reason—"oh, you absolute harlot, you filthy little sinner, Christ! Your pussy is always begging for a fucking, isn't it?"

"Yes"—her brow furrowed as if she was about to weep with the sudden force of his strokes; while he fucked her through those shorts her hip lifted to deepen his penetration and fill them both with tremors—"oh, yes, yes, Harold, yes, I need it, I love it, I love it when you fuck me—oh, so hard, so hard, just like that, harder, harder—oh, hurt me with it, Harold! Fuck, yes, yes, yes, it hurts, it's so hard, I want it to hurt me—"

He loved her! Oh, Jesus, he loved Dottie Shipman so

much. She was so emotive: as expressive of her pleasure as an alley cat, crying and moaning and sinking her nails into his flesh as if the ecstasy he provided her was some kind of assault against her rational senses that she needed defend against. Oh, and it was. He wanted nothing more than to truly fuck her senseless, yes—to fuck all sense and pride and, let's face it, wisdom out of her. He wanted to fuck her until she was fully amenable to the idea of their cohabitation; until she couldn't do without his cock the way he couldn't do without any of her. He could have printed up posters: DOTTIE SHIPMAN, WANTED DEAD OR ALIVE. Wanted, wanted, wanted. Wanted any way.

But the animation and beauty of her body alive was incomparably sublime. Her acrobatics were stunning to him: when at last she had her third orgasm and he gasped his way to yet another long-delayed one, it was devastating on an emotional level. Like reaching the end of a perfect theatrical production. His body tightened with the anticipation of a dog ready for a kick in the ribs. Time to go home, yes. Any moment she'd throw him out, rightly so, God, he was a clingy piece of shit.

Yet…such a moment did not come. Sighing low, Dottie carded her fingers through his hair and, when he lifted his face from her bosom, smiled. "I have to go to work in the morning"—her tone was never too tired to carry a teasing lilt—"and my boss is a real hard-ass for showing up on-time… but do you want to stay the night if you promise you won't get in the way of me making it into the office?"

"I want very, very much to stay the night…but I can make no promises like that."

2.

SMART HE DIDN'T. It did not take a psychic with a crystal ball to discern that neither Harold nor Dottie would be going into work the next day, Friday; nor did it take any elaborate forms of divination to declare that both Dottie and Harold received a better sleep that night than either had in six days, possibly longer. And it surely should have come as no surprise to anyone that, despite this very fine, very powerful sleep that descended upon both of them to bathe their eyes in the kind of peace only very lucky lovers know, Harold woke up once again around two in the morning.

But this time—oh, this time…this time, he awoke to a room smelling of Dottie, in a bed suffused with Dottie, and amid a sharp shock of pleasure he settled into the slow growing awareness of Dottie's naked body plastered to his side. There, against him. There, with him. Oh! Oh, Dottie. Never send him home, please! He couldn't take it.

As cold as her body was in her waking hours, she was just as warm in the night. Incredible, really. Perhaps it was only his own heat, absorbed and returned to him—yes, reflected to him. His little mirror-child. Oh…Dottie. What was Dottie? Was there any explanation for what she was? Any cause or source? Was she human? Did it matter? He couldn't make himself think it did. He sorted through his mind all number of mythological entities and found nothing quite like Dottie but had to admit that, as a man of business and alienated Catholicism, he hadn't devoted much of his time to thinking of far-flung things like ghosts and witches and all their paranormal friends.

But now his little witch curled in his arm, her naked body shifting with her breath, her mouth open to release the sighs of her sleep against his chest. How wonderful she was to hold! Even when sleeping in the same bed as his ex-wife, Molly, Harold had evaded her all throughout the night. The first few nights of their marriage, the husband's obligation having been achieved by a wide variety of thoughts too shameful to even recount in retrospect, he would force himself to hold her for oh, two minutes, three, then turn over and go to sleep as if he simply couldn't help it. In reality he was being avoidant; avoidant and, to his mind, horribly adulterous. He'd been obligated to have sex with Molly many times through their marriage and never once had he thought of her during the act.

It was for her own good that he hadn't, but it made him feel cruel. Even now his thoughts on Molly shamed him: what a cold word he had picked just now, "obligated." The duties of the marital bed should have been a privilege for him. Molly really was a beautiful woman, a pretty Brigette Bardot pout and Marilyn Monroe curls. Men and women alike were always crawling all over each other to hold doors and get chairs for her, but Harold would have done anything to see her dismembered and sealed neatly into a grocery store suitable package of beautiful woman-flesh, and his own thoughts sickened him so much that every sexual encounter with his wife had been absolute mental torture.

But there was no shame in having such a thought about Dottie. Absolutely none. She made his own thoughts feel so natural, God! Already he had begun to lose touch with how dangerous it was for him to feel natural, but he couldn't help it. It was addictive, feeling natural. After a lifetime of isolation, of alienation, internal horror at his own every waking thought and impulse, to at last feel not quite so abnormal was beyond relief. To think on it too long moved him almost to tears; and thinking on it there in the dark of Dottie's bedroom, her sweet-smelling head with its sleep-tousled hair resting on his chest, all he could do was kiss the crown of her lovely skull.

Christ! He had woken up hard as a marble column for that doll pressing to him, and each kiss he lay upon her primed him with an anticipatory jolt of pleasure. Gently, slowly, he eased the heavily sleeping girl upon her back, one hand running over her body while his mouth tended to her fluttering eyelids. Oh…her breasts were so delicate, so soft. He wanted to bite one off and satisfied himself as best he could by lowering his mouth to kiss it.

"Oh," sighed the girl, arching awake and up into his kiss. While his tongue worked against one responsive nipple, Dottie moaned and stretched beneath him, then seemed to realize, as his hands passed over her thighs, that she was awake. "Oh…Harold." There was a sweet sort of smile in her voice. "What time is it, Harry?"

"Just past two."

"Oh, Harold, I'm tired…ah…"

"Tired and wet!" He gasped to feel the lips of her pussy oozing such nectar already. He was used to morning wood, obviously, but as he had suspected, Dottie also seemed to be a natural victim of early morning cupidity. While his fingers eased gently over her soaking wet clit, her legs spread invitingly and his kisses began their descent. "Dottie, Dottie, oh, darling, I was right, Christ…yes, your little body is just begging for me—"

"Fuck! Oh, Harold, I'm so sensitive…oh, it feels so good—"

What a sweet little whine! Yes, ah—on the cusp of sleep, they both found themselves hyper-stimulated, and Harold was eager to take full advantage of it. His prick throbbed to see how she writhed under the careful glide of his hands over her body, and when his mouth lowered between her thighs to kiss and nuzzle the intoxicating font of passion hidden there, she swallowed back a keen of desire and rolled over to fondle his cock in the dark. Harold moaned against her pussy, spreading her lips with his fingertips to permit the rapid drum of his tongue against an adorable little clitoris he would have loved to bite off. Ah, Christ, maybe this weekend he would—cut off that perfect soft hand gliding up and down his prick like he fantasized about the first time he met her, oh, what a time.

At her urging, Harold rolled upon his back and the girl slithered upon him. An infernal succubus resting on his chest; while her head bowed back over his cock, the tip of her tongue sending electrical sparks from the head down the throbbing shaft, Harold gasped and opened his mouth to greet the drooling cunt that lowered over his face. Ah! Christ—oh, fuck, the next time she agreed to use him as her chair he would beg to serve her this way. He loved to be subsumed in those strong thighs, that wet pussy, that pert and yielding ass of hers. Eating her cunt in the metaphorical way made him think of literally eating the rest of her—of the head in his freezer at home, not even worth his attention as a sex toy since he'd cleaned it up and removed its tongue and cheeks. Those cheeks! So delicious—God, her meat was so sweet, so soft, truly addictive as no other substance on Earth. His teeth brushed her vulva and she moaned, shuddered, lifted her mouth from his cock to pet it as though it were a loyal dog.

"Careful, Harold…you may be stronger than I am, but with me on top of you like this, you could be in trouble…" Her pussy ground hard against his mouth and he groaned, lifting his face against it, wishing to disappear into her flesh and live forever in a state of cosmic pleasure. "It wouldn't be so hard for me to bite it off right here," she continued, producing a twitch from the cock she stroked up and down with that silky hand. "Or just hold you down and tie you up, see if I can fit you in my oven…oh, you like that, huh, Harold? Dirty Harry…oh, your cock is so hard, Daddy, I want it, I can't wait anymore—"

He moaned in sorrow as she lifted from his face—but how quickly his suffering yielded to sweet reward! Dottie's soaking tight pussy swallowed his aching cock whole and he almost sobbed for the sheer ecstasy of the pleasure. The intensity of it was somehow so great: perhaps for the dreamy hour, or for the night spent with her nude body always seeking unconscious union with his. She took to riding him, her acrobatic pelvis pumping and rocking around until she found an angle that produced an expression akin to pain in her beautiful face. "Oh, fuck!" The words emerged as another set of sexy whines while her smooth brow furrowed, her glassy eyes and parted lips seeking his while she arched her hips back to keep him grinding on the spot. "Oh, Harold—Harry, Harry, oh, Daddy, kiss me—"

"I love to kiss you, Dottie—oh, Dottie, I love you—"

"Ah! I love you, too—fuck, I love you so much I want to eat you alive, Harold—oh—" While his cock throbbed inside her and he cried out in ecstasy, she caught his face in her hands and stared wildly down into it. "Harold, Harold, oh, I wish you could do what I can do! Oh, God—I want to hurt you, oh, oh, you dirty, filthy old man. Yes, you gross old man—drooling all over me in my sleep, molesting me until I wake up, making me love your cock so much! I love it, I love it, I love it so much! Fuck, Harold, Harold, Harold, oh, you need to be punished—"

"Dottie! Oh, princess, I'm sorry—how vile I am, I know—"

"That's right." One hand lifted away so the other could pat a few times against his cheek; the patting escalating quickly into a series of light slaps that graduated to being not-so-very-light as she spoke through teeth clenched in her sheer desire to consume him. "Oh, you bad dirty man, thinking such dirty things about a nice girl like me—Harold, Harold, I'm a nice girl and you want to *kill* me, Harold! You want to eat me, oh, you're a monster, you're an animal, oh, it makes your cock so hard when I tell you that…yes, your cock agrees with me, Harry. Oh, this dick thinks you need to be punished, doesn't it?"

"Oh, Dottie, Dottie, it does—go on, angel, oh, I'm too wretched to deserve to be struck by such a creature—"

"That's right." This slap was a real slap and rang loud amid the obscene sounds of sex. Harold gasped, moaned, clutched her thighs and begged her to do it again. Once, twice, three times, each slap more confident than the next. At last, teeth bared in furious desire, the girl pushed Harold's face to the side and bent over him, forcing angry kisses against his cheek, down his neck, over his shoulder. There those kisses became biting. Harold cried out in real pain as her teeth penetrated his flesh. When her head lifted and she kissed his mouth the taste of his own blood upon her tongue brought him that much closer to the edge of orgasm.

"That's right, Harold," she continued at last, fire in her eyes as she fucked him, "you don't even deserve to be eaten by me. You're such a bad old pervert…oh, but if you *beg* me, beg me enough, maybe I'll change my mind. Beg me, Harold."

"Dottie, please—"

"Yes, yes, go on—"

"Oh, Dottie, please, princess, I want to be eaten by you so badly—Christ! Ah, slit my throat and dismember my body and lick my blood off of your beautiful fingers—ah, Dottie, Dottie, Dottie, please, swear to me, please promise when I die you'll eat my corpse—"

"Oh, Harold—"

"Say you'll do it, Dottie—"

"Harold, Harold, oh, of course, of course I'll do it, oh, I'll eat every last part of you! I'll suck the marrow from your fucking bones, Harold, oh, I love you—"

"Dottie! Dottie"—his eyes filled with tears and he grasped for her, clutched her down against his mouth, screamed against her flesh as he orgasmed—"Dottie! Dottie—Christ! Love isn't enough! Ah—ah—oh, God." While he shuddered up against her pelvis she watched each second in bright-eyed wonder, smiling tenderly upon him while trailing fingertips over his cheek. Gasping for air, Harold turned to kiss those wonderful fingers, then lifted his head up to suckle a few more drops of love from her mouth.

"Oh, Dottie," he whispered when the tremors receded and she began to roll off of him, "Dottie, no…the way I feel for you is so much more than simple human love."

When he thought of the love he had for Dottie the feeling was so overwhelming that he wanted to set himself on fire like a monk protesting the inhumanity of war. Oh! It was easier than being so overwhelmed by these emotions, by this desire! The passion of sex waned with the orgasm, or was intended to, but Dottie, Dottie—Christ, if he could have he would have gotten his dick right back in working order and plunged it into her again. Woken up all her neighbors with her screams. Fuck, he loved to make her scream with it.

It didn't seem like he even had to be inside her to achieve that effect. Splayed out against her headboard, Dottie moaned to reach down between her legs and press a pair of fingers into herself. He watched, marveling, moaning softly to see her savoring the sensation of his cum inside her. The thought of his genetic material inside her pussy rattled him with a new kind of pleasure and he knelt over her, pushing her hand away, sliding his own fingers in to work the wet fluid of their mutual arousals deeper into her cunt and over the welcoming flower that invited him into it. Impossibly, she had become even wetter—ah, what a lewd girl she was! He adored her body's slutty nature and how it all came spilling out for him, desperate to show off.

"Ah, Dottie—you love the thought of Daddy's cum inside you, don't you."

She shyly gasped, one hand lifting to her mouth while he fingered her. "Oh—uh-huh, yes, oh, I like how you make me into such a dirty, dripping girl…hm"—her hips arched up and her pussy tightened around his fingers, begging his cock to wake back up; he had to call Dr. Ernst about a Viagra prescription at this rate—"I love how you fuck me, Harold…"

"I love fucking you, Dottie…I could do it all day." While his middle and ring finger curled inside her to tickle that centerpiece of pleasure within her cunt, Dottie's sharp gasps increased. "I don't think you're in any condition to work, Miss Shipman."

"God dammit! I knew it—"

"You'd better take the day off."

"Hm—oh—fuck, Harold, no, no, I want to be a good employee—"

"No, no you don't—you want to be my bad little fuck-toy. You want to stay home and fuck your boss all day, Miss Shipman. Where's your phone?"

"*Now?* It's three in the morning—oh, oh, oh, and I don't want you to stop—"

"I'm not going to stop…and what more believable time to leave a message on the company absentee line than at three in the morning? Poor sleepless girl, up all night sick as a dog—yes, a dog, oh, my little bitch in heat, this little pussy of yours is really trying its best to get me hard again, ah, Dottie—"

"Mm! But—but everyone will know, oh, Harry! When you don't come in, either, everyone will know—"

"Let them!" He grasped her delicate jaw with his free hand, his other set of fingers working in her savagely while she gasped and shuddered and cried out beneath his snarl. "Fucking let them, Dottie, let everyone know it—Christ, Christ, I'll bend you over and fuck you in the middle of that fucking office, see if I give a shit, how's that for "Me, too—" Dottie, I'm so tired of hiding! I don't want to hide, oh, look at you! Look at you! I want to share you with the world. I want to show you off—I want to hold you in my arms, introduce you to everyone I know, show them, my God, say, "This woman loves me!" My God, oh, Dottie"—he slowed his motions, awed by the sight of her sudden orgasm and the convulsions it produced through the twisting limbs that grasped at him—"Dottie, Dottie…I didn't know it was possible to feel this way after only knowing a woman for a week."

"Ha—ha—oh, Harold—a week—a week, but three years—oh, and I feel—oh…I feel like we've been waiting for each other—Harold, please—"

She didn't have to finish her request. He kissed her, sighed into her, nuzzled her beautiful mouth and nose and rocked her close against his chest. Oh, yes. That was just what it was—like finding someone from whom he had been separated for a long, long time. Say, stumbling upon them one day in an art gallery and just—remembering.

Some passionate young lovers felt as if they'd known each other in a former life. That was close to the description of what Harold and Dottie felt for one another, but too reductive somehow. After she miserabled up the tone of her voice and added in a few sad scratchy coughs to go with her phone message, Dottie lay in his arms, permitted his petting, tolerated his gazing, abided every tender kiss and gentle exploration of his hands or mouth. He was just thinking about catching a few more hours of sleep when, admiring him through heavy eyelids, the girl murmured suddenly, "I feel like—I feel like something happened, and I should have been born sooner, and I wasn't."

Yes—that was what it was. He smoothed her hair from her face and said softly, "It does feel like a missed connection, doesn't it."

"Yeah…like I was supposed to be born as, like, your neighbor…or your sister." She smiled a little, faintly. "I'm glad I wasn't, though. I don't want to love each other in secret."

"Please quit the office, Dottie."

Sighing heavily, the girl hummed and rolled her head against his shoulder, her eyes turned away. "I guess I should look for another job, but I—"

"Please! You know you don't need to. I would be thrilled to take care of you."

"I know…but I don't want—I want sex to always be fun for us. Special, you know? I don't want it to be, like…an obligation. Something you feel entitled to because it's…like, part of an exchange somehow. Part of my duties, or something."

Ugh. Well—yes, he understood that, obviously. Harold drew her tighter into his arms, beneath his chin, and there bent his head over her to kiss the crown of her fragrant head. "I want to love you openly."

"Me, too…I don't know." She rubbed her eyes and sat up, apparently giving up on sleep around the time he was considering it. "Maybe now is the right time to try something new…I've wanted to draw a comic for a long time."

"Have you?"

"Uh-huh…I drew a couple of short series, but I haven't done anything with them. They're like my paintings, you know. I didn't sell them so I just got frustrated and gave up. But…I don't know, a lot of people have been having better luck monetizing, like, serialized *doujinshi* that get posted online on ad revenue producing websites. They get popular enough and publish real, bound editions of the comics…I've been thinking about it for a long time but I just haven't wanted to take the time away from the Dolcett community and talking with you. Now with you're here with me, though…"

While his head rested upon the sacred pillow of her thigh, Dottie fell into the gentle rhythm of petting his hair, stroking his ear, tickling her fingertips down his neck. "I guess if I'm not going to be making free art for them anymore I could just make paid art to appeal to them…maybe there's a way to leverage them into kind of a starting audience."

He shut his eyes beneath her caresses, sighing with

pleasure to feel how instantly his brain released itself for sleep with Dottie's soothing proximity. "You could come up with a comic based on us, sell it to the eroguro community…who would believe it's based on real life?"

Laughing, Dottie ran her thumb over the shell of his ear. "That's not a bad idea…something to start with, anyway. I'll think about it. Go to sleep, Harold."

"I usually get up at four in the morning…not sure why I'm so tired."

"Because you just spent all your energy fucking me senseless…it's okay, just go to sleep, I'll be your pillow. Not like I'm going to work today, right?"

3.

THE DAY WAS grand. Grand for loving; grand for driving. When it was spring he'd take Dottie for picnics—happy outings in the sunshine with lemonade and finger sandwiches. For now the grass was winter-dead on either side of the long highway to the slaughterhouse, their red-hot love-nest.

"I think I feel very wickedly disposed toward you today, Dottie." They cruised through the easygoing dips and curves of the country, his hand sliding upon her knee with far greater ease than he'd touched her with even the night before. The notion of being so much as en route to the slaughterhouse altered something in his chemistry in the first place, but to do so with Dottie—yes, oh, to be on the cusp of having Dottie isolated with him! Alone and helpless. His heart hammered in the fingertips he sank into her soft flesh. She gazed over, nibbling her lip, her legs (bared by those obscene short-shorts worn to torment him—clearly she was in need of a lesson on teasing him for those two long driving hours when she was inaccessible) swaying back and forth in pleasure at the caress.

He continued thinking aloud, breathless with the ecstasy of contact. "Yes, I think so…I do want to show you a nice time, Dottie, but you bring out the animal in me, and—ah—"

"Harold, oh—yes, you haven't been *really* mean with me yet. Please—I want to feel totally controlled by you."

"Then you'd better do everything I say when we're in my house, Dottie. If you don't obey, your last minutes on Earth will be very unpleasant."

"Oh, Harold!" She gasped: her right hand flew to her throat while her left slid down to caress the one that fondled her. "I'll be good, I promise—"

"You think I'm kidding"—his fingers sank deeper into her tender flesh and he choked back a gasp of shock to pinch her, to listen to her whine while he checked her viability for the kitchen—"oh, Dottie, I'm not kidding. You can be a good little lamb to my slaughter—a pretty doe, oh, my tender slice of venison—or you can be a bad, bad little piggie who goes squealing all the way to the killing floor. I don't mind either way. Either way I'll have my meat. So you'd better decide now if you're ready to die today. Because if you're not ready, it will be much harder for you."

"Harold"—the girl's voice was a whisper, tiny, desperate not with fear but lust—"Harold, please, will you pull over and fuck me?"

"No."

Shuddering, Dottie nuzzled against his arm, under it, trembled to be held against him. He drove within the margins of the speed limit only because he had the remains of her severed head in a cooler in the back of the car. She had insisted on staying in the car while he dropped by the condo and it drove him wild. He knew when she was at last there, at his real home, his lived-in home where he woke up during the week and existed in reality, then, then, then—then, then!—she would stay. She would stay forever. With him. Oh, God. With him. And she knew it too: knew the car was safer than throwing herself into domestic love with an old, old man as a twenty-four year old girl.

Oh, it depressed him. He hated himself for being so old. Perhaps it was not she who was born late—perhaps his soul had rushed ahead, insisted on blazing a trail. On building this empire to attract her. Yes—she was right. He had to be careful to avoid commodifying their sex in any real way except in the context of titillating play. God, God…whatever horrific things he committed against her person, whatever achievements of sin and depravity he orchestrated upon her lovely body, never let her doubt for even one second the depth of his love! Only a love so painful could engender imaginings so foul. He spoke to her kindly with her under his arm in the car ride to her death, his tone doting, oozing fondness he hoped she felt was more than just an effort to lull her into a sense of security.

"Why don't you keep real fish, Dottie?"

"Oh, those"—the girl laughed, her tone warbling with her anticipation of their profane intimacies—"I guess because I'd have to feed the real ones…I'm worried I'd be bad at taking care of living things."

"Goodness, you look at me with such gentleness—I'm sure you would be wonderful with fish. Certainly, fish for starters."

"That's nice of you to say…it's a lot of responsibility, though! What I'd really like is a cat, but my apartment is small. So, I let my pretend fish give the place a splash of color."

There was a plan in there for him. Harold made a mental note of it while pulling off the country highway and hit the button for the gate. As it swung wide, he assured her, "Well, they had me convinced…I'd like you to stay in the car, Dottie." He glanced at the clock, the numbers 10:33 nestled into the hard shell of the dash, then parked in front of the renovated slaughterhouse he was so glad he acquired. "Daddy will put your luggage away…and then you and I will play."

"Okay."

He bent his head over hers. "You know I adore you, Dottie."

"Yes."

"And that I'm doing this because I love you."

"Yes, yes—oh, I love you…" Her little mouth opened, the receptive vessel of his kiss, and he groaned to taste the supple interior of her mouth. With a sweet sigh, Dottie worked her lips against his, then slowly tilted away to admire his face. "But remember…you have to make me look in a mirror, Daddy, or you'll have to drive all the way back to my apartment to pick me up again."

Christ, good thing she remembered—all *he* could think about was what was going to happen. What was going to happen. Oh, God. What was going to happen? He kissed her once more and she told him she loved him, the words burning his brain with gratification. The girl's whisper was so small it was almost inaudible; his heart was seized with fear at its own ability to enact its desires—suppose he couldn't manage to do willfully what he did accidentally?—but oh, he couldn't resist his own impulses. It was amazing he had the foresight to think about putting her luggage away first, but it came natural. Give her some time to fret by herself in the cold car while he turned off the alarm, turned on the lights, admired the shining clean kitchen.

He had thought about this so many times over the past week. Thought and thought and thought. How to go about it? He had watched videos profiling the means and methods of slaughtering farm animals, done light research on serial killers, even cracked open his old copy of *The History of Torture* to get a little inspiration. Ultimately he felt it important to not get too exotic the first time. That first time, that first willful time that he killed her, he wanted it to be intimate. Yes, he was a romantic. He couldn't help it. His romanticism extended in all directions and afflicted even murder, even death, so that his relationship with his own mortality was bound up in the concept of beauty—and the notion of women's mortality was beauty, itself. Death was the ultimate masculine force, the final feminizer, the rapist of the human life that swept through and stole bodily autonomy for good.

Unless you were Dottie. Unless you were a pure, good, beautiful consciousness that came bounding back to life every time you were done in. Then, death was the ultimate lover. Death could be approached with mutual consent. Death could be embraced—death could be embodied.

Yes. As Harold opened the front door of the house, filling the doorway and coaxing his mouth-watering prey from the car where she sat in obvious, fidgeting anticipation, a very important thought occurred to him. Death was the body's bridegroom; in orchestrating Dottie's death, Harold himself became a manifestation of that archetypal force. Death. Hades. Mot. The Great Annihilator. Whatever you wished to call it, there it was in him. In the instant, Harold felt himself as more than human—and he blessed Dottie, blessed his cherished little victim, for engendering the revelation of his own immortality of the soul, even if he could not experience it in body as she did. She made the long passage from the car to the doorway and before she could step through he caught her by the arm. Harold yanked her into his house—Death's house—and threw her down upon the floor of the foyer while he shut and locked the way back out over the sound of her gasp.

"Oh, Harold—"

"Take off your clothes."

"Even my cute little—ah!" She cried out and tried to fend him off while he gripped her hair deep against the scalp. He shook her once, one sharp time like a dog breaking the neck of a rabbit.

"Every last scrap of fabric, now—so help me, if you add to my work, you brat, I won't even eat you."

The girl gasped sharply at that, feigning terror believably enough to make him hard while she grasped at his waist. "Oh, no, please, don't waste me—"

"If you exhaust me before I've even had the chance to butcher you up, I may have no choice—all the stress hormones of your struggling while I pull your clothes off will ruin your flavor. Be a good lamb for me, now…"

Gasping, she hurried to please him. Harold's body seized with desire as she scrambled to her feet and tore off her shirt, slid out of her bra, dropped away those irresistible shorts. In a few seconds she stood naked, glowing white marble in the center of his foyer. When he indicated the space before him, she uneasily crossed to stand at attention with her lower lip winsomely bitten; Harold caught her face in one hand and squeezed open her mouth while she cried out.

"God, this reminds me of fucking your severed head last week…shame it's in such poor shape that we have to bury it now. I've a supper idea for this one once I've killed you but maybe in the future we'll play some more games with other heads of yours. Let's see if your face is going to be worth the meat, though—"

She gasped as he reached a thumb into her mouth, pinching the flesh of her cheek mercilessly between thumb and forefinger. Oh, he was cautious for a second—then he remembered she was going to die. Yes, yes. He was going to kill her—oh, Christ! He was going to fucking kill her. Murder her. Yank the life right out of her beautiful, fuckable body. Oh! Dottie, Dottie—this effect on him was unnatural and the sheer, overwhelming force of his unnatural desire for her revealed itself at last. How he had restrained himself! He had not bruised or bullied her, had spanked her only in play, had carefully resisted his urge to grip her, squeeze her, hurt her until she cried out.

Now, all he wanted was to hear her cry out. Now he turned her around to push her head forward and tut at the still healing bruises on the back of her shoulder as if she had some say in it; now he grabbed the flesh of her ass contemplatively, criticizing in a tone of derision, "Awfully lean little animal, aren't you—where's all the fat? Am I going to have to control your diet?"

"Oh, I'm sorry, I'm sorry sir—"

"You should be. My God, I have to do everything for you, don't I—feed you, fuck you, kill you, you're a greedy little bitch. Why should I waste my time eating a girl so thin?"

"But please!" Gasping, whipping around, doomed Dottie clung to him while he tried not to look as pleased as he felt. "Oh, I know I'm not a very good little piggie! I'm too skinny and I just don't eat like I should, but please, please, you *have* to eat me—oh, it's all I want! All I've ever wanted, to be eaten by you—please, please, I have no other reason to live than to be your meat! Why was I born at all if my master can't eat me?"

Harold repressed a shudder, reaching down to fondle her thighs and slap that pale flesh he loved to touch a few sharp times. "Why, you're born to please me, of course. If it pleases me to waste your flesh instead of eating it, shouldn't you still consider yourself lucky?"

With a sad moan, the girl clutched all the tighter the fabric of his shirt and sought his face with those pleading eyes. Her desire to be killed and eaten was so burning, so real, that Harold fought the impulse to yield to it in the instant. "Yes, yes—yes, but it's all I've wanted since I was a little girl, Daddy! Oh, a little piglet—all I've wanted is to be eaten up by you! I think about my meat being chewed up by that handsome mouth and I just, oh, I get all warm and funny feeling inside—"

"A little slut, are you?"

"Yes, yes! For you, yes, oh, Daddy, please—please, I'm such a horny little animal, please, won't you fuck me before you slaughter me?"

"You expect me to eat meat I've defiled?"

Looking torn, the girl released his shirt to drop to her knees and tug on his belt. "Please, please, then let me suck your cock, please, Daddy—oh, please, will you eat me up if I do a good job?"

"Maybe, maybe…let's try and see what happens."

God! He'd never seen a woman so full of genuine enthusiasm for the sight of his prick; never known a girl could enjoy giving head as much as he did. Not only did she enjoy it, but oh, Dottie was good at it…it must have been a cannibal thing. Her lips and tongue moved over his cock with real concentration, those green eyes focused on his anatomy whenever she could admire it and lifted toward his face when she couldn't. Ah, and the soft little face she rubbed against his length—Christ, he wanted to smash her skull open right there on the floor—

"My, my…what a dirty little slut I've raised. Are you wet, slut?" She nodded around the cock in her mouth. He exhaled, pushed forward against her, rested his hand upon her dark hair. "Good…touch yourself a little, get good and soaked for me…you bad little temptress, you've convinced Daddy to fuck you after all. Isn't that nice…a nice last memory for you before you're nothing but a corpse-shaped pile of meat. Oh, Christ— my good little farm animal, my little piece of cattle, ah, you're going to be so many good meals, aren't you, pretty girl…oh, roasts and stews, briskets and steaks, my God, I can do so much…I could do so much more if you'd eat better, bad girl. I'll take my time and fatten the next body up just a bit—ah, Christ, Dottie, Dottie!"

He yanked on the back of her hair; she gasped as he pulled her off his cock and to her feet. "Come along"—he dragged her, still by his grip of that lustrous hair, off in the direction of the kitchen and the path beyond to the proper slaughterhouse portion of the property—"Daddy's going to spoil his brat one last time before he kills her. Aren't you a lucky little piece of pork?"

"Oh yes, Daddy, yes!" Her eyes were wild, utterly mad, and the expression incensed his desire all the more as he dragged her down the hall and shoved open with his free hand the door to the slaughterhouse bedroom. When he pushed her into the center of the room she gasped in time with her reflections, the three mirrored walls and a ceiling all reflecting their own beautiful replications, their own infinite series of splendid, naked Dotties. Which all of all these many bodies would be the next one her spirit inhabited? What would it be like? God, he was excited to see her return as he was to kill her, oh, he was a witness to the workings of the divine! Dottie! He loved her so much that he screamed inside. The wildness of her eyes changed to a kind of stunned realization, as if not until seeing the mirrors did she consciously comprehend the point—the intended apex of their sexual liaison. Turning those vast eyes upon Harold as he shut the door, the girl stumbled back upon the edge of the bed, riveted by his every movement as he strode over to take her in his arms and kiss her.

"Oh Daddy"—she gasped between his kisses, moaned beneath the touches of his hands—"oh, Harold, are you really going to kill me? Oh my God—oh, no one's ever wanted to before, oh Harold, Harold—"

He gasped as she clutched at his cock, guided it down to her soaking little hole; they both gasped at the penetration; she alone gasped while he slammed it deep into her immediately. "Dottie, oh, you haven't doubted, have you? Haven't doubted me? Oh, no, princess, no—ah, Christ, I'm here to give you exactly what you need. Yes, brought you here to bang those pretty fucking brains out"—she screamed, arching up against him at the brutality of his every thrust into the cunt begging for his abuse and growing wetter by the second from it—"and maybe blow them out when I'm done. Oh, Dottie, Christ, oh—let's do it a new way all the time, every time, as often as we can. Then, your favorite ways of dying, I'll perform them for you on birthdays—won't that be nice, oh, Dottie, I'll strangle you on our anniversaries—"

"Fuck! Fuck! Harold! You're so wonderful—"

He spat in her face and she groaned, producing a second, deeper noise of pleasure as he slapped her far harder than she'd hit him the night before. "Shut up, you boot-licking bitch. I'm not killing you because you want it. I'm killing you because *I* want it—fuck, because I look at you across the room and all I think is how delicious your flesh would be! How pretty it would be to see your skull naked and shining with blood in the light…ah, God! Dottie! Dottie—oh, you could ruin my fucking life, Dottie, Dorothy, oh, you little demon—"

It happened naturally, and faster into the proceedings than he had accounted for in fantasy—but everything unfurled faster than he accounted for with Dottie. Their love was a fast-moving love because of its intensity and therefore each rendition of the sexual act was an intense microcosm of their lust. It should have been expected that Harold's hands so quickly found her throat…but oh, what was never expected was the sheer, soul-inflaming pleasure of squeezing that delicate throat. Squeezing it as hard as he'd always wanted to squeeze a woman's throat: without control, without consciousness, without any need to stop. Just squeeze and squeeze. Pour all that desire, all that disgust at himself and fury at life and rage that Dottie should make him so pathetic with love, out into the clutch of hard hands around a fragile windpipe. He stared down into Dottie's face, her wide mouth and delight-filled eyes reddening under the pressure, and released her to let her choke herself back to a little oxygen. That wonderful cunt fluttered around him while she wheezed for desperate air, managing with a pained rasp, "Oh, God, no one's ever—" before he cut off her words with another sharp squeeze before she could fill her lungs.

"I love you so fucking much I can't stand it, Dottie—oh, yes—" He shifted his weight, bowing lower over her to give himself better leverage for thrusts deep into that desperate pussy. Her body seemed so wonderfully attuned to his pleasure. The change in position gave him a new capacity to clutch her throat harder; to feel with acute clarity every muscle and tendon bulging beneath her reddening skin. As her flopping tongue swelled in her mouth, Harold stared into her wild eyes and drowned in endorphins to see her life fade by the second.

Oh, so beautiful—so wonderful, so therapeutic. It was a way at last to yield to the urge of "cute aggression," the desire plaguing the human being when observing a small animal so cute one wished only to moderate one's emotions by crushing it, smashing it, biting off its fucking head Oh! He wished she was small enough to be chewed up whole—to feel all her little bones crackle and pop in his teeth. But this, this sensation of his hands tight around her throat, of his body being made into a weapon of his passion, yes, it was a reasonable alternative. Still a fulfillment of that aggressive urge inspired by emotions of love that were too overwhelming for the human mind to bear.

"Next time, Dottie, I'll suspend by your feet and slit this perfect throat, but this time, oh—I just want to crush you, Dottie, yes…ah!" Her hands scratched reflexively up at his but all the while her hips rolled up in greater welcome, taking his every stroke, inviting his renewed aggression. He shook her, savoring the bulge of her eyes, the purple hue of her face. His grip tightened, his thumb digging in against her artery to cut the blood off from the bran while his palm mashed down to crush her fuckable windpipe. The force produced some crackling attempt at a hiss, a protest rendered inaudible by the lack of air—and for a tiny, tiny hint of a second, a voice in the back of Harold's head asked, *What if she doesn't come back this time?*

But it didn't matter, did it? At this point, it didn't matter. He doubled down. He tightened more. He stared into her beautiful face, purple as the head of his cock squeezed equally tight by her begging cunt. Yes, oh, that body, this body, it wanted to live. But it did not want to live as much as Harold and Dottie wanted it to die. He bent his head to kiss that swollen mouth, savoring the limp thrash of her tongue against his; he watched those eyes, as he had not known to during her accidental death, and squeezed, and squeezed, and squeezed—

The body's eyes rolled up into its heavy eyelids, seeing no more. Harold gasped with sharply increased desire while the same final pound of pressure that crushed the life out of her also squeezed the piss from her body, the hot fluid rushing around his cock as though the death orgasm had made her squirt. With a groan, a gasp, Harold slowly released his grip, touched her limp face, moved her swollen head from side to side and watched with astonishment as, free of any internal tension of its own, it bobbed listlessly amid his cock's every thrust. Oh, it was so hard to stop! So hard, almost impossible, oh, he wanted to keep fucking that cute dead body until his seed was buried inside of it—but it was just a sex toy now. It was nothing, and he wished instead to behold with his own two eyes the greatest wonder of the world.

He had just pulled out and straightened up, swaying dizzily against the edge of the bed, when it happened. What happened? What happened…so hard to describe. Like watching light itself manifest out of nothing. No source—no lamp, no sunbeam, nothing but what was already in the room. But it was as if Dottie—his sacred Dottie, the queen of his heart and his mind and most of all his soul—yes, it was if she was somehow already in the room. Already alive again, standing there in the center of the mirrored walls, and his eyes simply had to…adjust to her presence.

It was so uncanny. He wondered if it was a phenomenon that could be captured on film—wondered if the phenomenon would occur beneath the camera's lens. He never wanted to test it. He never wanted to do anything that might somehow interfere with her ability to return.

Or…for her ability to re-present herself out of nothing again. When her body had fully resolved from the background of which it had seemed a part until the second it was separate, she jolted, gasped for air as if still choking—then cried out as, with a cry of his own, Harold caught her in his arms, swallowed up her kisses, screamed against her, "Dottie, Dottie Shipman! If you ever have to leave me, Dottie, please just kill me—oh, Dottie, I can't live without you, let me take you now, let me deflower this lovely new body, oh, Dottie, Dottie—!"

Dizzy, the nude girl could only laugh, could only accept his kisses and pet his face and turn away from his caresses to let his lips work over her mint-condition, feminine-fragrant neck. "Oh, Harold…how could I ever leave you? I'll never leave you, never ever…I've waited for you my whole life!"

4.

THAT MADE TWO of them. Waiting and waiting, neither one realizing what they waited for until they came together. Oh, Dottie. He made love to her beside her own dead body and when the act was over settled her down in the upstairs bedroom with water, food, anything she asked for. She laughed at him while he doted upon her, leaping to provide her every need, savoring the chance to once again feed by hand that lovely new mouth. How he loved to feed her…loved to make himself slave to that same little holy ghost he had murdered.

"You don't have to baby me so much," she told him sweetly, leaning against his shoulder to gaze into his face. "It was fun… and so hot. I feel so close to you, Harold. You don't need to make it up to me."

Oh, but he did. He absolutely did. His foul desires were to be atoned for and, much as he hoped she would someday come to accept that his interest in providing for her monetarily was a simple attempt to level the steep value differential between them (for how could a billionaire be worth even a fraction of the value of an immortal woman?), he also hoped she would someday settle in to this pattern of devotional recompense.

Even if she did not need it, he certainly did. It was vital, absolutely vital, that he treat her like a goddess directly after behaving as though she were nothing more than meat. Vital not to her perception of herself but his perception of her and the gifts she provided him. She was right. He could never let himself feel entitled to her. The simple nearness of Dottie was a gift to him. That she should let him perform such unspeakable acts was beyond parallel and required from him whole-hearted worship in exchange.

After a break for his fussing and his pleasure of watching her nap in his arms, the girl stirred, gazed up into his face with a flirtatious grin, stretched against his body. "So…aren't we going to do something with the meat, Harold?"

They were, they were indeed. Downstairs, he enlisted her help to move the dead body, first to the adjacent shower room where they rinsed it clean. Harold was flying deliriously high from his first deliberate murder. In the future he would have to make special time to appreciate the effect had by Dottie washing her own dead body, her eyes sometimes lifting to ensure he watched her hand briskly brush water off the carcass's rump or slip a few fingers into its sex cavity to rinse it free of waste. Oh…even without his full attention, however, even within his dreamy murder afterglow, he still had a great appreciation for the sight and still many times could not resist savaging her with kisses while she playfully complained about his bad habit of wasting time.

"You don't understand…everything else is wasting time, Dottie. Everything else in my life—I've just been frittering away the hours."

Take, for instance, Molly. The funny thing was that, before they were very nearly caught that day, he thought of Molly in a rather spontaneous manner while they hefted the body through to the processing room. Had to think about something to save his embarrassment. Oh, he sighed in memory to think of what a clumsy job he did of this second body, but it really was another first time. This was their first whole animal to separate into pieces and so, as the purpose of this particular instance was really more the intimacy of the death act willfully committed for the first time, the meat was not bled while its heart still beat. As a result of this emphasis on process rather than on product, the flesh was still not of the quality he would achieve with his later efforts at butchery—but Harold did have to admit that in the end it was even more splendid and tender than the fruits of the first slaughter.

Anyway, this was all to say he thought of Molly while watching the waste products and the blood they manually pumped out of the animal's still veins go drifting down the slaughterhouse disposal trench, off, off and away. The wild creek guided through the house and tamed briefly into the concrete gutter was visible through a broad window along the northern wall. Its every pane was sealed except the one through which he gazed and he feared that although keeping the window shut loaned the room a gloomy, ponderous horror movie quality, he really couldn't afford to open even that pane very long. The property was gated and private but it would have been just his luck for someone to pick that day to wander past. "You know," said Harold while they lay the carcass out upon the block for further processing, "when I took Molly on a tour of this house, the first thing she said to me was that she just couldn't understand why somebody would want to buy this property to live on it…the second thing she said was that this room was useless."

"Have you ever loved anybody, Harold?"

"I cared about my mother very much," he said while considering the industrial-sized bone saw intended for the manual bisecting of cattle. In modern slaughterhouses machines did the hard work: here Dottie was employed to assist him by holding her old shoulders down, and he severed her head. Harold occasionally dared to look up from his work to enjoy the lust-inflamed features through which she hazily watched him, cuckolded for his attentions by her own corpse. Oh, Dottie! It was agony to be unable to drop everything then and there and fuck her, but sawing off her old body's precious head was its own unspeakably deep, intimate brand of pleasure, and he felt as if each passage of the saw grinding back and forth between the bones of her vertebrae bore a harmonic similarity to the thrust of his cock into her. The symmetry was too natural to require pointing out to her. She looked as if she felt it.

Once the head was gone she helped him break the shoulders and hips, laughing in morbid, insane fascination at the process of destroying her old body's big joints to make the removal of limbs and eventual skinning that much easier. What hard work! They were both covered in a combination of sweat and blood, the two of them conjoining their knowledge to come up with a passable job. All week he had poured over *Gray's Anatomy* and watched instructional videos concerning the slaughter and butchering of various types of livestock, mostly beef and lamb; Dottie, required by her interest in art to be a careful student of the human body, consulted with him in the occasional helpful suggestion. After some time, with the torso skinned and his dick as hard as a rock, Harold had to take a break to beg Dottie for as many caresses as she was willing to tolerate from his blood-soaked hands. She let him bargain a few kisses from her pouting mouth before he got too fresh and she put him back to work, saying, "You horny old goat, I'm hungry! If you don't finish processing this meat, I'll roast *you* up."

Only motivation to work slower, really. God, he loved Dottie. And she hit the nail on the head when she was in the process of realizing who he was: his ultimate dream, the only way he could ever even bear to contemplate his own death, was to be murdered and eaten by a beautiful woman. A wicked little witch, like a devil girl out of a fairy tale.

He worried every once in a while that he was dead. That

he had suffered an aneurysm at his desk and that Dottie was his soul-mate in the sense of being a manifestation of the ethereal anima, the match to his dreams that made all his long-ignored and struggled against fantasies permissible. The thought frightened him at first, but after contemplation, after studying the world around him—the tangibility of the body he bisected upon completing the hard work of removing the spine—Harold had to wonder if it really even mattered. If this was death, and life in death was still so real, and events in death were still causally linked, well…then it didn't matter, did it. If anything, the explanation that he was already dead was just too good to be true. Where once they had been hiding separately, Harold and Dottie now had the dubious privilege of hiding together. Were Harold in heaven, say, they wouldn't need to hide a thing.

But this was the world they were in. The world with its very serious consequences. With the task of bisecting the body complete, Harold and Dottie worked together to wrap up the dismembered limbs and chill them to be dealt with at a later time. The head needed firming up. But as for the torso, Harold was keen to get a move on at least cutting a few steaks out of the shoulders—oh, it made his stomach rumble just to think of it! When they had lain the meat down on the kitchen counter he was on Dottie with kisses again, miserable with his obsession for her, agonized as she fluttered out of his grasp with a laugh and a push against his chest. "Go on!"

"If I don't kiss you, I'll be tempted to eat a piece of your meat, instead…then we'll really have to drop everything. From what I can tell it's much more potent when it's fresh."

"Harold," she began—

And the house intercom system rang.

Harold's arms tightened around Dottie, his ears on keen alert. After looking down at himself, his mind scrambled across the wide variety of explanations for the intrusion and could find nothing—no supposition of who could have made it past the gate. The housekeeper came only on Thursdays and the only other person with a remote to the fence was—

"Stay here." Harold hastily washed his hands in the nearby sink, looked down at himself, tsked, slipped his bloody shirt over his head, then looked with far graver irritation at the stained undershirt beneath. After snatching up a nearby apron and using it to cover himself, he responded to the intercom by hurrying out of the foyer and answering the front door for Molly.

"Harold," she said with an only slightly strained smile of pleasant surprise, falling back on her heel, looking at his apron. "Oh, I caught you cooking—I'm so surprised to find you here!"

"Not as surprised as I am. Very good to see you, though."

Oh, and it was so very good to look at her without the horror and shame of his old compulsive thoughts, not cured by Dottie so much as semi-safely sublimated—although he would have much preferred, say, bumping into Molly at the Met Gala once he and Dottie had settled into a fine partnership. Introducing them at a point where Molly could see Dottie as an enchanting young equal (in intellect, if not in status) to her ex-husband, rather than a slutty little rebound. Dottie was *his* slut, thank you very much, and certainly no mere rebound.

"What are you doing here, exactly, Molly?"

"Oh, well—I don't know, it's almost spring, and I've been putting it off and putting it off—I mean, my clothes are still up there, aren't they?"

Approximately one sixteenth the woman's total sprawling wardrobe. Blast it! She'd had three years—three years to collect her things. To come by at any point in time, fetch her clothes and be gone. But instead she had waited, and waited, and lived her fancy-free life and waited some more, and she had chosen now, the exact worst possible moment, to come by for them. Molly added nervously to see Harold's hard expression of displeasure, "I—I didn't expect you to be home today, not that I'm not happy to see you—oh, it's been months."

"You could have called first."

"Well, like I said, I expected you to be at work today…can I just get this done? It won't take long. It's been on my mind for weeks now."

Christ…at this point, turning her away was far more suspicious, but—good God, what was he going to do? Had to watch her like a hawk, shepherd her far as possible from the kitchen. And naturally (Damn the contemptible woman! This instinct of hers to go precisely where she wasn't wanted was what ruined their marriage before it even began) the first thing she asked when within the foyer of the house was, "So what are you cooking? This is new! I've never even seen you boil water."

"Never too late to learn…just working on a roast. You know where the bedroom is."

And he turned, about to leave her, but God damn it—

"You don't have to be so cold to me, Harold." Her tone was the sullen one: the pouting, girlish one that did have a way with him. He sighed with his back to it and her as she went on, "I know—I understand that I wasn't enough for you—"

"Molly, please."

"But I just mean, I wish you'd make the least effort to be my friend. You never tried to be my friend, Harold. Not even when we were married. You're nicer these days than you were but—well, right now for instance—"

"It's a bad time, Molly." He faced her again, arms spread in irritation. "There's such a thing as a phone, as I said. Forgive me for being a little taken aback, I was up to my elbows in a project and—"

The kitchen door opened and he withheld a gasp as Dottie slipped through, calling as if oblivious, "Harold, I just put on some—oh, hello!" With a soft smile, the half-naked (and swiftly cleaned) girl closed her robe more tightly around herself and hurried to Harold's elbow. "Who's this?"

"Ah—Dottie, this is my ex-wife, Molly…Molly, this is Dottie." He stared Molly down, defying her to make a comment as he hurried through a series of possible titles for the girl before she hurried forward, extended her hand to Molly and offered the simplest one with a brisk smile.

"Hi! I'm Harold's girlfriend."

"Oh! Really!" Eyes wide, then blinking rapidly, Molly did a bit of a double-take at Dottie and after a few seconds took the girl's offered hand. "Well! I—goodness! It's nice to meet you, how unexpected."

"Like I said," Harold continued, willing Molly to leave as hard as he could, "a bit of a bad time."

Dottie, on the other hand, seemed delighted as always to meet someone new. "Of course it's not a bad time, Harold—I'm glad to finally meet you, Molly, he's told me so much about you! Did you come by for lunch?"

Harold swallowed back the non-consensual pulse of lust that struck him at Dottie's question. Oh, the little tease. An audience gave her a whole new power over him—it was unbearable to have to pretend with her in any way, at any time, but oh, most especially at home, where they were supposed to be liberated from ridiculous pretense and able to collaborate in their elaborate fantasy life. And here, in the twilight zone of almost-private interactions with others outside of the context of the office, she was free to disrespect him as much as delighted them both. As she would never have in the workplace, he could see now that out and about in the world the little wanton was going to be stoking his compulsive cannibal fantasies about other women.

And to think he was just for the first time in his life getting his thoughts under control! Getting them more focused, anyway. Less painful to think on and more adjusted into an accessible realm. Opening the way for him to start thinking about women other than his magical sweetheart, now that was a recipe for trouble, and by God, Harold was going to have to keep very careful track of his own impulses if he was going to keep himself from dying in prison.

After the women had some cheerful discussion (No, not for lunch, only to collect her clothes and a few old CDs—oh what CDs? Etc… Charm on, Dottie, charm on), bright Dottie, brilliant Dottie looked at he front door and volunteered with a helpful hand wave, "Did you bring some boxes or something?"

"You know," said Molly, smiling thinly, "I didn't! I thought about having somebody come by to help me, but in the end I just came by myself." While Dottie peered at Harold, who stared back in smoldering lust only she could identify as such, his ex-wife continued, "I gave my valet the day off. You know, I'm so embarrassed—I'm in such a fluster—" Molly waved her hand in a short way and tacked on a sprightly laugh that always brought to mind his vision of Daisy Buchanan. Oh, Molly. He did love Molly, of course! She caused him a pain that was not as intense as the pain caused by Dottie, but it was still a very rich pain—and unfortunately that pain triggered the same crisscrossed impulses of his unspeakable lust.

But now that he wasn't married to Molly anymore, she was safe for him to speak to as a peer; and, moreover, now that he had Dottie for an outlet, he found he could actually look at his ex-wife longer at a stretch than he ever had. In her flustered posture, in the way she tugged the white fur around her shoulders and used an over-bright tone and had brought neither valet nor security detail nor movers to help her with her things (Imagine an heiress like Molly packing and moving her own clothes! She was as transparent as his office window), Harold could tell that Molly was crushed to have come upon him with a new woman. She had in fact never intended to take her clothes but instead come to try once again to appeal to Harold.

There was a little part of Molly that clearly hoped he would reform. She prayed the prostitutes would just vanish overnight and the first thing Harold would do would be to ring her up and say, "Honey, I've done it, I'm all better now. I can look you in the eye, I can touch you with abandon, I can be intimate with you in mind and spirit. Let's marry again."

That blasted Catholic upbringing nailed them both. It installed an unjust sense of shame for their failure to live up to the lifelong monogamous standards of the Church. Harold had always found chastity fetishism dreadfully dull.

To Harold's relief, Dottie said helpfully, "Why don't we have some coffee and hang out a minute? Maybe then I'll help you get some things packed up—is there any kind of storage room around here, Harry? A few empty cartons, anything?"

"Oh, there's something…I'll look. Are you sure you don't want to come back another day with some movers, though, Molly?"

"Maybe that would be for the best." With a pained, awkward laugh and a blue eye that struggled against gravity and Dottie's choice of dress—that was, one of Harold's robes—Molly waved her hands and looked at the door over her shoulder. "I really don't mean to intrude, I—"

"No, no, it's okay! I'm the one who should be sorry, go on, I'll bring you some coffee. You sit in the drawing room over there! I hate to think of you coming all this way…" After letting Molly take a few steps in the direction of the indicated room—steps taken under Dottie's gentle direction that first time out of social obligation more than any real desire to engage in the situation, no doubt—Dottie turned to look at Harold in a significant way. She whispered hastily, "Are we open?"

Speaking of monogamy. Nice of her to ask—he'd been pondering that very subject himself just the day prior. "I'm open if you are, for now…but let's discuss the minutiae later. Give me a few moments with her and then keep her—"

Molly paused on the threshold of the drawing room with a pained look over her shoulder for the lovers whispering in the foyer. Harold forced a smile at her and Dottie hurried away to get the coffee, keeping the kitchen door as shut as she possibly could.

Then, there he was: across the drawing room from Molly, wishing he had the ability to die on the spot. The time in this hateful purgatory gave him a good chance to appreciate the checkered tile of the lovely floor, though, and the comely shape of Molly's high heeled shoes upon it. Looking a bit neglected, actually—the floor, not the shoes. The shoes, like everything about Molly's aesthetic, was immaculate.

"So, Moll"—she perked to hear the closest they'd ever gotten to a petname, returning the gaze he forced himself to level with her inquisitive eyes—"how'd you suss out that I'd be home this weekend?"

"Oh, that. Giorgio called to ask if I had any work to pick up—I figured that meant you had given him a couple of weeks off, but you know, he's so professional… It just wasn't worth asking."

Yes, God bless the man. Harold hadn't needed to check the safe to know the housekeeper hadn't even looked inside it: it was an honorable man, God-fearing, and Harold knew he could trust the fellow when, having made an honest mistake and come in on a Thursday when he wasn't scheduled to, Giorgio walked into the kitchen, found Harold fucking flour-covered Simonetta over a cutting board while another, much more bored girl filmed. Giorgio turned right back around and promptly walked out without so much as a word, took care of the rest of the house, left a note asking if Harold wanted him back next week, and never brought it up again. Got a good raise for his shut mouth. Harold wished Giorgio kept his mouth even more shut than that—as in, Harold wished he could have induced Giorgio to also divorce Molly—but a man did have to make a living. Harold couldn't blame him for phoning one of his former bosses to pick up the slack on weeks he wasn't needed at the country place.

Restraining his sigh, Harold spread his hands. "Well,

again—you always could have called. I would strongly advise it."

"Oh, I know. But I wanted to see you Harry. I wanted to talk I—I'm just so surprised. I wasn't expecting something like…like seeing you with someone."

"It's been three years, Molly. Do you want me to take Holy Orders?"

"I— I guess you're right. It's none of my business anymore."

He knew what was next. Wait for it: here it came. The turn, the fulcrum, the—

"But—"

Aha! As predicted. She had glanced aside for a second and now pinned him down with her stare, her brows knitting quite theatrically.

"Don't you think this girl is a little—I don't know. I mean, I know I just met her, but she comes off a little—"

"Poor?"

A few rapid blinks. "I was going to say "young,"" Molly claimed, unsteadily enough to draw a snort from Harold.

"You're fairly young yourself, Molly. Not much more than ten years her senior, wait, let's do math, I think it's twelve… So you may have intended to say "young," but really, inside your heart, you meant "poor.""

"Well," said Molly with a flat glance of two seconds at the doorway, "isn't she?"

"You've always been able to tell. I suppose that's because it's important to you."

"Oh, *please*, Harold. I'm not trying to horn in on your Eliza Doolittle fantasy—"

"Eliza—" He scoffed and crossed his arms. "Please. Don't project *your* obsession with changing *me* onto my relationship with Dottie."

"I'm not—" Molly shut her eyes. "I am not. Here. To fight. In fact, I'm really hoping to do the opposite of that. I've been *trying* to do the opposite of that. And I hope that, now that you're in a relationship with—with somebody else, maybe we can work things out between us. But I'm just worried to see you with some…you know."

"I don't know, Molly."

"Don't make me say it, please. I just don't want to see you taken advantage of when you're feeling emotional. You're such a sensitive man, Harold."

"Don't tell me what I am if you're not going to have the balls to back up your vague accusations by saying the words "gold-digger.""

She had goaded him into being the one to say it and lifted her eyebrows in a certain smug way that he absolutely always hated. *"Well?* Look at you! Look at who you are! You're out of your mind—who is this girl? You were in *TIME*'s most influential people. I don't know if you're thinking straight."

"Rest assured, whatever your kneejerk reaction is to walk in here and find your proverbial position filled by some beggar, you're wrong. She's the Queen of Sheba in the rags of an orphan. My God, she is. Ah! I don't want to be cruel to you. I'll spare you the details—you wouldn't know the first thing about it even if I told you. No, don't try to argue. Even if I told you everything you couldn't possibly understand. You would think me madder than ever. But I—I care about this girl very much." He fell back in his seat upon realizing he had leaned forward so steeply.

"Well, I don't doubt that you care about her." Molly's eyes grew very sad once she overcame the shock of hearing her meek ex-husband speak with such poetic obsession for this young woman. "My God, I don't think you would have defended me like this if somebody was saying something about me—it's true." He shut his mouth and let her finish. "And I don't know if I've ever seen you…I don't know, look at me or whisper to me like you just were…out there. With her."

Flush-faced, Molly glanced away and reflexively stroked the white fur around her. Harold was thunderstruck, he had to admit—Molly was obviously the jealous sort but for her to still be jealous now after all this time was really something else. Even so, she was wrong, and he wished so badly to show her the flaw in her own thinking. "You see, your problem"—he spoke as if she had asked him to tell her what her problem was and she immediately flicked a displeased glance in the direction of the nearby lamp—"is that you've never worked, Molly. Not a day in your life."

"That's not true—I've volunteered my time. I've done charity benefits, and things."

Photo ops, she meant. "But you've never had a steady job filling that time. Volunteering is a luxury, you see? A privilege. Not everyone is even capable of making the time for such activities. Why, when I was young, my mother made me get a job at a convenience store. 'I don't want you growing up to be lazy like these Americans,'"—a parody of his mother's stubborn German accent came out of him with his memories—"'so you must get a job and learn to work. Perhaps when you are older and you can convince me that you've learned how to work, I'll invest in some project of yours.'"

"And she invested in your project with Byron, right? Your company." Molly delicately pulled an eyelash from the corner of her eye and examined it against her fingertip.

"Yes, that's right, God rest her soul. But the point I'm trying to make is that while I worked in these retail positions—and there were a few more—I learned something important. The kindest people were the "poor" ones every time. The college students and the prostitutes. The customers with drug problems, especially: oh, the friendliest, most polite customers were the junkies. Meanwhile after the standard work hours were up I'd have businessmen blustering in, the rudest people you've ever seen. All demanding I hurry up to get them their cigarettes or charge their gas that much faster. Whenever I had problems it was with somebody in a suit or holding a designer purse. Nobody with real problems in their own lives would have dreamed of adding to mine."

"That's nice," said Molly with a sniff, sitting forward, refusing to see his point. "I'm not saying being poor is a character flaw, Harold, I'm not saying that all. I'm just saying—"

"Knock, knock!" Dottie pushed the door open with her hip. Harold had the very clear impression she'd been listening and had by now simply tired of Molly's bad attitude. More power to her. He was dying to deal with the body in the kitchen and rose as Dottie hurried to set the tea service down. "Sorry to interrupt, and sorry that took so long! A watched pot never fills with coffee."

Just like that, all skepticism was replaced with girlish charm. Molly leaned forward to take her coffee mug, saying with a smile, "Oh, it's no trouble, thank you so much! Gosh"—a sound of incredible shock as she took a sip—"what kind of coffee is this? It's so good!"

"Just some cinnamon—I was a barista for a while in college and I learned that a little cinnamon really brings out the taste. You can put sugar in the coffee grounds, too, but I didn't know what you liked in terms of sweet to bitter ratio."

Someone was either eavesdropping or very timely. While Harold glanced significantly at Molly, she laughed in an awkward way and asked, "Is that so? How interesting, I never would have known a thing like that…"

"If you ladies will excuse me"—Harold vacated his seat as Dottie filled the couch cushion beside Molly with a totally organic brand of over-familiarity that clearly made the rich woman uncomfortable—"I just need to see to a few things in the kitchen, myself. Back in a jiffy."

And with a new shirt. He glanced down with a grimace to see his apron was beginning to absorb the blood from the undershirt beneath. Molly hadn't noticed, at least. He barged through into the kitchen, preoccupied with the task of removing his apron to put it away, and somehow felt as if amid day-to-day dramatics he had almost forgotten the dissembled carcass lying semi-prepared on the kitchen island. The sight shocked him, thrilled him beyond all reasonable measure—God, to think this was here while two rooms away the women were chatting over coffee as innocent as anything! He tried not to get too worked up over the perverse idea, though he couldn't help but sigh and pat a few times a glistening red shank not yet differentiated from a few other mouth-watering cuts of Dottie flesh. So many possibilities, oh, so much to explore together.

All the more reason to ensure he wasn't caught. After kicking around, he managed to loosen the brake of the kitchen island that was, strictly speaking, mobile. Intended for entertainment, of course: put a big birthday cake on it, wheel it out, stripper pops out and makes everybody laugh. He preferred the version where a skeleton popped out of the stripper, he had to admit. Or where the stripper doesn't jump out, because she's baked into the cake. Ah, reminded him of that old Tom Petty music video—that was one of Dottie's favorite songs, he knew from their Internet chats.

Dottie, Dottie! Boy, she'd really fucked him up, for lack of a more eloquent term. There was just nothing else to describe it. Here he was, his ex-wife in the same building while he pushed a kitchen island bearing human remains down the hall of his renovated slaughterhouse—and all he could think about was what Dottie liked, what Dottie was like, how much he liked Dottie. Love really was very similar to mental illness…though he had to wonder if it was a personal problem of his own. Harold pushed Dottie's second corpse through the abattoir and into the cold room beyond, where more meat from the first Dottie still waited to be used. Pausing with his hands on his hips to study the appetite-inspiring image, he thought to himself that it was a damn good thing Dottie's meat possessed such a potent psychedelic effect. How fun it might have been to play Tantalus and slip a little flesh into the meals of the ignorant! No wonder so many serial killers, real and fictional, had tried out the routine.

But how much more fun it would be to gain actual consent! Harold pondered the notion while exiting through the exterior door of the cold store, rounding back to the front of the house and then sneaking back in through the foyer to creep up the stairs without catching Molly's notice. He had always been so taken with the thought of a woman throwing herself at him and begging to be eaten that he had not spared thought to the notion of, say, seducing someone into the dark aesthetic of Dolcett. What love was like the love he and Dottie had for one another, after all? What was even comparable to this all-consuming fire, this desire each had to feed the other? God, God, for just a hint of Dottie's powers—for just one chance to feed her his own flesh without consequence.

Harold stripped off his shirt and hopped quickly into the shower, rinsing the blood from his body and stroking his aching cock once or twice to the thought of feeding Molly a little bit of his new beloved. Would Dottie's tender meat have as invigorating an effect on a woman as it had on Harold? Why, refined Molly might take a nibble and transform in the instant to a feral, fuckable harlot like he'd never seen. If he could keep control of himself—resist a taste of Dottie flesh to retain his senses—he and Dottie could have reduced that buxom ex-wife heiress of his into their personal pet. A hot little bimbo eager to be stuffed in more ways than one. Ah… Christ. All right, the blood was off him, leave the shower. Calm down, old boy.

Briskly drying, quickly re-dressing, Harold took the stairs two at a time and swung himself about the banister with the momentum. He felt positively boyish. Ah, it was so good to think his own thoughts without a bleak overhang of shame! So good to let things drift in and out, knowing they meant nothing. When he could pour himself into an outlet—into Dottie—he could think whatever he wanted. Yes: Dottie was fantasy realized, rendering the rest of the world fantastic reality.

Occasionally, however, the two conditions interlinked. He strolled into the drawing room and his pleasant smile widened quite genuinely to see the girls together—and his filthy mind conspired in the instant to present him with as many helpful suggestions as he had dollars to his name. Weren't the girls lovely together? Oh, compare and contrast! A collage of pretty white and bronze and black and gold and pink and red. Dottie sat against the heiress to hold her palm upright beneath the light of the nearby Tiffany lamp.

"—and you must be an art collector like Harold is—or, maybe, do you model?"

"Oh my gosh, I do! I used to model for paintings all the time, years ago. How did you know that?"

"This finger is shorter than—oh!" Beaming up as Harold returned to his seat across from the ladies, Dottie said with a shy tone and a grin as pleased as if she hadn't seen him for hours and hours, "Hi."

"Hello." Kiss her? Don't kiss her? Ah, she tilted her head up expectantly toward him. He couldn't deny her, courtesy be damned—it was an important message to Molly, anyway, and an unexpected thrill when he lifted his head from his brief, bright contact with those ultra-soft lips. The heiress watched slyly, as unsubtly as Harold himself no doubt watched Dottie at the office while believing his behavior unimpugnable. When they made eye contact Molly turned her face away, eyes downcast toward her demure hand in Dottie's. Harold saw no reason to sit in his old seat and instead settled beside Dottie. The younger girl pushed her glasses atop those billows of dark hair before leaning down to resume nearer scrutiny of Molly's palm.

Harold did not believe in magic before meeting Dottie, and he still did not believe in parlor tricks like palm-reading. Not then, anyway. He watched Dottie bending close against Molly's furs, admired her caresses the heiress's ringed hand amid announcements of many things that could have been easily gleaned from *Forbes* or Wikipedia. It was an amusing little game, this cold-reading…and it was the routine of a pick-up artist. He had to admit he admired Dottie's abilities.

It did make him think about things, however. Even as he slid a hand down Dottie's waist and held her—with a flash of lust to do so before Molly—it occurred to pragmatic Harold that so much about himself and his ex-wife was readily available to anybody with time and an Internet connection. Yes, he tried to be private, but business stories were key parts of his industry and it was natural for the human mind to study successful individuals. There was much that was out there about Harold Fleetwood; much about Molly, too, and their marriage, and even details about Harold's life going back to his childhood thanks to the odd biography or business memoir.

But Harold knew nothing—an absolute big, blank, white null set—of Dottie. He knew just a little of what she could do. One thing. He also knew other things, too. That she was funny. Wildly attractive. Very, very smart. And seductive—willfully, intellectually seductive. He knew also that Dottie was not the name with which she was first born. And he had to give Molly an honest point. All these qualities tended to be red flags. Indications of some kind of con when present in a normal person who had only one death to die.

But watching Dottie cold-read his ex-wife's palm, Harold wondered how much of her witchy, shyster veneer was there to obscure some real magic being accomplished behind the scenes. Some molecular effect of pheromones and unknown energies yet to be distinguished and measured by science. Oh, he wanted to torture the truth out of her…break her fingers and pull out her tasty little tongue until she gagged out the truths of what else she could do, how exactly she came to be in his life. The thought made him throb with pleasure and he stroked that waist against which his hand had come to rest, draping his other arm around the back of the couch behind the women. Dottie went on and on, looking through the lines of Molly's palm as though for something. Then the girl emitted an abrupt laugh.

"Why, you're just like Harold…no wonder you two were married! You're both so repressed."

With a bashful gasp, Molly pulled her hand away and hid her palm against her heart as though to keep her secrets from Harold's little seeress. "I'm not repressed—"

"You are. You just want to have fun but you can't make yourself. How come?"

"Well, I— I— I do have fun—"

"Catholic upbringing," answered Harold helpfully to Dottie, who made a noise of understanding as the heiress sputtered.

"It has nothing to do with that…why, I have plenty of fun. I can't imagine what you mean."

"See! You can't even admit you know exactly what I'm talking about." Dottie turned to pout irresistibly at Harold and he, unprepared, froze completely beneath her smoldering eye contact. "You didn't tell me poor Molly is as shy as you are, Harold."

Heated with all kinds of vulgar fantasies at that, Harold said with a careful look into Dottie's face, "Why, I didn't know Molly was as shy as I am. She always seemed very extroverted in our marriage."

"Extroverts can still be shy about sex." At Molly's little scoff of semi-alarm, Harold and Dottie both looked. The girl continued to the heiress, "Well! You are…you're even embarrassed by the word."

"I just think—"

"Like—you've probably never even thought seriously about trying two people at once, I'll bet."

Amazing. In all the time of their marriage—even in their courtship—Harold had never seen Molly's face grow so red; never seen her eyes so animated by shocked blinks or such a fluster of erotic turmoil. Somehow Harold had never talked to Molly about her fantasies, maybe because he wanted so desperately to avoid the subject of his own. But audacious Dottie went tromping right into Molly's mental space, knocking over precious objects and propping her pretty feet upon the furniture. Harold held his breath and looked into Molly's face, for once able to observe her shame and feel none of his own. Oh, it was grand—the humiliated flicker of her eyes toward the door made him want to fuck.

"I'm old-fashioned, I guess," said the heiress, reflexively smoothing her hand over her fur but not yet rising from her seat. She did however glimpse at Dottie leaning against her, and then, more conspicuously, at Harold's hand upon Dottie's waist. "Yes. It's fair to say I'm shy about…public displays of affection."

Dottie tipped back her head and laughed gaily, her glasses falling off her hair. Harold caught them with a fond smile as she said, "Oh, I'm not! Not with Harry—you should watch us fuck sometime. You'll see how not-shy I get when I'm all turned on."

Oh, Christ. He needed to marry this girl before she got away from him. She was too good: too hot a sexual partner and too expert in her dealings with other people. Some Catholic or ex-Catholic men would have been very stubbornly offended by a suggestion like Dottie's, but any minute granule of shame Harold felt was so remote compared to his normal, true shames that it only served to enliven the already very scintillating imagery. While Molly batted her eyes and sputtered, "Excuse me?" Harold found himself playing along. Worth a shot, anyway.

"She really is a very liberated young woman, Molly. Much less self-conscious than either of us…perhaps it's a generational difference."

"That's one way of putting it! I—I have to admit I'm a little shocked—"

"That's because you're turned on and you're trying to pretend you're not." Leaning away from Molly, Dottie sagged back into Harold's embrace and delicately extricated her glasses from his clutches. She extended a long arm in the direction of the coffee table to slide them upon the tea service. This process left the robe hanging open a few degrees more and revealed the edge of one rosy pink nipple at which Molly visibly struggled to avoid staring. "I don't know why people resist their own feelings…it feels good to watch people making love. It feels good to have two people making love to you—you should try it."

"I—I don't—I wasn't—"

"Well, I won't pressure you into anything…not that I could, of course." Dottie smiled admiringly up at Molly. "What am I beside somebody like you, after all…just a nobody. Just some crazy girl who loves Harold. But I guess what I'm trying to say is…it's okay if you still love Harold, too, Molly. Maybe now that you're not married anymore he'll be more reciprocal."

Sad to say the girl was right, but there was no time to agree. She tilted her head back with that look of fiery desire for him and Harold had no choice but respond with an appropriate kiss. Or inappropriate, depending whom you asked. Didn't matter. The girl sighed with pleasure as he eased his tongue past her lips, the desire to consume her rising within him. Oh, Christ. Not just to consume the Dottie in the freezer, the dead Dottie he had killed that very day (if only you knew, Molly!), but this Dottie, the living one. He wished to assimilate every part of her, of this scrumptious body over which his ravenous hand ran as if Molly wasn't in the room. He had forgotten all about her, in fact, until, parting their kiss with a flush-faced gaze of desire into his very soul, Dottie lifted her head to find Molly watching, still as a bird on a fencepost, her eyes glazed and her lips parted with shock.

"See," said Dottie, smiling over at the heiress while Harold lowered his head to kiss that exquisite pale neck. The girl cooed and arched into his lips, moaning softly, asking Molly, "It's nice to watch people kiss, isn't it?"

"I—maybe." His body so roared with pleasure to hear

Molly admit such a thing that he couldn't help himself; he drew open the robe and slid Dottie's naked body out of its fabric, into his lap. Moaning to feel the aching protrusion in his trousers, Dottie lifted a hand to caress his cheek and display herself with a sigh. Molly, apparently no longer seeing any reason to not look, stared in faint shock and what Harold had to note was a not insignificant amount of desire. As Harold similarly felt no further need to restrain himself and ran his hands over Dottie's soft breasts, Molly said with a soft hint of jealousy, "I've never seen you like this before, Harold."

"Don't be mad at him for being shy, Molly." Sweet Dottie, tender Dottie, she wiggled in his lap and sighed beneath his caresses while going on. "He loves you still. I can tell by how he talks about you—but not everybody can let themselves go with other people."

"Then why can he let himself go with you?"

"Because we have so much in common…" He sank his teeth into her shoulder under auspices of laying down a kiss and she gasped, thrashing in his clutch, spreading her legs as his hand trailed down her twisting tummy. "And because I encourage him to experiment…shy people need somebody who's not shy with them, see…so they can—oh, Harold!"

He hadn't been able to stand it: his fingertips had traced over her labia to find her wildly aroused. "My God, you naughty girl…you love to show off, don't you."

"Uh-huh…oh, Harry, I love to show you off…you're so good at fucking me, I just want to show Molly what she could have if she'd come play with us."

Her face a passionate red, Molly covered her mouth with the back of one absent hand and dreamed on at the avid caresses of the couple before her. "Why would things be different now just because we're not married anymore?"

Harold gazed into Dottie's face as he answered, dying to tell his ex-wife the truth and lap up her reaction. "That's not why…it's only part of it. The truth is that Dottie is right—I have more in common with her than I do with you. Mutual interests—a shared aesthetic. For instance…you like the slaughterhouse, don't you, baby."

With a grin and a nod, the girl gazed up into his face. "Yes, uh-huh, D—Harold"—her grin widened and so did his, especially as one finger eased into her flowing channel to find it desperate for him—"I love your slaughterhouse, I think it's hot…I want you to fuck me in your abattoir…oh, God, kiss me if you're going to do that, Harry, oh—"

"Ah, another difference, little Dottie loves to be kissed." While he indulged the girl, Molly emitted a hurt gasp.

"I love to be kissed—"

"Oh, please, you're always whining. Casual affection alarms you, you complain—"Not here, Harold, my lipstick. No, Harry, what if someone's around to take a picture." Yes, what if! God forbid a married couple be seen canoodling on the town."

"If you felt that way"—leave it to Molly to argue with him like his fingers weren't lodged up a naked girl's insatiable cunt—"I don't see why you didn't just talk to me. If that kind of affection was all you wanted, why didn't you talk to me instead of going to—"

"That wasn't all I wanted, Molly. You can't possibly imagine what I want—you're too sheltered, too gentle. Look at this girl."

Fire in his eyes, Harold snaked his arm from over the back of the couch and caught Dottie by the gasping jaw. He wrenched her face toward his kiss and she hungrily accepted it, reaching up to blindly tug at his hair and the collar of his shirt. All the while his fingers worked in and out of her with new intensity. The soft cry she produced was so satisfying that it was a struggle to keep himself clothed, to keep from savaging her then and there. His teeth clenched and he tightened his grip enough to bruise while Molly cried out with terror for Dottie, "Harold—!"

"Look at her," he continued, working pleasure from Dottie's quivering pussy while lifting his eyes to meet those of his ex-wife. "Whatever I want to give her, she doesn't just take it. She begs for it. She thrives on it. She sees me for what I am underneath the money and prestige and power. Don't you, Dottie—a wolf dressed up in sheep's clothes, yes, you know. Oh—"

He smacked another furious kiss to her pouting lips and gasped as she cried out, that trembling voice mounting a pitch he had begun to associate with the irrevocable nearing of her orgasm. While his fingers drew from her to tease her a little and massage her labia rather than that well-attended silken glove, his hand relaxed from her jaw. Now it covered the column of her throat, lightly, a reminder to them both how quickly and easily he'd taken her life that very same morning, and she moaned at the beautiful memory.

"Dottie's a wanton little slut," he said, looking into her gauzy features, restraining a smile as her hips bucked against his fingers to lure him back in. "Yes, a pure, uninhibited daydream of a girl. I can hit her with anything—metaphorically or literally"—he lifted his hand to lightly slap her cheek and she gasped, harder still when his fingers penetrated her again, God, she was so wet his heart seemed ready to stop—"—and she'll accept it, try it. Love it. And even if she doesn't love it she'll still try it. Won't she, Dottie?"

"Yes, yes, yes, yes! Harold, Harry, oh, do whatever you want to me, fuck—please, harder—"

"Precious little beggar…that's all you beg for, isn't it, darling. Sex, sex and attention. Don't worry, baby…Daddy has both for you." He felt Molly's rapid glance into his face but didn't care; he was captivated by Dottie, by her trembling limbs and sudden tensing beneath the crushing weight of the orgasm he could bring about with the well-timed use of one word. Amid a little keen, his name on her lips like a bird call, Dottie tugged at his hair, pleaded up into his face with that beautiful furrowed brow. Wanted a kiss, his angel. He forced her to wait for just a few seconds while he admired her panting orgasm. Then, at her urgent whine, he smiled and gave in, the sweetness of her mouth somehow intensified by her height of pleasure. Oh, fun idea. Yes, next time he'd wait until the very second of orgasm: time her death to the peak of her ecstasy. The most delicious meat of all, no doubt.

Gingerly sliding his fingers free, Harold drew the robe over Dottie's unbearably beautiful body and wondered how it was that Molly managed to bear it without Harold's fits of exquisite agony—perhaps she was only better at hiding them. Certainly had been hiding an adventurous streak all this time…ah, it was almost a pity, but if they hadn't divorced he might not have had this insatiable, invigorating love of Dottie. "Perhaps we should wait for more," he told her softly, kissing the corner of her still softly gasping mouth as she re-adapted to reality without his fingers in her. "Don't want to shock poor Molly…it might be a little much for her to watch me fuck you all at once like this."

"I guess so," said the girl with a dreamy grin, a gay little laugh, the sound and the sight of it all somehow snapping Molly from her stupor. Blinking, blinking, coming out of it, shocked at herself, Molly looked around and Harold wondered if there had not been some hypnotic technique applied during the palm-reading. Surely not. What a fool he'd been with his Madonna/Whore complex—he'd been so afraid to approach even the basic elements of what constituted fun with Molly that it had been safer to pretend she was a somewhat frigid, controlling little shrew who just wanted to horn in on his fun with his working girls. Now, ironically after bringing his (yes, much younger) new woman to orgasm in front of her, he somehow realized for the first time that his had not been the only sense of isolation within the frosty realm of their doomed marriage. Much as there were all these aspects of himself that he had never dared show Molly, perhaps Molly had been holding back some things of her own from him.

And like that, he was interested in his ex-wife again.

"I'm sorry about what happened between us, Molly," he told her, one arm draping over Dottie's shielded bosom to keep her comfortably embraced to his body. "Dottie's right, and very forgiving of my disloyal heart—I do still love you, even if it's in a different, perhaps somewhat more patient and formal way than the crushing things I feel when I look at this—oh, this little strumpet." He caressed Dottie's hair and basked in the sparks of her gay laughter beneath the forceful kisses he applied to that comely brow. With a hefty sigh and the urge out of his system, he looked up again to see Molly watched him in not jealousy or sorrow but true, flat-out astonishment.

"I won't be so deluded as to think I could have my cake and eat it, too, but…I'm not the man you married, Molly. I've changed—no, perhaps it's more accurate to say that I am changing. Engaged in the act of change."

"I see that."

"And because I've changed, the ways in which I interface with the world—with other people—are beginning to change, too. If you would be open to occasionally spending time with me, whether alone or with Dottie—especially with Dottie—you would find me quite different from how I was during our marriage."

Still apparently at a loss for words, the normally poised heiress glanced between the lovers' faces and futilely attempted to produce meaningful sound with her open mouth. After a few seconds she managed, "That's—that's quite an invitation—"

"You don't have to feel obligated—"

"I didn't"—Molly looked away and lifted a hand, glancing toward the open door of the room again—"I didn't say 'no,' I just—"

"Have to process," supplied Dottie helpfully. At the heiress's nod, Dottie said, "We understand! It's no pressure, really…we're just getting to know each other on, like, a real level anyway. So take your time. I'm sure whenever you're curious we'll be down to hang out."

With a little laugh, a strange noise of semi-shock (perhaps at herself more than anyone else in the room), Molly asked Harold, "Um, can I—can I ask how long you two have been... going together?"

"A week," answered Dottie. Harold laughed and so did she as Molly sputtered on.

"A week! The way you two talk, I thought—goodness, to have already brought her here, Harold—"

"I had known Byron forty-eight hours before I was sure I wanted to secure him as a business partner until the day I died. Now we're two of the richest men on the planet. When I make a snap judgment on a long-term investment, it's for a reason."

"It must be," said Molly, eyeing Dottie, who gazed up at Harold, who studied his ex-wife. "Yes, I guess it must be. I—I think I'm going to go, uh—"

"Hey wait," said Dottie, nudging the heiress's valuable knee with her bare foot as the woman rose. The girl demanded of the older woman, "Let's swap phone numbers so I can complain about Harold to you," and the man in question found his gaze naturally directed down the plump curve of Molly's calf. His stomach rumbled and, hearing it, Dottie recited her number while nuzzling the top of her catlike head against Harold's aching, inhuman jaw.

"All right, well...this was all very interesting." At last liberated, Molly cleared her throat and looked with a red face down at the still entwined pair. "I'll just...let myself out, so don't get up. Gosh, this is so unexpected."

"Sure you don't want to bring some clothes with you, Moll?"

"Wh—oh!" Very slick, Molly. She was never good at lying directly and laughed, waving a hand. "Gosh, no, I don't really care...I was just worried about you, Harold."

"And whatever gave you cause to worry?"

She caught herself in the middle of being too honest and

grimaced, clamming up a little, glancing at her pocket book, opening it to remove her keys. "Oh, just—"

"Who's been talking to you, Molly?"

"W-e-l-l"—she had an adorable way of drawing out such words when childishly 'in trouble,' her eyes averting and her shoe's pointed toe scuffing against the expensive floor—"I just thought it would be good to see how you're adjusting…and I think I see. You learn more by listening than by talking, right?"

Ah, Pearl. Of course, he should have guessed. Pearl knew Harold throughout the duration of his courtship and marriage to Molly; and Pearl, like most middle-aged to older ladies working in American offices, was something of a notorious busybody. Bribe or no bribe, she no doubt felt it her duty to ensure the welfare of her boss and save him from being manipulated by some saucy little minx. Well, he'd set her straight when he had a chance—that was not going to fly. Nobody would pry Dottie out of his clutches and if they tried, God help them. He'd be dead in the cold ground long before he bent to any external pressure against their relationship.

Her sunglasses on to blind her from the depravity, Molly said with a forced smile, "Well! Nice meeting you! I'll be sure to call before I come by next time."

"Don't feel you have to," Dottie cried after her, delight further brightening her post-orgasm glow. "Just walk in any time and see what you find!"

The front door shut; Dottie laughed uproariously while Harold bent his head to kiss with savage lust that ruby mouth. "If you tease her too much, she might not let you call her 'Mommy.'"

"I don't know if that's what she wants, exactly…" With another, more cryptic chuckle, Dottie glanced off in the direction of the door. Guiding Harold's hand, she urged his palm beneath her robe, over the slopes of her breasts and back down to that alluring fertile crescent of hers. "Say, Harry…"

"Yes?"

"Do you think"—she pressed his fingers to her cunt and gasped, her other hand reaching back to fondle his throbbing member through his trousers while she used his fingers to masturbate—"we could convince Molly to feed herself to us?"

Oh, tyrant! Tyrant of his heart and soul and sexual fantasies, oh—evil Dottie. He throbbed, gasped, gave her one hot little swat right on the sensitive folds he otherwise caressed. While she moaned with toe-curling pleasure, he remonstrated, "What a wicked thing to suggest…you shouldn't tempt me like that, Dottie."

"Oh, but you like it…I know you've thought about it, what she'd taste like, oh! Fuck, I bet she'd be all tender and buttery sweet, all those pampered years—"

"Not as sweet as your flesh, little cow—God, ah, Christ, that was so close." He shuddered, clutching his beloved's living body all the tighter while contemplating the dead one. "You think it's funny to put my life at risk, do you?"

"I like to see you panicked…you're so *together* most of the time, after all. It's good for you to sweat a little—ah, oh! Daddy—yes, oh, please, keep spanking me there—"

He did, biting back a groan as her hips bucked into the rapid swats he lay against the wet flesh of that bare pussy he was coming to worship. As he resumed drawing his fingertips up and down the valley between those throbbing lips, he told her, "What an evil girl I love—trying to convince me to eat my ex-wife, then trying to get me into trouble for a murder that isn't even really a murder…talk about bad girls, Dottie."

"You love it, you pervert…I feel it." Her searching fingers at last located his zipper and eased it down; seconds later he gasped and pressed his face against her hair while she eased his cock out of his pants. That gentle hand worked over it. "Oh, yeah. I know it's all you think about, all the time, whenever you're looking at a hot girl—oh, Harold, you want to know how she'd taste, how her corpse would look in all these pieces floating in a cauldron—oh!"

He pushed her out of his lap only to stand; then, kneeling her upon the couch with her forearms gripping its back, he finally satisfied his urge to fill her up. She gagged on the sound of her moan, the pleasure slightly stifled by the tension of her new pussy—deflowered but not utilized more than once. He couldn't imagine what that was like to get used to…no wonder she was such an avid masochist. She had no choice.

"It's true," he told her, wrapping one hand in her hair to keep her face pressed against the couch's back while the other braced her hip for her pounding. "It's true. I look at any beautiful women like Molly or Simonetta and thoughts rush through my head, oh, cutting out a shoulder round and feeding it to Molly, God. What I've always really wanted was to feed Molly to herself—ah, Christ, but I can feed you to yourself all day, all night, Christ, ah, Dottie, Dot, oh, no one could ever know what a—wild, scrumptious, irresistible little nymph you are—"

Forty minutes later Dottie lay in Harold's arms, her mouth open with the sleep into which she'd slipped once their mutual pleasure had combined in that deadly peak. Oh, Dottie. She was so beautiful. He had wanted to get right to cooking but it was so much better to simply watch her sleep…and better still because she had such a soothing effect on his mind. Even after planting such insidious seeds within it.

Fantasy, of course. All fantasy. Part of the game of dreaming of Dolcett. Why, Harold lived in the real world, after all. Dolcett stories and drawings were all set in fantastical societies where murder was regarded somewhat differently, and legalities were no obstacle between a hungry man and a delicate morsel of his choosing.

But this was reality. And Molly was very well-known. And, this day aside, she usually traveled with a retinue of valets, guards and assistants. Harold and Dottie would therefore likely never get another chance (oh, surely not, God, You would not tempt him like that) to even dream of such a thing as teaching Molly what a pleasure it was to be eaten for love. Of course…if anybody was capable of teaching that notion to someone else, it was certainly Dottie Shipman. Yes, Dottie Shipman; convincing, alluring, capable of draining the pus of shame from the open wound of his mind. Now all those ugly thoughts, that festering wound of his imagination, it was all exposed to air. It all had such dangerous possibility of coming into the world…and Harold did not want his thoughts to come into the world. He wanted to be a good man.

But, oh…there was so very much he longed to experience with pretty Dottie.

Delicately, with fingertips so light they might as well not have been there at all, Harold dared to touch her dreaming mouth. He marveled at her sigh. Ah…her flesh was so much softer alive than dead. So much warmer. So overflowing with love.

If he didn't find a way to convince her to move into his apartment, Harold was going to literally lose his mind.

IN THE NEXT VOLUME OF DOTTIE FOR YOU

Dottie, Dottie. Harold loves Dottie. Sad as it is to think that a Fortune 500 CEO can be reduced to an absolute simp for his own fresh-faced secretary, that's the truth of it. But given the taboo proclivities both he and Dottie share, the fixation held by this capitalist pig for his immortal dream-girl is fairly understandable. The whole cannibalism thing, well, that might not be quite so much—not for the world at large, anyway. Not even suave billionaire playboy Leo Byron, Harold's oldest business partner, could understand this side of him.

But Harold doesn't just have to protect himself: he feels an increasing urge to protect Dottie from the world, or at least to keep her at near him. After sensual acrobatics lead to a trip to the doctor for a nice new set of stitches, Harold can only see himself taking on an increasingly caring role in Dottie's life—which is why, when Leo sweeps in hoping to poach the pretty secretary for his new tech start-up, Harold is more determined than ever to see DOTTIE DOMESTICATED. If he can't have her at work, he wants to savor her haunting presence at home: and the thirsty CEO would do anything to prove his devotion.

Even give the twenty-four year old minx
total control of his wallet.

OTHER WORKS
FROM PAINTED BLIND PUBLISHING

REGINA WATTS

INDUSTRIAL DIVINITY (2020)

WILD GIRL RUNNING (2020)

THE BURNINGSOUL SAGA (2021-)

I WAS AN OP DEMON LORD (2021-)

BE MY BULLY (2021)

SEDUCED BY SABINE (2021)

MAYHEM AT THE MUSEUM (2021)

IDOL (2022)

M. F. SULLIVAN

DELILAH, MY WOMAN (2015)

THE LIGHTNING STENOGRAPHY DEVICE (2017)

THE DISGRACED MARTYR TRILOGY (2019-2020)

ADA DART

THE RIFT BRIDE (2022-)

ABOUT THE AUTHOR

Regina Watts is the penname of M. F. Sullivan, founder and flagship author of Painted Blind Publishing. From her cozy home a few universes away from this one, Watts transmits Sullivan stories that are then transcribed and published. Her available titles range from transgressive erotica to psychedelic fiction to horror to romance. Be sure to sign up for her mailing list at hrhdegenetrix.com!

ABOUT THE PUBLISHER

Painted Blind Publishing and its erotic imprint, Painted Blue Publishing, are the brainchild of author and devoted editor to Regina Watts, M. F. Sullivan. Founded in 2015 while Sullivan resided in Tucson, PBP is a house dedicated to bringing readers the finest in consciousness-expanding fiction. Be sure to check out the wide variety of essays available for free at paintedblindpublishing.com to learn more about the company, Watts, and Sullivan.